THE CRAZY TRUTH

For my sunshine, Poppy.

THE CRAZY TRUTH

GEMMA JUNE HOWELL

SEREN

Seren is the book imprint of
Poetry Wales Press Ltd
Suite 6, 4 Derwen Road, Bridgend,
Wales, CF31 1LH

www.serenbooks.com
Follow us on social media @SerenBooks

ISBNs
Paperback – 978-1-78172-752-2
Ebook – 978-1-78172-759-1

A CIP record for this title is available from the British Library.

The publisher acknowledges the financial assistance of the
Books Council of Wales.

Illustrations on pages 52, 116 and 117: Poppy Abigail Howell.
Concrete poems: Illustrations based on originals by Dan Broughton.

Printed by 4Edge Limited, Essex.

This is a work of fiction. All of the characters, organisations,
and events portrayed in this novel are either products of the
author's imagination or are used fictitiously.

Everyone should have the opportunity to create, share & consume stories that reflect their cultures & communities, so that we all feel equally validated.

– Bernadine Evaristo, 'Manifesto: On Never Giving Up.'

VODKA

The night was over.

The clingfilm skin-and-bones of Girlo lay on a state issued mattress. Lungs ablazin' from the *weekend sesh*, she snatched her breath in scanty gasps. Her tongue cracked. SLAM. *Where the fuck wuz she?* The ripe stink of piss gave her an inkling. She opened one velcroed-with-mascara eye. Her toes flinched, feet scabbed and glass-crusted. She'd gone barefoot again. Sleep-walked into another attempt to fill the rotten void, which over the years had become fertile land for the perverse appetites of more powerful others. TAP TAP-TAP TAP TAP-TAP A tympanic tapping… a *tap-tap* tapping echoed through the pipes. She tried to block it out, but it travelled—got under her skin and into the nerves like the promise of a panic attack. The tapping tiptoed through a fog of thought and resurfaced as *Vodka—taste it—taste the numb.* A fragment of refrain—came to repeat, to regurgitate… *taste the numb* bubbled, belched, then marched on like the souls of foot-soldiers in a lost war. *Vodka—taste it—*sounded like a slick advertising slogan. It took hold, rhythm inching in, beat in her veins, rattled her bones, marching in, forming something of a line: *Vodka—taste it—taste the numb—bite—my—bum.* SLAM *Damn!* She lost the run of the line. TAP TAP-TAP TAP TAP-TAP TAP TAP *Want to cum—Want to hit, want to run.* SLAM.

"Shut the fuck up with that tapping! Yewell nevuh ge' out if ewe carry on wivah shit!" SLAM. "LEMME OUT! I need tuh see a doctor. I need my medication! I know my rights. Do you yere me? I know my fuckin' rights, I doo!" TAP TAP-TAP TAP TAP-TAP TAP TAP-TAP TAP "Wait 'til I ge' my 'ands on you. Gunna fuck you up good un proper, you tiny tapping cunt."

The copper on duty bashed on a door, shouting: "you shut the fuck up or you'll never be getting out-tuh yuh, d'yew yere me?"

TAP TAP-TAP TAP TAP-TAP TAP TAP-TAP TAP "I know my rights! I know my rights!" SLAM "Shurrup, ewe crazy bint!" SLAM. *Want to hit, want to run, just for—fun.* TAP TAP-TAP TAP TAP-TAP TAP TAP-TAP TAP

Girlo lay down to sleep herself elsewhere. If she kept her eyes shut long enough—and imagined it hard enough, then maybe, just maybe, she could be at home with Nannie Pearl— all safe and sound in the antique bed, with its rattling, mis-fitted baubles, and old planks for slats, and the familiar sound of the telly in the other room, and the smell of family. Instead, she had the *tap-tapping* and a sinkhole where last night was meant to be. This was no place for quiet reflection or artistic inspiration… or was it? Girlo peeled her face off the plastic mattress. Her brain almost fell out of her earhole. She smoothed her cheek to make sure the skin was still there. She stood up. Her left leg seemed shorter than the right. The window jerked inside the cell's flecked walls. In the corner, a chrome toilet bowl advertised a large black skiddy from an intrepid alcopoo. On the water's surface, a crystallised layer of crud had formed. Her pee was the colour of cooked skag, and as it hit the crust, like a spoon cracking the burnt sugar of a crème brûlée, it released a stench so fucking potent that it almost singed her eyebrows off. She was bleeding but didn't think she was due on yet. There was no bog-roll. The chain wouldn't flush. *Fucking fucksake!*

Then came that twatting tapping again. Someone still bumping off uppers or a headcase pissing the pigs off on purpose? She tried to get her head together. *How the fuck had she ended up in here?* VODKA VODKA VODKA Girlo rocked herself in the foetal position. The sweat of her grip slipping down bare knees. "Let's just try and get my story straight," she whispered into the blanket, which smelt like it'd been used as a fanny rag.

Gobbets from the night before meandered: little lost orbs or pickled eyes, slowly bopping, escaping the grip of the cerebral spork with which she tried to capture them. She knew that for the rest of the day these blots of memory would scurry up to the surface and POP against the skull membrane, letting

8

her know, between blackouts, what happened the night before. POP *High Street* POP *Saturday night* POP *Summer break, 2005* POP *It was coming...*

That's where she was: stampeding with the rest of the sex-charged herds of hedonists. She had finished work and headed into town. The cattle were buzzing... hens, stags, gangs of fancy-dressed skirt and clumps of blokes wearing identical shirts. She recalls being stood at the edge of his bar, all kitted-out in heels and an orange Lycra dress. "Orvuh there luvlee girl," he said, pointing with a sovereign-ring-squished finger. She called this guy the Snot, and not just because it rhymed with his real name, Scot, but because he was a sleazy bastard who'd plied Ruby with a whack of charlie, before telling her to ride him on his leather recliner for three hours straight! At the time, Ruby had no choice... skint and stuck in the middle of nowhere, he said he'd pay in coke. She saw a darkness behind his eyes, like he'd topped somebody, so had no choice but to comply.

Girlo was never backward in coming forward, and if she didn't get the gig, at least she could wangle a few free drinks. Deep down, she enjoyed the sexual power and justified it as feminist research, having recently started a course in creative writing. Her slicked back red ponytail whipped her shoulder blades as she strutted her stuff up towards the stage. She mounted the podium, and as the urban beats of Faithless began to pound her soles, she slipped a hand up-and-down the pole. *Watch me ride her,* she mouthed. "Grind those hips luvlee girl," shouted the Snot. The quart of vodka she'd downed in the bogs was starting to kick in and her inhibitions were melting away as she swung around the pole like a pro Go-go girl.

Koko Bar was a creepy dive of a place. From the podium she could see the cubbies filling up with the razor-burned necks of twatty blokes, eager to blow their poxy call centre 'dollar' on shots, sniff and pussy. The place stunk of sweaty-palmed porn addicts and sports-socked feet, riddled with long-term yeast infections. After half-an-hour, Girlo was beginning to think that this wasn't an audition at all. The Snot wasn't even looking. He was shouting down the phone.

"Right! That should be enough 'en!" she shouted, as Britney Spears' tits burst onto the screen behind her.

"What uv we go' by yuh then? Yewer uh feisty one, in ewe? Yewell finish when I tell you to dahlin'... now carry on dancen, like a good girl."

"Time's up 'Luvlee Boy.'"

After a longish pause, tapping his repro Rolex, he said, "not what we're looking for dahling,"

"Ruby wuz right, yewah a fucken prick!"

"Yewah a fiery one, in ewe?" He was chuckling, as she stood, hand on hip, a wet pout smudged across her chops. She jumped off the podium and took out her phone.

"I got better places to be than this shit hole." Her battery was dead.

"Oh, woah woah..."

"No, fuck you. Fuckin' dragged me down yer for nuffin." He slipped his arm around her waist. His Paco Rabanne was blinding.

"Tell ewe wha', why dun ewe go and sit up at the bar and owuh new barman will mix you up a couple of cocktails. 'Ows about that swee'art?"

What she really wanted to do was take off her stiletto and slit his big-fat Playdough nose. He pulled her body. She could feel the heat of his lob-on pressing into her thigh.

"Yew like a bit uv tha', sexy girl?"

"Nah, yer alright. Ruby said yew were no bigger than her little finger... she was tha' bored tha' she fell asleep when yew were in 'er. Yew cun shove yer fuckin' job and yuh cocktails and yuh little cock up yer arse!"

"Trust, yewell av it one day luvlee girl, believe me... yewell 'av it!"

DAMAGED GOODS

The glass brick windows were sucking up the angry sun outside, spluttering murk all over the walls, onto the floor and into Girlo's head, which churned the line 'how will you pay for it now, little woman?'

Then *he* crept in—scorched the corners of the cell. Half-formed memories came like old-skool overexposed photos. She could feel him. Hear his gibber. Her palms gushed. Palpitations flicked up through her throat. Then, it all rushed back: that night in the flat, ten years ago; she was seventeen again. It was a school night and she'd acted all high-and-mighty when one of the boys placed a cloth taxi moneybag of magic mushrooms on the grotty coffee table.

"I'll do us a brew," she'd announced, even though she'd never done them before. She didn't give a rat's arse about revising for her exams the next day. *How will you pay for it now, little woman?*

The kitchen was an inferno, radiator belting and a gang doing hot-knives on open gas flames. She filled a pot with hot water and began to toss the shrooms in by the handful. A bottle of rum circulated and before long, the facial features of the boys started to curl into thin wisps then fall away like the slain vampires of Tarantino's *From Dusk till Dawn*. A strange synchronicity ensued as they found themselves in Super Mario Land, climbing virtual stairs within the chip-board walls of the council flat. The lounge was submerged under sea level, with the rag-rolled walls undulating around Girlo. She was in the eye of a tornadic waterspout. *She needed out.* Then an amphibious face tried to mouth something she couldn't hear as if from underwater. She needed to swim up. Breathe. Be free. So, she pushed open the window, and through the fine-mist rain, over the leather rooftops—there—in the distance, was the football pitch: the fresh, wet grass beckoning her. The rain, kaleidoscopic through her teary eyes.

She could smell the earth of her valley.

She had the urge to fly. Strip off all her clothes and dive into the mud. Slide over its entire length. She gripped the slippery fin of a shark smoking a spliff.

"Drive me a drag." He placed the tip into her open mouth, and she nipped it from his grip. "Sorry, but I need this for where I'm going." She mounted the windowsill and put her hands in her cardigan pockets—stretching them out, like wings, behind her.

Next thing she was scrunched up in a clapped-out camp bed with some demented prick humping her leg. *Stay in the light. Stay in the light.* The naked bulb from the landing light cast a triangular beacon across the Artex ceiling. Loops of luminescence moved, smooth, in the grooves like the bioluminescence of a giant squid. *Stay in the light. Stay in the light.* Even if the slightest wisp of shadow touched the trusted light, then he would reappear: the red-eyed monkey, and with serrated teeth, he'd gnaw on his own arm, before laughing wildly and doing backflips. *Stay in the light.* She focused hard. Double vision. *Stay in the light.* Then came the blur. Iridescent contours of bubble elephants gently bopped and merged on contact. Her body softened, melded with the figures for what felt like hours, days, years even. BOOM. Brought back to shitty reality with a bump. She was still on the camp bed but the horny leg humper had fucked off. From the shapes passing over the landing light—in came the **BLACK**—and with it the BOOM BOOM boom-box, drum & bass beating the thin walls. The camp bed started to pull her down into its fusty folds where she sweated. Fast breath. Paralysed, she searched for something, a beacon. Beyond the folds, it squinted, like a tip of a pen torch in a far-off forest. *Come follow me, come follow me.* The torch turned into the gold-capped molar of her Nannie Pearl, which glinted as she threw back her head to laugh. She was joking, smoking, socialising in a red wine glow. Girlo called to her, and she stopped.

"Over here," Girlo cried, "I'm here." A fungi tentacle slid up her oesophagus, then back down to coil around her innards, constricting her thrashing heart. A ripping belch—Acid fireworks—BOOMS. Blooms. Fucking mushrooms! BOOSHHH *Find the light, find the light.* Dissolving clouds of glittery dust. *Stay in the light. Stay in the light.*

In a sneaky crack of black, *he* was there, sat slobbering and gibbering—that was the first time she saw The White Monkey. He leapt up, and with his bear-trap teeth, clamped onto her cheek. She jumped up: slapping herself. But the little fucker wouldn't let go! She rushed to the bathroom, but it was floor-to-ceiling flesh—sweating, pulsating griege skin—slashed to expose pink, bloodless wounds. The door was gone. She pushed her palms into the wall. All she could feel was cool clammy flesh and her own waning heartbeat. She had to get in the bath—at first it worked—she felt safe as a baby bean stuck to the wall of a womb. She even drifted off into a comfortable kip until she remembered her Nannie Pearl's story about Dirty Don who'd lured a poor girl to a skag den where she OD'd and died alone in an empty bath. The girl was there for well over a week. People came and went, but no-one even noticed and when the undertakers lifted her corpse, half of her face ripped off and stuck to the bath like undercooked fish skin.

Girlo got the fuck up.

The White Monkey had gone.

The door had come back.

She splashed her face, but in the mirror she saw the face of age—her old-woman-self. Her hands were wrinkled, knuckles coarse. She tried to shake it off. She flicked her fingers but her chipped nail varnish came alive, spurting blood into the air until it turned into a smattering of broken countries. On one thumb there was a country shaped like a pig's head, riddled with decay, and on the other, a city… trains and motorways of micro-people, self-contained and state-tamed, who believed they had *very* important things to do and *very* important places to be. *She had somewhere important to be.* A waft of golden Ganga smoke spiralled in. With it came the softness of her Nannie Pearl's 'tumps-of-love' cwtches. She recalled the slowness of her silver-ringed hands, deliberately rolling and folding a pristine deck. Herby smoke. Synapses snapping the fizz of thought. An easing of gasp and kiss of imagination transcending. A fairy-lit tree beside Nannie Pearl's hearth where time stopped for a moment—just for them—to honour the tales of their times, told in a wealth of shared belly-laughter.

SEX ON LEGS

Ruby waited in the Cop Shop. Her legs hinged over the counter with the crease of her perky little arse peeking through her fringed denim cut-offs.

"She's not suicidal, officer. She's a twenty-two-year-old student whose got pissed and locked up!"

"And does she need her medication for the Manic Depression, ADHD, Anxiety?" The officer scrolled down his screen. "I cun go ask her if you like."

She pierced his gaze with her baby-blues until he shied away. "Oh! Hang on a minute... I know you."

His face turned a shade of pink.

"I don't think so, Miss." A strip of moisture broke out on his brow while Ruby tongued the temple tip of her Gucci sunglasses.

"I never forget a face, or a fetish." She winked, the roots of her lashes flashing a diamante trim. (This copper had recently paid her a routine visit where, in exchange for his silence she'd satisfied his mysophillic inclinations). "Don't tell me you can't remember the naughty lunch we shared?"

He shuffled some desk papers.

"Don't tell me you can't get my girl out... for your favourite—"

"Take a seat please, Miss. I'll see what I can do."

Ruby lifted her cleavage off the counter, sauntered towards the seating area and parked her arse.

"There's a good boy," she laughed.

SLAM

Back in the cell, Girlo paced the floor. The walls were closing in, thoughts overflowing as she circled the tiny floorspace. *Come tomorrow, little woman, and I'll tell you then, what I have decided overnight?* The bolt on the viewing slot unlocked. She rushed to suck some air from the corridor, but the blackhead-studded nose of a copper appeared.

"Calmed down a bit now then uv you love?"

"Why am I in here?"

"All I know is that when they brought you in, you tried to make a run for it but went the wrong way and ran into the cells. Me and the boys had a right ole chuckle this morning."

"I think something might've happened to me last night."

"Righteo. D'you wanna cuppa?"

"Am I allowed my phone call please?" Her plan was to ring Ruby. She wouldn't involve her Nannie Pearl in this—she'd fucking kill her after what she'd put her through last time.

"Not much point. You should be out within the hour, now."

She could smell tobacco on his breath.

"Can I have a fag please?"

"Dew! You don't want for much, d'you?" The copper went to close the slot.

"Sorry, one last thing: I'm bleeding, I am. Don't suppose ewe got eneefin?"

He blushed. "Er... I'll send a female officer over as soon as she comes on shift."

"But..." It was too late. He'd already shut the slot and she was left with *The Dread* again. *How will you pay for it now, little woman, when your husband is on strike?* He wasn't a bad copper though—not like the last bastard who nearly snapped her arm the first time she ever went clubbing in Newport. There was a ruckus, and she was only looking out for her dick-head boyfriend, who stupidly decided to start on the bouncers. They smashed his head through a six-foot solicitors' window. He'd started on a gang of Pyll boyos because apparently, *she* was getting too much attention.

Girlo didn't want to think about all that now, she was meant to have left that life behind her when she started university. She was meant to be proper now. *How had this happened again? Why was she so stupid?* With thoughts of self-hatred ruminating, she tried to force a kip but the booze was wearing off and the nuggets

16

of glass in her feet seemed to be growing. Lost gobs of memory began to rise again... POP *ankles shackled* POP *fingernails bend right back* POP the stench of Paco Rabanne POP *hair drenched in backstreet slashes* POP *knees, torn, hands, raw...*

She had scraped herself up off the floor, onto the wall, then stumbled through the glass of a broken Beck's bottle that had been smashed in a despotic display of rage. She didn't feel a fucking thing, but that was the point. Her stilettos were off, but the ankle straps were still attached, shoes swinging underfoot. They tripped her up as she ricocheted between the walls of piss-alley. Her purse, fag-box and dead Motorola flip-phone skidding into the puddles of piss. She felt her wrists for the amethyst bangles Nannie Pearl had given her for sobriety but they'd snapped off. As she fell out of the alley, she could see the Retro's sign: it was a safe place because it played songs from the good old times. She sat on the kerb to pull her shoes on. They pinched her ankles like the weight of a dancing chain, and with every step, the balls of her feet felt like they were being carved with a carpenter's hook knife. Swathes of men jacked-up on testosterone and wombling women populated the street to set the scene for a night of animalistic hedonism and extreme inebriation. To her right, she saw a woman whose skirt had ridden up so high she could see the folds of her flabby labia as she bent over to vomit, while a bloke nearby took a dump in the gutter. *Is this who we are?* She had reached the philosophical level of drunk where epiphanies blossomed like sea anemones. She supposed this was bound to happen: her youth had prepared her for this. Across the nation, kids just like her would be getting bolloxed on white cider until they passed out. With Blair's golden ticket of *education, education, education,* the fledgling adults were living hard and fast with wallets full of Promised Land credit cards, and who could blame them? She found a cigarette. The cork was wet with piss so she tore it off then lighter-dried the rest before sparking it up. Nothing like a fag to sort you out, she thought, as she sprung up at the bar and downed two dog-rough shots. The fire coursed through her and hit the synapses like the explosion from a long, drawn-out orgasm.

BANG

She was back. *Don't see—Don't feel—Don't breathe*—All me—
All FUCKING ME. She'd schmoozed her way in through the
bouncer-clad doorway of Retro's. Totally off-her-fucking-face, she
was surprisingly on form! Just going with the flow, she tried to act
mega chilled... super cool... taking to the dancefloor when 'The
Time of my Life' started playing. She'd watched Dirty Dancing so
many times as a kid. The boys would do the final lift with her in
the pool, just like Patrick Swayze and Baby did in the lake.

"Ready? One. Two. Three. Now I've had the time of my
life." She'd launch herself at them in her itsy-bitsy bikini, their
bony thumbs digging into the crevices of her prepubescent pelvis.
But they never managed to lift her all the way up. Even if they
did, they couldn't hold her for long.

In the packed club Girlo slinked through the strobe lights like a
jaguar beneath a parapet of rainforest Silva in a Catatumbo storm.
She was suddenly infatuated with the idea of recreating those
virtuous swimming pool days when she needn't worry about opening her legs for validation. The song continued, *Now, I've finally
found someone.* Time was running out for the Big Lift. Unknown
dendroid torsos became mottled in the depths of the dance-floor
distance as the myopic lights encumbered her quest to find the one
who could hold her mid-air! Her feet became unsteady as her
stupid stilettos skidded through the slime of the blighted floor. But
there, beyond the swathe of heads and arms prickling like a puddle
pelted by a rainstorm, was a stage! And there was a mob of skinny
guys, like meerkats in aloha shirts, awkwardly perched on the edge
next to the steps. Girlo resumed her she-cat status and, gripping
the helping hand of a pimple-faced fresher, stepped up onto it.

"Will you *dirty dance* lift me?" Her request was like magma
being poured into his ear. He may have misunderstood, but thought
it sounded sexy, and maybe she could be the one to alleviate the

very painful hard-on he'd been nursing in his pants all evening.

"Go down there." She pushed him down the stairs and pointed to the centre of the dance floor, where he was meant to await her descent and prepare for the big finale. "There! Ready?" *This was her time.* The time of her life! The song had reached the part where Baby is lifted off the stage and glides towards Swayze like Odette from Swan Lake. 'This could be love—'

Unfortunately, this wasn't the movies. She clumsily alighted the stage, falling to her knees, then pulled herself up on the arm of a bystander. Under the strobe light she skated blindly towards the poor chap who looked like a bemused toddler lost in a supermarket, waiting for his mother to come back.

"Ready? Ready?" she called "BECAUSE! I've haaaad..." She thrust her entire body, and her open mouth, into the guy— ripping open his dimpled chin with a set of ultra-violet incisors. They both ended up in a tangled mash on the floor, blood pissing everywhere! The guy cried into the crowd of shocked onlookers: "Stupid fucking cow! What the fuck was that?!"

In a flash, a bouncer lifted her up and hoisted her out the door BOOSH.

The cold air hit her like a Geordie kiss. She found herself in a mangled mess in the gutter, the bouncer kicking her aside like a used chip tray.

"My bag! I need to get my bag," she pleaded. "Can't let you back in now, love. You're too drunk. *State*, like!" He laughed in the face of his leather-jacketed friend.

"But, but... how am I meant to get home? I need my purse. I haven't got any money to get home like. Please can you just let me get my bag? I'll be straight in and out." Girlo had been in this situation many times before, so she liked to think that she had some valuableexperience talking the bouncers down.

"Can't love. Manager won't allow it. Watch out the way." A gaggle of tinsel-eyed totty wafted their feather boas in her face, *here come the girls! Girls, girls.*

"Oh, watch where you're putting that love!" snapped Girlo. The bouncers towered over, a leather wall of folded arms.

19

"Iss alright for them to come in, buh no' meee like? Iss-iz fucksen rudicoolus iss iz. Wha' about them?" The bouncer pinched a girl's bum as she sprang over the threshold.

"They are not off their fuckin' 'eads, on their own in town, uh they?"

Girlo looked down at her bloody knees and flicked her piss-drenched hair.

"Now, outtuh the way!"

Another gaggle of twenty-somethings approached.

"Evening Ladies," the bouncers drooled.

"You gonna chuck her out as well 'en?" shouted Girlo.

"If needs be. Unless I fancy's takin' 'er ome like." The bouncer laughed at his dickhead mate again. Girlo turned around and a big gang of men had rocked up, wearing rugby jerseys.

"Oi, Oi... wanna suck on this babe?"

"I'll take you home gorgeous, you can ride this all night!" one of them said, grabbing his crotch.

"This fucking prick won't let me get my bag."

"Not our problem, love."

"I'm not drunk. I slipped on their soaking wet dancefloor, fucking elff 'azad, tha' iz!"

"You are only ouwer problem when you are in yere."

"You just chucked me out!"

"Clever Girl! Now, move out the way. ID lads?"

"Fuck you, CUNT!" Girlo hacked up a large phlegmy and gobbed it straight in the bouncer's eye.

"Stay there, I'm ringing the fuzz! Cheeky little slut! Grab her, Moosh!"

SLAM

Back in the cell, she was still bleeding. Red spotted the floor like pixie kisses. She was feeling mega grotty and her gums were starting to rot. The air was thinning and her mind was playing tricks on her. *He* was back from the dark place. He was doing somersaults in the shadows of her cell, and beneath his paws, the red was spreading—multiplying like bacteria. She was weak with worry; paper-thin and petrified. The not-knowing was crippling. She felt clipped—SNIP-SNIP little scissors cutting shapes from her mind, until it felt like a botched snowflake hanging by a dusty thread. SNIP-SNIP She smoothed the bruises on her wrists. She deserved this. *A nasty little whore. Little bitch.* SNIP-SNIP A dangerous woman. Loud-mouth bitch. SNIP-SNIP *brought this on yourself.* Little bitch. SNIP-SNIP. She rested her eyes and, as the words began to drift, the snipping surpassed and silence, a black canvas presented itself in her mind's eye, with the words, *need to be alone, want to be alone, should be alone. I am Vodka*, staple-gunning themselves into a new line. After some time, the slot slid open and a sanitary towel, the size of a life raft, was pushed through. It hit the floor with a PUDD.

"Wait! Do you mind if I get my phone call please?"

"If I had a pound for every time I heard that?"

Girlo looked through the slot. She was confronted by a new copper, a woman. She looked like Cogsworth from Beauty and the Beast—square frame, short eyebrows and thin lips. Her nice copper had been replaced with a *clock copper.*

"Could I possibly have something to eat?" She tried to come across like an innocent schoolgirl, but the copper would not be fooled.

"What d'you think this is, a five-star hotel?"

To Girlo's surprise, ten minutes later, the copper shoved a cardboard box of microwaved curry through the bean chute. Tasted like puke. She really wanted to protest that it was her legal right to a phone call, but she'd made a similar mistake before, singing the entire Tracy Chapman album, emphasising all the lyrics slating the police. *It won't do no good to call—the poh-lice...*

"You should go on Pop Idol," the police mocked as she'd bashed the door with all her might. The aggressive approach was lost on these pigs, she needed to keep her mouth shut and wait patiently. They couldn't keep her in for more than 24 hours—she knew that at least. She needed to keep sane, keep tapping out rhythms, lines, words of reproach, poems of power, songs of freedom. *How will you pay for that, little woman, now your husband is on strike and full of the fiery language?* She scratched her head to stimulate the flow and searching her scalp for scabs of text and lyrics, she discovered a bobby pin lodged in the dread-like mass of her hair. *Full of the fiery language.* In the still of the cell, in the blank-canvas silence, she scratched a poem into the state-owned mattress, and, as she wrote, told herself that when she got out she'd spray paint her fiery language all over town—all over the big-dick statues and skyscrapers.

She might not have her freedom, but she could still write.

I AM VODKA

Vodka
Taste
the numb.
Bite
me.
Want
to cum.
Dumb
my clit.
Throw a fit.
Fight or flight.
Want to hit then run
with until I'm done with

VODKA

Feed me with VODKA. Need to be alone. Should be. Would be could be. On my dirty knees, love me. Tease. Push me. Hate me please. Fake me. Can't see. Be. Don't feel. Can't be them, you, nor me. I'm breathing in

VODKA

Profound surround sound. On a rebound, unfound. No-one around. Unbound in the love of VODKA. Clarity of VODKA Running-through-your-veins VODKA. Blocking-out-the-world VODKA. Only friend, VODKA. ALL FUCKING ME. MY

VODKA

Taste it, taste the numb.

I AM VODKA

PRINCESS

When Grandmamma called Girlo her 'lickle princess' she never felt so special in all her life! Grandmamma was a very particular woman who ritualised every task. For breakfast she'd fold porridge into Pyrex bowls then dunk a 'special' commemorative silver spoon into the Lyles Golden Syrup tin. With one swift twist she'd scoop just the right amount to drizzle over the steaming bowls. From the corner of her cashmere elbow Girlo waited with delight. Grandmamma would always give in to her demands to have "just one spoon of Chree-ckul?"

"Just the one, then… or you'll spoil your porridge," she'd say, rolling her Rs.

"Thank you, Granma."

"I am not your Gran-ma. I am your Grandmamma," she'd say, accentuating the D. Then, after pouring on just a *smidge* of milk she'd serve it to Girlo, who relished the act of seeking the golden pools of treacle nestled between the silken oats.

As a woman of the 50s, Grandmamma had a very high standard of appearances to keep up. She never forgot her manners and made sure Girlo didn't either.

"Don't speak with your mouth full, Princess."

"What?"

"What? I think you mean *pardon*—not *what*."

"*Pardon*… sorry, Grandmamma." And, when Girlo coughed, Grandmamma would remind her to put her hand in front of her mouth. When she burped, Grandmamma would always say: "pardon you for being so rude…"

"…it was not me; it was my food. It only popped up to say hello…"

"And now it's gone back down below!" they'd recite in

unison. When Girlo asked to be excused to use the toilet, Grandmamma would remind her to "use only one square of toilet paper." She was religiously thrifty.

"Ok, Grandmamma… but, what if I need a poo?"

"Don't talk about number twos at the table please!"

Above the dining table there was a plaque engraved with words Girlo preferred to sing rather than recite. *Christ is the Head of this House. The unseen guest at every meal. The silent listener to every conversation.* At every mealtime she sang those words out loud so he'd know she was paying attention and would look after her. Grandmamma went to church *every* Sunday and did her bit for charity, 'helping the blind'. She had a big old grandfather clock which, just like church or school, dominated the living-room like a Headmaster with a searching, probing eye. He bellowed every hour on the hour. BOING-BOING he went, never failing to make Girlo jump right out of her skin. Grandmamma wound him *every* morning at 9am, and despite his omnipresence, his steadfast tick provided a sort of stability where each second seemed to last a lifetime. Of all the things in the living-room, it was the china cabinet that was Grandmamma's pride and joy. It housed a large collection of Charles & Diana memorabilia, and under no circumstances was anyone even allowed to *look* inside, because *looking* meant *touching*—and then the breaking or losing of her most-precious-of-things. Girlo loved the replica gilded carriage from the Royal wedding.

"Oh, please? Please. Please. Please, Grandmamma. Please can I have a look at the carriage?"

"You can *look* with your eyes," Grandmamma called from the pantry. Girlo pushed her kitten-nose up against the glass; breath obscuring her view of the titchy, filigree wheels and crests adorning its bodywork. As she sighed, the mist grew heavier, and in her mind, she shrunk right down to the size of Thumbelina and saw herself gliding along in the plush Royal carriage—her crown jewels winking with every *jejune beau geste*.

"What is Princess Diana like?" asked Girlo.

"She is the People's Princess... so kind, and beautiful and generous—just like yew."

"I think she looks sad." Girlo peered in to admire the Princess; her crown too heavy for her head and her big poufy sleeves making her arms look like ivory toothpicks. "I wonder if I'll marry a prince one day, Grandmamma."

"I'm sure you will, my Cariad, I'm sure *you* will."

"Tell me about her dress again."

"Her dress? Well, her dress was the most beautiful dress..."

"Made of silks and satins and diamonds?" They had rehearsed this conversation many times before.

"Yes. It was made of the finest silk and satin, and the sparkliest diamonds."

"I wish I was a *real* princess, Grandmamma."

"You are a real princess! You're my lickle princess."

"Did you want to be a princess when you grew up?"

"All little girls want to be princesses, Cariad."

"What did you do before you made porridge?"

"I used to work in service. Before that I was a Land Girl."

"What's a Land Girl, Grandmamma?"

"During the war, while yewer grandfather was away fighting, us women had to work in the factories and on the land. We had to keep the country going while they were away, see."

"Who made the porridge?"

"We did. And we carried on cooking and cleaning and mending and looking after the children."

"What did they make in the factreez?"

"Well, they made bombs to help win the war."

"Did you make bombs?!"

"No... I worked on the land, digging up lovely potatoes to have for supper, and picking juicy apples from the trees, then I cleaned a big grand house for a well-to-do family in the city.

"Can I have a toffee please?"

"After yewer dinner, fanakapan!"

BOING-BOING

At twelve o'clock sharp they'd have a full cooked dinner: potatoes boiled with onion, thinly sliced runner beans and sticky sausages all washed down with lashings of thick gravy. Grandmamma doused her dinner in vinegar, then soaked up the remaining gravy with a bit of bread, slicing and forking it into her mouth in a most gentile fashion. She had a very precise way of laying the table and went to unprecedented lengths in its adorning for lunch; using a selection of table coverings, including a base table-cloth of starched cotton to protect the wooden top of her drop-leaf table, then a decorative, crochet garment placed on top, followed by two folded tea-towels, rested beneath their placemats. The faces of the Renaissance angels on the placemats looked lovingly up at Girlo as she patiently waited for her dinner. After saying their prayers, they ate in silence, placing shiny forkfuls of gravy-smothered fried onions into their mouths. *Pure heaven.*

"Grandmamma, could I have a glass of pop please?" At Nannie Pearl's they'd have 'Council Pop.' This was how the adults sold the idea of tap water, always a disappointment because pop is meant to be fizzy!

"Eat a little bit more of your potato first," Grandmamma would insist, before bringing a glass of crisp lemonade in a frosted glass that reminded Girlo of Cinderella's slippers. At Nannie Pearl's they were lucky if they could find a cup.

Girlo gobbled up Grandmamma's strict rules, stern scheduling, and endless supply of toffee. Grandmamma was in remarkably good condition for her age, with all her own teeth and the most flawlessly smooth skin, which she'd maintained with a lifelong skincare regime of Oil of Ulay and Nivea cold cream. But in the middle of her cupid's bow was a small blood blister.

"What's that, Granma?" Girlo asked, looking up as she lolled in her tartan lap.

"Grandmamma!" she'd corrected.

"What's that on your lip, Grandmamma?"

"A naughty little faery princess bit me."

"But she didn't *mean* to—" Girlo could feel the uncomfortable heat of guilt seeping into the nape of her neck.

"It was only by accident, she got carried away kissing me."

"Can we sing the song?"

"There was a little girl, who had a little curl..." Grandmamma began.

"RIGHT in the middle of her fohm-head."

"Forehead," Grandmamma corrected, rolling her R. "When she was good, she was *very*...

Girlo straightened up with a toothy grin.

"But, when she was bad, she was horrid!" Grandmamma concluded in a very stern tone, tickling Girlo's ribs.

Girlo never did have a curl in the middle of her forehead. Instead, she had a feathery fringe and an arrow-straight parting, which Grandmamma had etched into her head before curling her fine hair into pink foam curlers before bed. Grandmamma ritualistically curled her own white hair every night too, and her great-grandchildren always laughed at her because she'd use a pair of her full briefs to protect the curls.

"Why do you wear knickers on your head Grandmamma?" Her grandkids would mock.

"To keep my curlers in at night!" She'd snap. Grandmamma was usually a very patient woman—she'd have to be with four unruly grandsons—but she had a sharp edge to her. Girlo's father, Eric and his brothers were often threatened with The Tickler—a cane she kept in the pantry. But Girlo was a good girl. She never got The Tickler and lived quite happily with Grandmamma after her mother had 'fucked off and left you with me and Grandmamma,' as Nannie Pearl put it.

BOING-BOING

Girlo remembers the day when she was ripped away from Grandmamma's summer lawn. She was five years old. She was helping Grandmamma with the weeding, wearing her ruby red shoes (which were so grown-up and *princessy*). They were about to tuck into some freshly pulled rhubarb with sugar when there was a rumble of car tyres on gravel and her mother's voice calling up from behind a large butterfly-dotted Buddleia.

"Come on! We've got to get going."

"Crystal, what a surprise!"

"Thanks for having her, Alice, but we've got to get going now."

"Get going where?"

"I've found us a lovely place by the coast…"

"Not too far then?"

"In England. We're gonna have a fresh start. Just the three uv us."

Image-wise, Crystal modelled herself on Madonna: a back-combed hairdo, clumpy blue mascara and a New Romantics black dot puncturing her right cheekbone. She wore tight, tie-dyed cropped tops to smother her big boobs, with high-waist leggings to hide a ladder of scars that had weaved itself up from her belly-button. Her stretchmarks were 'the kids' fault.' Everything was.

"I want to stay with Grandmamma. I want to stay here. Granma, please don't let her take me." Crystal grabbed Girlo's hand. Girlo could feel her nails digging in as she dragged her away.

"No. No. I like it here! I want to stay… Grandmamma, can I stay?"

"She's your mother, love. You'll have to do what she says."

Girlo screamed and tried to run back but her mother had a firm grip on her.

"What about her things?"

"Dolly! Dolly!" She'd been given a beautiful doll with black hair and a *magic* iridescent dress.

"You can send them on—"

"Come on, Crystal? Come on in and have a cup of tea. Let's all calm down a bit, shuh we?"

"She'll be fine in a minute. Once we get going, she'll forget all about it. We've got the new house to look forward to. She'll be excited... won't you, love?"

"Grandmamma, I want to stay with you. Please. Please! Please!"

"Does Eric know?"

But it was too late, Crystal shoved Girlo into the back of a battered blue Astra with a strange man sitting in the driver's seat. Crystal was magnetic to non-committal arseholes who seemed to prey on her pain. Men just couldn't resist her wounded bird act. Once-upon-a-time she'd had a spark but over the years booze and disappointment had slowly killed it off.

Girlo seethed with anger.

"Where's Eddie?"

"We're picking him up on the way."

"On the way *where*?"

"Shush now! Put your seatbelt on."

Girlo flung herself back so hard that she whacked her head.

"Where's Eddie gonna sit? I can't even sit proper with all this stuff. Who is that man?"

"Come on now, you remember me, dun ewe?" the man said in a jovial tone. "I'm your Uncle Groggy. I live with your Auntie Beryl."

"We're going to stay with them for a while."

"What about Dad? Does Nannie know? I don't want to go!"

"You will dooo as yuh told!"

Girlo screamed so hard that Grandmamma ran over to the car and started hitting the window. "Are you ok, Princess? Don't worry. Just listen to your mother now. Be a good girl, won't you?"

"She's fine!" Crystal hissed. She slapped Girlo's legs.

"Oi! That's enough now!"

"It's not fair!"

"Life izunt fair!"

When the car pulled up at Nannie Pearl's, Eddie was playing in front of the raspberry bush, wrestling Tyson the Alsatian with a big stick. When Crystal jumped out of the passenger seat, Grand-dad Miles appeared in the doorway.

"Where's Pearl?" Demanded Crystal.

"Nipped out for some milk. Everything a'right, Crys?"

"We've come for Eddie. Where's his stuff?" Eddie wore a Roland Rat T-shirt and no nappy because the weather was still warm. Crystal swept him up into her arms and pushed past a gobsmacked Grandad Miles.

"Whoah... hold your horses, Crys—Pearl'll be back now in a minute."

"We've got to beat the traffic, Miles." And just like that, they were gone.

As soon as they got onto the motorway Girlo and Eddie fell asleep and when Girlo woke up, she was in an unknown bed that smelled of mouldy onions. A strip of light came from the crack in the door and lit the side of a flaky radiator covered in thin black socks—in the darkness it looked like someone had trailed a tin of black paint along the top. She heard a creak from the landing and the footsteps of someone who was not her mother. The door swung open. Her eyelids flickered open and closed. Through the slits she could see the bitty outline of a man tiptoeing into the room. Then he paused and took a step back over the threshold. *What was he doing?* Then he slipped fully in and softly closed the door behind him. The doorknob squeaked. He took off his jeans. The change from his pockets tumbled onto the bare floorboards beside the bed.

"Shh. It's ok," he whispered. He unpeeled the covers and climbed into the bed. Eddie was asleep, the rise and fall of his baby ribcage pulling at the quilt. Girlo just lay there. Stiff. Bolt-awake in the lumpy bed of the pitch-black room, pretending to be asleep.

That was the night that Girlo lost her princess status. She knew that this was it: she'd no longer be sleeping under Grandmamma's Welsh quilt in her queen-sized orthopaedic bed with lavender-scented pillows and a starched top-sheet gently warmed by an electric blanket. She just lay there, still, picturing the portrait that hung above Grandmamma's bed; of the Lord Jesus, holding his lamb and a crook, watching over them both as they slept.

INVISIBLE

Girlo and Eddie burst into the rooms of their new Georgian house. It was a world away from their tiny council house in Wales.

"This is my bedroom," called Girlo.

"My, mine," copied Eddie.

Then Crystal lead them down to the basement, where she opened the door of a store cupboard.

"You'll both be in yere for the time being kids. Just until something better comes up."

The house was full of smugglers who'd fled the starving valleys to make a few bob from across the channel.

"It's a squat, Ber," Crystal said to her sister, kicking a double mattress on the floor of her new bedsit.

"It won't be long Crys. There's people moving out all the time. Something better will come up, I promise."

Girlo couldn't sleep that night. She could hear shrieking laughter, the thud of feet and music playing, and the front door slamming all the time. The bunk bed she slept on was like something from a prison; tinny metal frame with a chain-fence holding the mattress in place. It made an ear-splitting squeak every time she or Eddie turned over. She got up. On the top floor she stood by a draughty window, scraping the black gunk from the corners of the frame with a bobby pin. In the darkness below, she saw something. *Was it human?* He scampered around a fire, hunched over—ape-like, with flecks of flame glinting in his eyes. Just then a cat popped up from behind the brambles and trotted along the high wall, before plopping down next to the figure. The tiny fire blazed under the ape-like man's watchful eye as he sucked on a skinny roll-up, then flicked it in the fire. He jabbed at the cat with the tip of his steel-toe-capped boot. The cat nuzzled in, thinking he was being affectionate.

33

"Fuck off, you mangy bastard!" he said, kicking the poor thing in the face.

"Don't, Uncle Groggy!" Girlo cried, but it was too late, the terrified thing shot into the darkness. Groggy drained his can of Tennent's and threw it into the flames. As he did an unexpected wind picked up one of the embers, flicking a pearl of fire straight into his eye.

Groggy was a dogsbody. Heavy-set, with a 'beer-belly' paunch. He always wore a khaki army shirt with the sleeves rolled up to reveal his hairy, blue-inked arms. His eyes were dead black beads. He hid his mouth behind an unkempt, spiky moustache streaked with bits of gloss paint and yellowed from chain smoking. His nails were thick, brown, and seemed to grow around the tips of his fingers like claws. He was always trying to get paint off his hands. "When you've run out of turps, get some butter… you need a good bit of butter to get the bastard stuff off," he'd say, pinching a pat of grease, fingered from the butter dish. Auntie Beryl thought she was artsy because she wore throwback 70s print shifts with matching bandanas. She blended into the background like a two-dimensional paper doll, cut-out from a dog-eared copy of Bunty, a thin, anaemic-looking woman with an insipid voice: "How's your eye now, love?"

"Speak up, woman!" bellowed Groggy from his throne-of-an-armchair. "Can't hear a bluddee word yewah saying!"

In Crystal's lounge-come-kitchen-come-master bedroom, a black-and-white television with a coat-hanger shoved in the back hissed static white noise.

"Give it another go, will ewe babe?" she called to Girlo as she prepared Spam and beans. Girlo crossed the room to wiggle the make-shift aerial, while Eddie sat at the squat plastic table with a snotty nose. "And wipe his nose for me, will ewe, love?"

Girlo twisted and turned the aerial until she got a picture. A very strict looking woman came on the screen.

"Who's that, Mam?"

"She's the Prime Minister." Women weren't meant to be Prime Ministers, thought Girlo, that was a man's job.

"But she's a woman!" Girlo could just make out her blue jacket and pearls.

"Yep. Turn it up. Let's see what the witch has got to say for herself."

A stern, posh, school mistress voice filled the room: "These are the most impressionable years of a child's life when the seeds of goodness are being sown. I teach my children all the best things in life," she said, "because then I know they will remember the best things when they are older. Those of us who have happy homes have a duty to teach our children the best."

Crystal slopped the food onto two scratched plastic plates.

"Eat up, kids!" She didn't have a stove—just a plug-in table-top hob and a kettle. She kept the milk in the leaky hand-basin in the corner of the room. She kept an ice-cream tub under the U-bend to catch the drips but always forgot to empty it so they'd all end up with ice-cream-flavoured socks.

"Mam, my socks are wet again!"

"Take them off and put them on the radiator then."

"It's not on!"

"Leave them on then… they'll dry out soon enough."

Beryl and Groggy had a much better set-up upstairs: a *whole* kitchen and a bathroom all to themselves. Beryl's cat used to do his biz under the furniture, and the kids would often encounter what Beryl referred to as 'little sculptures', while crawling around on the floor. Groggy had left his 'older model' with a brood of seven, but Beryl was childless.

"He likes kids. He's just like a big kid, himself," Beryl would say, "we dun mind having them for yew, do we, Grog?" So, the kids were told to 'play out of the way', in the cupboard under the stairs, while the adults got wasted. They made it quite cosy in there with a couple of cushions and their Happy Meal toys. Girlo liked to scratch pictures and words into the paintwork with a rusty nail.

"Ohm… I'm tellen," said Eddie.

"You fuckin' dare!" Warned Girlo, as she scratched a picture of a pregnant doll into the wall. Eddie was still a baby really. His

35

pudgy face looked like he had only just got out of the womb. Crystal said that he nearly killed her, 'split her in half!' during childbirth.

"Ruined my body, he did!"

Girlo was jealous when he was born and once scrawled his name on the wall with her left hand. "Eddie done it!"

But when they moved things changed. Crystal had to work, so Girlo became Eddie's Mammy. She changed his nappy, which hung like a hammock of jelly between his red-raw thighs, did his bockie and told him bedtime stories. There were people in and out of the house all the time. To Girlo they all looked the same: sunken jowls, missing teeth, sketchy eyes; all covered in stubble and stinking like a pub carpet. She never really understood what they were saying as everyone seemed to speak in code. Crystal covered her ears most of the time. Girlo tried to lip-read which was quite difficult when their faces were so warped and worn. The familiar door slam and a thud of feet climbing the stairs must've sent the kids off to sleep and Beryl and Groggy must've forgotten about them. But then Girlo woke abruptly to a slam and a gruff voice shouting: "Wuz me gear?" *What was this 'gear' they were always talking about?* Girlo thought. "Am clucking, I yam Beryl… and av paid oop-froont!" Eddie woke up.

"Shush. It's just the telly, don't worry." Girlo covered his ears and he started shoving matchsticks into the air-holes of a vent. Then she heard the backdoor swing open and Groggy shouting: "I just told yew to fuck off!" He turned to Beryl, "what 'ave I told yew?"

She tried to get up from the beanbag, but the polystyrene beads sank beneath her and before she could get away, he thrust himself at her. She fought under his weight, the fringes of Groggy's s biker jacket lashing through the air. Girlo heard the sound of slapping.

"Stop! Stop it!" cried Beryl, whacking at his studded shoulders, hands turning bloody. Girlo was too terrified to speak. She held her hand over Eddie's mouth.

PRETTY AS A PICTURE

Beryl never said nuffin. She never noticed nuffin neither. She never noticed when Groggy slurp-flicked his tongue at other women. She never noticed that he always wanted Girlo sat on his knee. And she certainly never noticed when he'd disappear for ages to 'tuck the kids in'. Girlo hoped she would notice something because she *really* loved her Auntie Beryl, and her paintbox eyeshadows and sweet lipsticks that didn't come in tubes like from her mother's forbidden cosmetics, but from a compact palette that tasted like petals instead. One day, when the snooker was on the telly, Girlo snuck into Beryl's bedroom. Everything was hard to make out because the curtains were closed all day but in the bottom of a drawer she found her Auntie Beryl's lipstick palette. It was shut stiff, so she opened it with her teeth. As she was digging her fingernail into her favourite candy pink, Beryl appeared.

"Woah, woah, woah, whatcha doin?" She slapped Girlo's hand so hard her fingers smudged the colours.

"Jus' trying on some lepsteck, Auntie Ber."

"Well, don't dig your finger in like that, use this." She took a teeny-tiny paintbrush which looked like something a mouse might use. "Which colour?" Asked Auntie.

"Pink!"

"You love pink, dun ewe. All little girls love pink!" Beryl carefully daubed the brush, "you are—let me do it for yew. Go like this…" She made an 'O' shape with her mouth. "First, we do the cupid bow… then the lips… good—that's it. Now, pucker up!" Girlo was absolutely loving this: she felt like a real woman. "Then you suck your thumb, like this…"

"There, you look pretty as a pic-chuh!"

"When I grow up, I wanna be just like you, Auntie Ber."

Beryl looked in the mirror.

"Grog? Come un 'ave a look," she called.

Groggy, who was lurking outside, popped his bald head in.

"Mmmm, good enough to eat girls!"

Why did she have to call him in for? thought Girlo, as she tried to get off to sleep that night. Her mam was going out again, so she was already tamping. This should've been one of her 'sleep nights', where she didn't have to layer up with tights, and knickers and pyjamas then lay awake in the ache of silence, waiting for the plod of his footsteps. She'd worry all night long, thinking of little songs or poems to keep her mind occupied... *Bright eyes, blonde hair, rosy cheeks, happy grin. Pink dress, hair a mess, yellow teeth, legs all thin.*

The next morning was a Saturday, and the Wide-Awake Club was on Auntie Beryl's telly. Timmy Mallet made Girlo squeamish when he stuck out his tongue and went "blurgh!" She didn't like tongues. She didn't really like Jim'll Fix It either, but he made kids' wishes come true, so she often thought of writing in to see if he could take her away and make her safe.

"Mam, can I write to Jim'll Fix it? He could get us a nice big house all to ourselves."

"Weyull see…"

"Mam? Can we get some sticky-back plastic, then?" was the usual retort. Girlo loved Blue Peter and they were always going on about sticky-back plastic. They only had Sellotape, and she thought she would never be able to construct the ambitious models without it. Sticky-black-plastic was superior to plain old ordinary Sellotape.

"Mam? Can you make me a birthday card and send it in on the telly?" Girlo also liked watching the birthday card segment before Playdays. She'd wait eagerly to see the face of the birthday girl or boy behind the little flaps of the homemade cards. It always made her sad when they read out the birthday wishes though. *Happy Birthday Gemima, lots of love from Mummy, Daddy, Baby Jake, Grandma and Grandad and Kitty the Cat!*

"Weyull see," replied Crystal, who reckoned only children whose parents worked for the BBC got their cards on TV.

"Can we get a cat and call it Kitty"

"Bugger off!"

Anyway, on this particular morning Girlo and Eddie were up while everyone else was still in bed. There wasn't any cereal in the cupboard so Girlo found a few soft biscuits in the bottom of the barrel. Her feet were like blocks of ice and she tried to keep them warm under her nightie, stretched over her legs. Her mother had slapped her on the thighs loads of times for doing this.

"You'll stretch the neck out... you think I'm made of money?"

Timmy's big square head jolted all over the screen as he bashed his pink and yellow mallet on the heads of two small children. Eddie shoved his Sippy cup down the back of the couch.

"Eddie! Wha' you like?" Girlo put her hand down the cushions; scratching at some gritty tobacco, scrunched up foil and spare change until she finally got to the ripped hole right at the back. Arm deep, face pressed into the stinky cushions, she searched blindly for his cup. Then, she grabbed something and pulled it out through the hole: a sports sock. She flicked it in Eddie's face.

"Smell that!"

"Ewww. My eye!"

She dived down again and this time found a tin. "Oooh, what's this?"

"Put it back!"

"Oh, shut up will ewe, Eddie! Let's ave look shu we?"

"I'm tellen!"

"I'm tellen. I'm tellen. I'm tellen! God, you're such a baby Eddie." She picked up a cushion and whacked him on the head. "Whack-a -whack-a!"

Eddie copied her, and they hopped and dived on and off the sofa, hitting each other with pillows. "Whack-a -whack-a!" until the tin fell off the arm and hit the tiled floor. Girlo picked up the tin. It was a battered looking thing, full of dents and scratches. She tried to pull off the top, but it was jammed from where someone had trodden on it. Eddie was overexcited with the game and continued to hit her over the head. "Whack-a -whack-a!"

"Shush, now Eddie. Let's see if we can get this open."

He hit her again with the cushion.

"We need a knife!" Girlo left Eddie playing the lava game, throwing himself from one sofa to the next and went into the kitchen. On the worktop she saw the handle of a kitchen knife the size of her arm. On her tippy toes she managed to grab it, slipping it from the sink and bringing it back into the living-room—holding the blade upright. Girlo thought nothing of it, her mother could use knives and she was a big girl, so so could she. Once, when Crystal was hungover in bed, the kids thought it would be a good idea to fill up the paddling pool in the living-room. It took them ages! They blew up the inflatable rings round the sides, then brought in saucepans and cup-after-cup of water to fill it.

"It's a magical pool! Let's dive in Eddie. We'll be safe in here, away from The White Monkey!"

When Crystal eventually dragged herself out of bed, she found a trail of sodden footprints and sloshes coming from the kitchen to the living-room and her two kids in their bathers having a splash in front of the telly.

"Are you for real?! You gotta be kidding me?! Get out of that FUCKING. Pool. Now!" She dragged their pool into the bathroom, and in a *super-strength* temper, pulled it up into the bathtub. "Right, that's it!" she shouted, and marched into the kitchen. They could hear the clash of the cutlery as she opened the drawer and rifled through it.

"What are you going to do Mam?"

"I'll show you what I'm going to do now!" Then she appeared with a massive kitchen knife.

"Please Mam, don't. We're sorry!" they cried, clinging to each other. "Please don't kill us! We're sorry!" They'd never seen their mother so mad. "No, Mam, no!" With gleeful rage, she stabbed the paddling pool over and over. It laid like a dead baby dolphin in the bath for weeks after.

WHACK-A-WHACK-A

Eddie was still going nuts. He flung a cushion onto the floor and face-planted it. Girlo jammed the end of the knife under the lip of the tin and started jiggling it about.

"And… WHAT DO YOU THINK YOU ARE DOING?"

Girlo's hand slipped. She nearly took Eddie's ear off!

"Gimme that knife!" Crystal shouted. "Cuh-righ-st Almighty! What is the matter with you? Can't leave you for five minutes! First the paddling pool, and now this! Two of you… get dressed… and take your brother out to play fuh five… Fuckin kids!"

GOOD GIRL

Groggy had generously given Girlo a pink kidney-shaped dressing table as a gift for nothing.

"What's that for?" she asked.

"That's for being a good girl."

She loved it, but it had to be stored away until a bigger room became available. She couldn't wait to arrange all of the special little ornaments her Grandmamma had given her on it; a figurine of a little girl who looked like Miss Muffet and a gold and bright green brooch in the shape of a beetle they'd named Kermit. By the time she got a bigger room, and arranged all her knick-knacks, she hated the dressing table! She didn't recognise herself anymore when she looked into its mirror. She had big sunken bags under her eyes. She'd pull at her eyelids, gauging at the flesh—tearing the tears out of her eyes and scratching them down her face, leaving dirty scram lines. One day when her mother was meant to be going out, she dragged the dressing table out onto the landing and booted it down the stairs. The glass smashed everywhere as it hit the patchy Melksham tiles at the bottom. Girlo's mam said she was an 'ungrateful little witch', and Girlo had given her the finger when her back was turned. Groggy laughed it off, claiming that he'd get her a new one, which he never did. Instead, he bought her a can of Coke for one of their many 'lovely walks' to the Smugglers' Caves.

It was a sunny day and Eddie wasn't well. Groggy pounced on the opportunity. She didn't want to go, but Crystal had had a guts full of Girlo winding Eddie up and jumped at the chance to get rid of her for the afternoon.

"It's a lovely day, look! You don't want to be cooped up in here all day, d'you? Go on, go with your Uncle Groggy."

Groggy took her by her clammy hand, meandering down the thin footpath leading away from the promenade. Girlo watched as the lacy friezes of the bandstand dissolved into the glare of the sun. As they got towards the caves his grip slipped on her sweaty palm. She knew what was coming. She searched for signs of life ahead of them; a few dog-walkers and a woman pushing a pram. Girlo thought they must've looked odd; a topless, tattooed man holding the hand of a six-year-old girl in white pelerine socks. She wanted to shout. Scream. Something. Anything. She heard the screech and groan of the cliff lift in the distance.

"Can we go on the cliff lift, Uncle Groggy?"

"Another day, beaut."

His hard belly overshadowed most of his face and when she looked up at him, all she could see was a disgusting crab ladder climbing up from his waistband.

"Where are we going, Uncle Groggy?"

"To the Caves, I told ewe… to hunt for the smugglers' gold!"

"I don't want to go to the caves. I want to go on the lift to the seaside."

"If you come to the caves, you can have this…" He pulled a can of Coke from his bum-bag. "A treat just for you." Those huge cans were always too big for her little hands, and far too much for her little bladder. But Girlo was getting hot from all the walking in the sun.

"Will you open it for me?"

He snapped back the sharp ring pull and flicked it into the bushes.

"Drink it all up!" They were getting closer to the caves now and the woman with the pram had gone.

"My shoes hurt. Can we go back?" Girlo's toes were aching: her school shoes were too small.

"Let's have a quick pit-stop by here, shall we?" He lifted her onto a nearby wall. "Do you know this one?" He began to sing: "Five and twenty ponies, trotting through the dark, Brandy for the Parson, 'Baccy for the Clerk." His moustache, like strands

44

of Drum tobacco, twitched and his black eyes burned into her.

"I need the toilet, Uncle Groggy, can we go home?"

"Can you hold it until we get to the cave?"

"I want to go home!"

"Well, it's closer to the caves than home now, so if you're that desperate for a pee then the caves are your best bet!" They kept trudging down and down, until Girlo could see a strip of sand and smell the salty sea air. She could just make out families picnicking and making sandcastles.

"Can we go to the beach? I can take off my shoes and socks and have a paddle."

"How many times have I got to tell ewe? We are going to the caves to look for the gold." He squeezed her hand so hard she felt his grubby nails dig into her flesh. "Here we are," he said, as they stopped at the mouth of the cave. "The Smugglers' Cave!" The stern tone in his voice shifted. He became childlike and animated as he pointed out the quartz stuck in the walls.

Maybe he wasn't going to do anything today, she thought. falling for it.

"Wow! They look just like diamonds." She ran her fingers over the shards.

"I bet there's Viking gold hidden in there somewhere... shall we go and see, beaut?" He took her hand and led her deeper into the cave where she could see a ledge the height of a bench.

"I don't like Vikings, Uncle Groggy,"

"Do you still need a pee? I'll take you down here for a pee, look."

"I don't like Vikings, or gold, I want to go home."

"You need a pee though, don't you?" He pushed his hand onto her bladder.

"No." But she really *really* needed to go.

"Don't be daft! Go down by there. I'll keep an eye out for you." As Girlo peed, she could feel his footsteps moving towards her. "I haven't finished, yet, Uncle Groggy. I haven't finished."

"That's a lot of pee for such a little girl," he said. "Must've been all that Coke you had." He was getting nearer and nearer.

She could hear his boots crunching on broken glass as he approached. "You can sit on the little rock bench and I'll make you all clean," he said.

"That's all right Uncle Groggy. I'm all right!" Girlo was peeing on her shoes, pushing it out as fast as she could. She could feel his minatorial presence; the familiar shadow of his heavy shape pressing on her, like a—

Just then a dog came bounding into the cave, its owner calling after it.

"I'm so sorry. Benji? Benji!" The dog snuffled its way down to Girlo who was making her way out of the darkness.

"Oh, I am sorry, I was just trying to… Benji?"

"Is he friendly?" asked Groggy, the dog jumping up on him.

"Yes, yes, he's friendly," smiled the dog-owner. "Well best be getting on. C'mon, Benji? Time to go home."

When they got back, Crystal had taken Eddie to the doctors. Girlo had to sit on Groggy's knee while he cracked open a can of Tennent's lager and watched the snooker.

"It's only a game, so put up a fight, I'm gonna be snookering you—snookering you—snookering you tonight," he sang.

DOLL

Girlo had a best friend called Bambi. They were best friends because they shared the same Christian name. Bambi earned her nickname because she was the baby and 'could get away with *anything* with those big brown eyes'. She lived in a Victorian house, with an oval front garden and whimsical, flower-lined path that led up to a shiny green door with a brass knocker in the shape of a Lion's head. In the front garden the shrubbery included dwarf pampas grass, which reminded Girlo of paint brushes. The litmus paper hydrangeas in ruddy pinks and denim blues looked like artist's rags that had mopped up the coastal sunset.

Girlo didn't have a front garden. But she had access to the back of Auntie Beryl and Uncle Groggy's. It was a shit garden. It had stingies taller than her and empty pots of paint collecting rusty rainwater. In the centre of Bambi's back garden was a handmade tortoise hutch and a lovely, manicured lawn which her dad and tortoise kept nice. In the centre of Groggy's back garden was a bald patch of earth, scorched from a succession of bonfires. A boy they met at the harbour had thrown an old lighter into the fire's dying embers and it had exploded, leaving him with a melted face.

"Now, that's what happens when you throw lighters in fires, kids!" Crystal had warned.

Bambi's older sister liked to make miniature elves with an expensive kind of plasticine she'd harden in their aga, before placing them around the garden at night—they even had little lanterns that actually lit up! Girlo's back-up babysitter was the closest she had to a big sister, a girl who wore stonewash jeans and was obsessed with new ways of bleaching her hair. She leapt in and out of Girlo's life like a glittery bouncy ball. One day, she turned up with a bottle of Sun-In.

"You just spray it in, sit in the beer garden with your pint, and before you know it… blonde! Easy-peasy, lemon squeezy."

"Ower very own Debbie 'arry!" Groggy interjected, slurp-flicking at her with his tongue. After that, Girlo never saw her again. Bambi's mother liked to call Girlo, Poppet.

"Come in, Poppet," she'd say, as she welcomed her into the warmth of her home. Girlo liked being called Poppet. Their house had seven-bedrooms which *all* belonged to the family—one of which was reserved for Bambi's China doll collection. Bambi was allowed to choose any room she wanted for her bedroom. She'd change it every few months. Girlo's family only had one room between them. Bambi's mum and dad didn't like Bambi going over to hers, so Girlo always played at theirs after school. It was for the best really. Bambi had *so* many lovely things to play with including the entire Sylvanian Family collection, which Girlo really wanted and asked Santa to bring every Christmas, but never got. Crystal said that she had to be a 'good girl', but when they were at Toys 'r' Us, she'd always dismiss Sylvanian Family as 'a bloody rip off!' Girlo's mam was a very dismissive person. When they asked to go on school trips, she'd say no, and then ring up to check whether it was compulsory, before handing over the fee. She dismissed Ribena, in favour of Ki Ora—which left a starchy residue on the tongue. And even though they'd rather have a bowl of Coco-pops, Girlo and Eddie got Weetabix. With their rationed splash of milk it became a brick of wet cardboard, painful to swallow. It almost felt like it would come out of their ears and nose, like Playdough out of a Mr. Potato Head. Crystal had a blanket ban on all sweets, claiming they were 'full of eez'. Girlo never knew what *eez* were, but by the way her mother always went on about money, maybe her social security wouldn't stretch to such luxuries—especially if they were going to make her hyper-kids bounce off the walls. But Girlo and Eddie loved sweets! As entrepreneurial children of the 80s, they'd find *any* opportunity to make a couple of quid. They washed cars, cleaned windows, swept driveways, and walked the dogs of posh people who lived in their suburb. But, by far the best place to make money was in the pub. Drunk people would give *anything* to be left in peace to get even drunker, so they had a steady stream of income, as they were practially brought up there. Then, on the weekend they'd venture up the cobbled street, full of tourists, and watch the confectioners roll out gigantic worms of soft rock dough. If they had enough money they'd buy a rock each. Girlo would take her time eating hers, licking off the glossy pink, then sucking the peppermint core and slowly digesting the engrained lettering. Eddie would chomp at his until all he had left was the sticky cellophane and a chewed-up picture of the HMRS.

Instead of Sylvanian Family, Father Christmas brought Girlo a Fashion Wheel. The lady from her Learning to Catwalk class had encouraged her to fulfil her ambition of becoming a fashion designer. She never liked Catwalk. She wanted to go to Ballet, Tap & Modern like the other girls in her class, but Crystal said that the uniforms were too expensive, so she had to make do. Bambi treated Girlo like a real-life doll and Girlo didn't mind, she was tired of being the oldest. When she was with Bambi she felt like a little sister. She felt at home in Bambi's house. Safe. Bambi's mum encouraged them to play at the kitchen table whereas Girlo and Eddie had to keep all their toys in their room because Crystal couldn't 'cope with the fucking mess!'

Bambi's mum was a vegetarian, which meant she did not eat meat. She cooked something called lentils, which looked like dead frogspawn, and braised purple cabbage, glazed with butter. She had a massive fruit bowl that was forever filled with clean Granny Smith apples, so clean they stayed white inside after you bit into them. The apples Crystal bought were a dirty yellow, and the flesh would turn brown after the first couple of bites. At Bambi's house, they sat around her mother's oak table and took it in turns to trace the outlines of the fashion models on the wheel.

"I want a polka dot top and a miniskirt on mine," Bambi said, as she turned the wheel to trace her figure.

"I don't like miniskirts. I want trousers on mine. Black trousers."

"My sister wears miniskirts, and she shaves her legs."

"I thought only boys shaved."

"Girls do too!"

"Do they?"

"Yeah, and they shave their privates." Bambi giggled but Girlo was horrified.

"Her privates? But privates should be *private*. That's why they're called privates!"

Just then, Bambi's mum entered carrying a steaming antique terrine of something nutritious. Girlo blushed.

"Come on my aspiring fashionistas, wash hands. Dinner's ready... Darling?" She called to her husband, "dinner is served, my sweet."

After dinner, Bambi asked if Girlo wanted to see her mum's studio. As they climbed the stairs, Girlo felt uneasy; the studio was like her house, cold with bare floorboards. A splinter caught on her sock as she went to look through the sash window.

"It's cold in here."

"Mummy likes it that way. Helps her do her best work, she says."

"And what's this?" Girlo had noticed a leather-bound book, daubed with paint splodges.

"Oh, that's *Jane Eyre*. Daddy calls Mummy the mad woman in the attic, whatever that means." *Bambi's mother wasn't mad,* thought Girlo.

"I write poems sometimes."

"Don't lie!"

"I do!"

"Read one then. Go on, read me one of your *poems*!"

"I—I can't, I wrote them on my wall..."

"You're allowed to write on the wall?"

"What's *Jane Eyre* about?"

"I dunno. Who cares! Anyway, I'm an artist! Look..." she pulled a hessian cover from a canvas perched on a dinky easel. "It's Crow's Nest up the Smugglers caves."

Girlo recognised the place instantly and froze. As she stared at the painting, Bambi's sunny paint strokes turned gloomy, slashing into the white of the canvas.

"I think I need to go home now."

That night Girlo had strange dreams. She dreamt she was all on her own in a big deep forest. But she wasn't scared. Everywhere she looked there was a tree trunk blocking her view. The tree trunks were ancient and rough; all covered in trails of moss. Then she could hear her mother laughing. She couldn't see her but when she went to look for her, the tree trunks moved, and a great moonbeam appeared. It persuaded the branches to sweep her up into the treetops and carry her across the starry skies. She could still hear her mother's laugher, and the murmurings of other people somewhere. After some time the sky subsided and she found herself on the ground again. In the distance she could see the glimmer of fire; it flickered as shapes moved over it. And as she moved closer she could feel the beat of a drum. Her mother's laugh still pierced the night as Girlo stumbled through the thicket. In a clearing, she saw a tribe dancing around the fire. But they were not human. They looked to be half-monkey, half-man. And on a throne, watching over them, was a white monkey, wearing a crown. He held a magical staff which he thrust like a composer's stick. He had a smug look of satisfaction on his face. Auntie Beryl was there too, dancing around the fire with her mother and some other women who were pregnant. They were all dressed in white wedding gowns, twirling and whirling around the neanderthal figures. Girlo called to her mother but she was oblivious.

I am Doll

Bambi's doll has glass eyes curly hair Pink dress China cheeks happy grin

my doll has rats tails for hair always a mess Dirty dress

found in a jumble sale bin

FLUFF

When Girlo got back, Nancy Random was still up, still *on a mad one*, partying with a couple of randomers she'd picked up.

"Where did you get to last night?" called Nancy, who was blasting Dizzee Rascal with Jeremy Kyle on mute in the background. "FIX UP. LOOK SHARP," she rapped, as Girlo poked her head in.

"Is that wine?" It was 8 o'clock on a Monday morning.

"Aye, breakfast wine!" Nancy was a heavyweight and would stay awake until the sun came up, talking shit, swigging dregs of what was left; month-old cooking wine always tasted

"fine" in the early hours.

They lived in a skanky flat above the corner shop in Studentsville, run by a notoriously corrupt landlord called Mr Khan, first name, Sher. Girlo was not supposed to be living there, but bin liners full of her stuff were dotted all over the place which, as well as Stella the dog's presence, instigated a constant source of interrogation.

"Iz that a dog I can smell? Iz that dogmess? Iz it? Who do those bags belong to? I know she's living here!" Girlo didn't have a flat nor did she have a job. She'd failed at uni and the old saying: you can take the girl out of the estate, but you can't take the estate out of the girl was beginning to ring true, but at least she wasn't up the duff, she thought. Nancy was Girlo's saviour; she was from the valleys too. They both fell prey to the demon drink and allure of wrong uns.

As soon as Girlo sat down, Nancy threw a newspaper at her. She'd circled an ad in red: Clean Queens Hiring Cleaners. It was a little minimum-wage cleaning job. She could easy do a cleaning job. As a kid she'd go with Crystal to clean posh houses. She'd taught her how to do everything from Brassoing the fireplace, to hand-brushing the stairs; making beds 'the quick and easy way' and scrubbing the under-rims of the toilets so 'you could eat your dinner off um!' She even designed a special rota where each job was charged at 50p, and after completion, her mam would inspect the accuracy of her work.

"Come downstairs, please... see this?" she'd say, holding up a fork plucked from the cutlery holder. "Filth!" she said, pointing out a string of chicken hammocking the prongs. "That's fifty pence to be knocked off." Then she'd trot off and strike fifty pence from the rota.

"I'm sorry, Mam. I was rushing to go—"

"You won't be going anywhere until you've finished all your chores, Girlo."

"What about Eddie? Has he finished his—"

"Never mind Eddie. He's nipped over the shop for Doug's Auto Trader."

"It's not fair. He'll have the change from that, as well! It's not fair. Just because he's a boy."

"Life izzunt fair."

Girlo was a good cleaner and over the years had built up calluses from sweeping and had even burned her fingerprints off with so much neat bleach, a bonus for fingerprinting at the station. She could do a cleaning job standing on her head!

"I've got you into the agency," Nancy said. "There's a couple of numbers by the phone; our first clients." The first number was for some guy called Earl Newman. "He's probably some ninety-year-old pervert," laughed Nancy. "He'll be lurking about trying to get a look up yer skirt when yer doin' the feather dusting"

"We could capitalise on that," said Girlo, "Cleaners in the Buff! We'll make a bomb!"

"That's not very socialist, Girlo!" Nancy joked.

"Not when I haven't got a pot to piss in, no!"

"We'll call ourselves Fluff in the Buff."

"I'll be *his* bit of fluff!" laughed Girlo.

"Not very feminist, either… Eh, you might end up giving him a heart attack if you bend over too much. Just make sure he falls in love with you first so he can write you in to the will." Her dirty cackle turned into a hacking smoker's cough.

"Shush, now." Girlo dialled a number. There was no answer so she left a voicemail on his answer machine. The second number picked up on the third ring: "Ruby's Retreat!"

"Er… sorry, have I got the right number? I'm calling from Clean Queens. I'm your new cleaner."

"Oh, right. Uh, yeah—"

"They asked me to 'touch base' and see what times work for you."

"I'm in a bit of mess here to be 'onest… jus' go' back frum The Big Smoke. Cun ewe pop over this afternoon? You know the Indian takeaway on the roundabout in town? Yew know… opposite the Potters? I'm above there. Cun you come down, say, twelve-ish? I'll warn you though—everything's in boxes! Got lots of work on for you, I have… so, I'll see you at twelve? Is tha' ok? Sorry, but I've got so much on this mornen, uvuh-wise I'd say come now. Is twelve all right, above the Indian? This afternoon?"

"Er… yeah! No worries. I'll be there."

"Catcha ina bit! Mwah, mwah!"

SUGAR

When she approached the Indian, Girlo could see the restaurant was closed. She looked up; the exterior was covered in a cloudy composite cladding, the windows blacked out. *What kind of a place is this?* she thought, as she banged the door. An old guy wearing dirty chef whites sprung from somewhere.

"Can I help you, Miss?"

"Yeah, I'm looking for Ruby?"

"You're a pretty one, aren't you? She's up there, luvelee gurl."

"Is there a doorbell?"

"Just WHACK WHACK, like this…" he bashed the door.

"Yep… nice one."

"Tell Sugar Tits I'll be up to try you out for m'self aff-tuh." He stuck out his turmeric tongue and flicked it. Girlo had no idea what he meant but after hearing a long aerosol spray, the door wafted open to present a tanned leggy blonde wearing denim cut-offs and a distressed Levi T-shirt. The blonde, presumably Ruby, ushered Girlo in through the foyer with a manicured hand, before leading her up a gloomy flight of stairs. Her heart was in her mouth. *What had she walked into?* She followed Ruby into an office with a spotless cream leather sofa next to a glass table with a vase of dragon lilies. *Was it a funeral parlour, perhaps?* Ruby left her to 'sit and wait.'

BUZZ BUZZ-BUZZ.
BUZZ BUZZ-BUZZZZZZ

An electric drill reverberated through the walls. Girlo's head couldn't take the sound of repetitive noises, especially skull-splitting buzzy ones. On the desk a monitor displayed a gallery of

Ruby in sexy lingerie. She clicked on a picture of her wearing nothing but furs and a pair of over-the-knee Ugg high-heels. It was a nice shot and seemed to have been taken on location in some snowy woods somewhere. Suddenly she twigged. She did know what kind of place this was. As she carried on clicking through the pics, words sprung to mind, *her eyes painted bright blue, dazzled like diamonds in snow, as she made his member grow.* The phone rang and Ruby slipped in from a secret door to snap up the receiver.

"Ruby's Retreat... yes, Darling, no I haven't forgotten you, Darling..."

Girlo scooped up an album and absently began to leaf its pages while Ruby spoke in her best sultry voice. She was looking at a portfolio of a girl named Lolli, who looked very much like Ruby, a 'curly-haired cutie with pink nipples and a gold nose stud.' Her vital statistics were printed on the first page: 'Nationality: Welsh, Age: 22, Size: 8, Waist: 26in, Height: 5.2, Bust: 32D. The description continued over her pert left breast and down the hip of her girlish figure, posing pig-tailed with an oversized lollipop. Hair: Platinum Blonde, Build: Slim and slender, Personality: Bubbly, Services: FGE.' *What was FGE?*

"Lovely, Darling... I will see you then. Toodles. Mwah. Mwah!" Ruby turned to Girlo, "a fashion shoot, that is—"

"Is it you?"

"Before I had these done," she grabbed her tits with both hands and pushed them up.

"How old were you?"

"Dunno, seventeen, eighteen..."

She had some guts, thought Girlo.

"Right, follow me... As you've already guessed, I am Ruby, the proprietor of this establishment... Come through here." Ruby led her back from where they'd come, past an ominous door, over the landing and into a black-tiled galley kitchen that had the same type of cupboards you'd find in a council house. The window faced a raw concrete wall. The floor and every other surface was stacked with boxes, most of which had been ripped open and were spilling out an odd-sod assortment of Ruby's life —all packed up in a panic. There was stuff next to them, stuff underneath them—fucking stuff everywhere! Girlo looked at it all—then at Ruby.

"Right, yewer job is to put all of this crap away."

"Where to?"

"Anywhere you can find for the time being. I've got a massive cabinet coming tomorrow morning, and I've got all these drawers in yere and the drawers in the office… don't just shove it all in as it is though. I want you to organise the whole fucking lot. Put it away tidy like."

"Yes Suh!" saluted Girlo. She scanned the enormity of the task sprawled out before her.

"Madame to you, and don't get fucking cocky, you're a cleaner f'fucksake. Know your place! Oh, yeah—and before I forget—when that cycle has finished, can you pop the clothes in the dryer with two Bounce sheets? Everything has to smell clean and fresh at all times."

Girlo made space on the floor to start 'the big sort'. She opened the first box to find a selection of lighters—some with no gas, some with too much gas, others with no flint—some with the metal bits bitten off in a last-ditch attempt to get them working again. There were ripped-up Rizla packs, old film reel cases dusted with skunk, a swirly glass pipe tinted with brown. On top of the fridge was an old Roses tin used to house all the smoking stuff. At the bottom of the box, under a silver-framed picture of a nude Ruby, was a pile of tightly folded letters. Girlo had a nose: credit card bill—two grand, catalogue—£2,500, rent arrears—six grand! And so it went on. Girlo placed the letters in a carrier bag hoping Ruby could afford to pay her.

BUZZ BUZZ-BUZZ.
BUZZ BUZZ-BUZZ.
BUZZ BUZZ.

In the next box she found a large purple dildo—*was there a giant dildo buzzing away somewhere in one of the hidden rooms at the end of the corridor?* This one was wrapped up in a patent leather G-string—clean, at least. She switched it on; it was a powerful one. She was tempted to place it on the tip of her nose. According to Ann Summers, who she'd worked for as a representative in previous years, the end of the nose has the same heightened nerve-endings as the clitoris, which after buying her first pocket pleaser and spending at least two hours a day experimenting she decided was absolute bollocks! BUZZ BUZZ-BUZZ. BUZZ BUZZ-BUZZ. BUZZ BUZZ. She buzzed the dildo in time with the drill. The words *lip-glossed crack, turn you on, turn you round then on your back,* sprung to mind. She buzzed away, using the dildo as a drumstick and then a mic. Once she was bored of that game she went on with her task.

She found a few scrunched-up tubes of lube alongside three crinkled packets of instant rice, a plethora of free condoms from the GUM clinic, nubs of lipstick, and a load of crumpled up pantyliners. In the adjoining bathroom she found a wicker basket for all the toiletry stuff. Above the bath a selection of expensive lingerie and bikinis drip-dried on the shower rail. She had a quick pee while she was there. When she returned to her space on the floor of the kitchen, the washing machine had stopped. Girlo dug in the cupboard under the sink for the Bounce sheets, then yanked the contents of the washing machine out onto the floor. It was all aubergine towels; they flopped out like a foal from its mother's womb. She shoved them into the dryer and started it up. Christ almighty, it was fucking loud! It sounded like the belt needed replacing. The buzz of the drilling had stopped now but it had been replaced with the bastard tumble dryer. FUH-LUMP.FUH-LUMP.FUH-LUMP.FUH-LUMP.FUH-LUMP.

As Girlo unpacked another box of kink, the beat of the flumping drum conjured the words, *a place to cum, a lucrative hell.* FUH-LUMP.FUH-LUMP.FUH-LUMP.FUH-LUMP.FUH-LUMP. She wondered about Ruby's profession. *Was it un-feminist to be a prostitute?* Sex was the best feeling in the world so why not make money from it? But what would people say if they saw her coming out of there? She could keep it a secret. Plenty of women had secret sexy jobs; she had a friend, a festival dancer, who'd ended up working in a strip club, but the job was fucking dire; the clients sleazebags and the other girls so competitive one of them had smashed her windscreen. The management weren't any better, they didn't even pay for the girls' taxis home. Company policy was once you leave the establishment, you are responsible for your own safety, despite grinding your hips in a potential serial killer's face for the last few hours. Any fucker could've snatched them off the street, stalked and killed them. And the law wouldn't bat an eyelid. *Prostitutes don't get protection in the patriarchy.* Girlo wondered if Ruby looked after the girls who worked for her or was she just like everyone else—in it for the money and fuck the cost to human life. She must know what it's like to be a vulnerable young girl on the game. *Was she a victim or a warrior?* Girlo tried to imagine why she had to leave in such a hurry; maybe a nasty pimp was controlling her. Maybe she owed too much money. Maybe a punter had got too heavy with her. No matter what had happened, in the rubble of Ruby's life, Girlo felt useful. There sorting all her shit out, Girlo felt needed. FUH-LUMP.FUH-LUMP.FUH-LUMP.FUH-LUMP.FUH-LUMP. *Fishnet's itch, toes bleed, need this hole for mouths to feed.*

MAM

Crystal was laid up for a legitimate reason: she had broken her leg. That said—the accident hadn't happened because she'd attempted to dampproof the ceiling of their basement flat, nor during a botched compo job or even from a suicide attempt off a bridge. Crystal had been hit by a reversing car.

It was surprising she didn't try to make a claim but she would have struggled to present a plausible case since she was paralytic drunk from her own home-brew. Her streak-of-piss sister was not impressed.

"You were only supposed to sample it, not drink the whole demijohn. Groggy seen ewe galloping down the high-street in the middle of the afternoon!"

"I only had a glass. Bluddee car come out uv nowhere, honest!" Crystal spewed into a scuffed-up washing-up bowl. "Stuff is fuckin' leeth-ul!" So, she was bed-bound. Nothing out-of-the-ordinary as this was usually the case with her perpetual hangovers. On weekends she'd evaporate in bed—her dank pit, like the inside of an empty wine bottle. Girlo often wondered how she even got onto that mountain of stinking mattresses: all piled up like used teabags slopped on the corner of the kitchen sink.

Girlo and Eddie longed to sleep on the Mattress Mountain but 'unless it was a matter of life or death', they were forbidden to disturb their Mam. Reaching her on a weekend morning was like a something from G.I. Jane. After tackling the world's ricketiest cushion bridge, then climbing over the world's snappiest crocodile pit, they'd swim through a deadly moat of stilettos and studded leather before arriving at the door to her lair. Eddie was to cover Girlo as she'd inch open the bedroom door. The sight of Crystal's flickering red toes in the mirror flagged danger, and at that point the door would certainly squeak... FREEZE! Poised in paralysis, they'd yearn for the next sign of life, then, with her heart firing like a machine gun, Girlo's wet grip on Eddie's hand would sharpen. And she'd whisper, "Quietly." She'd whisper, "Shhhhh—you first."

"No, you—"

"You, soldier!"

Eddie was always sent in first. He'd slip in sideways, trying not to trip the squeaky hinge, then drop onto his hands and knees and scamper through a debris of tissues blotted with lipstick kisses, curls of cellophane from cigarette cartons, blister-strips of pills and wineglasses and Lucozade bottles dropped like bombshells around the perimeter of the Mattress Mountain. Beside the plume of a bulging ashtray, Girlo's Mam's handbag hung in the gorge between the mountain and the bedside table, above it an ebony statue of a pregnant woman who surveyed the room, wide ivory eyes staring down at Eddie as he edged in for the target.

"I can't... the woman... she's watching."

"Don't be sh-too-pid! She's not real."

"What if Mammy catches us?"

"She won't... You want biscuits, don't you?"

"I'm starving. My belly 'urts."

Girlo slipped in, did a quick tuck-and-roll (just to show off) and snatched the handbag. Social Security Day was always a Friday so they were certain there would be some surplus left over from the binge-fund. After pinching Crystal's last-couple-of-unspent-quid, Girlo squirrelled it into her sock. Then she and Eddie'd scale the side of Mattress Mountain. Crystal moaned as she felt the gentle rock from their measured climb to the raggedy top. They slotted their freezing hands and feet into the gaps of each squalid layer; and, like hungry spiders scurry up to their mam, who, like a bluebottle, languished in the webbing from her uncovered duvet.

"Mam? Mam? Wake up!"

"Arghhh... Kids? What's the time?!"

"We're hungry. Feed us. Feed us. Feed us." Whining repetition in unison was a proven tactic.

"Ah-right! Juzz five more minutes. Where'z my fagz kids?"

"If we get your fags then will you feed us?"

"Yezzzz. Pass um up here!"

But this particular bed-bound stretch was different. Instead of telling them to 'get the fuck out' when they'd brought a pretend breakfast on a hand-me-down Bluebird Kitchen she beckoned them into the gloom. Her hair, dark and wet with sweat, slicked around their worried-little-faces as she paired their heads together and wailed into their scalps.

"I'm so sorry kids, so sorry this has happened to me." As she sniffed and sobbed, a slip of sun sliced through the gap in the curtains and lit up the side of her face. Her mascara had bled into watercolour weeds. She looked like a ragdoll with broken eyes.

"This was meant to be a fresh start, a new beginning. This is all yuh fuckin' father's fault... fuckin' bastard as he is! Leaving us like this yere!"

"But we left him, Mam."

"I wanted a better life for us. All I wanted was a better life..."

She continued to sob. Instead of the victorious mountaineers they'd initially envisaged becoming, they felt stranded now. How could they stop their mammy from being like this? Maybe they should buy her something with the money they'd nicked. Little steam-breaths puffed from their lips as they shivered in the damp and mildewed room. They jumped under the covers to cwtch up to their mammy, but she felt like an empty pillowcase.

"Shall we make you a cup of tea, Mam? We'll make one with the hot-tap."

"There's no money on the meter."

"I tell ewe what: when my leg is all back to normal, we'll go for a picnic in the park. Just the three of us."

But it wasn't just the three of them. And they didn't go to the park.

WHORE

Downstairs the front-door slammed and there was the stomp of man-feet climbing stairs. Girlo knew that sound. Her heart began to fire rounds. Another door slammed and Ruby's stilettos skedaddled across the laminate. She heard the thud of something being thrown against the wall. All went silent. *Should she venture out of the shit tip?* Eventually, she got herself up, smoothed down her tabard, then pulled open the fire-door. The dryer had reached its maximum and sounded like it was about to fly out of the fucking kitchen window!

"Hello," she whispered into the corridor.

"I told you I'd get it for you, din I? I've rung him." Ruby's voice sounded shaky from behind the door.

"You better had or I'll fuck you up, whore!" Boomed the voice of a man. Girlo couldn't catch much more—her heart was racing in time with the turn of the tumble-dryer and a waft of fried chilli had crept up the stairs to scorch her eyeballs. Ruby opened the door.

"Er—and what the fuck do you think yewer doing out by yere?"

"I just heard banging. I was worried and I—" Girlo sniffed and wiped away a tear from the burning chilli.

Ruby paused, then quietly closed the door behind her.

"No need to worry. It's just my boyfriend. He's acting like a bit of cunt he is. Dun worry... I'll sort that dickhead out, now. How's the kitchen coming on?"

"I might need to start putting some stuff in the office soon, but, getting there..."

"Why don't you come and take a break? Come on, come in here. You can meet my fella then."

Behind the scabby black door was a luxurious boudoir, the focal point, a four-poster bed draped in ivory silk and aubergine satin. At its foot was a full-length, floor-to-ceiling mirror (pristine, without a smudge) lit with mounted candlesticks made of twisted wrought iron that seemed to grow from the glass itself. A chrome pole had been erected in the centre of the room and beyond it, a shiny-topped bar stocked with three optics: Jameson's Whiskey, Absolut Vodka and Three Barrels Brandy. Next to the bar were two leather barstools, one of which held up the dirty crackhead arse of Ruby's boyfriend.

"Ooz iss 'en?" he mumbled.

"The cleaner."

"Ar, right! You gonna open tha' Corky's 'en, sugar tits?"

Ruby reached down behind the bar for three shot glasses, then filled them with electric blue liqueur. The blackout window was ajar, letting a cool sun spill in. Ruby raised her glass.

"Here's to Ruby's Retreat. To new beginnings!"

"New beginnings!" Toasted Girlo. The boyfriend threw back his shot and smiled, revealing his drug-rotted teeth, like smashed toffee. Girlo winced. She often wondered how the fuck people let their teeth get so bad. One of her most recent ex-boyfriends, nicknamed Balboa on account of his bare-knuckle boxing heritage, used to love his pills. He'd leave two to sizzle away on his back molars while he threw several more down his neck. Or, if he had whizz, he'd scoop it up and rub it into the back of his gums so that it would get into the bloodstream quicker. His back teeth were like shale and gave him a pain that could only be suppressed with copious amounts of gut-exploding ibuprofen. Her and Balboa had had a dramatic breakup; she'd smashed a giant lamp over his head in a hotel room on New Year's Eve, the climax of an ongoing row regarding her whereabouts after a night out eight months prior. After much coaxing she'd finally told him the truth.

"Why didn't you tell me before? I knew I could feel something on you that morning! I thought you fucked him behind my back. I thought you were a lying slag."

"I didn't want to rock the boat, especially after what happened to me when I was a kid! I didn't want to dredge up the past. I didn't want to not be believed again."

"Why the fuck didn't you tell me? I knew something was up, I knew it."

"I didn't want you to go over there and get into trouble with the police."

"Tell me what happened again."

Girlo told him about how he kept buying her vodka shots every time she ordered a bottle of Archers alco-pop, and how a hard-faced bitch was picking on her for being in university, taking the piss and making trouble. She couldn't get a taxi so she had to walk and all she could remember was walking and walking on that long road in the rain... how he caught up with her and offered to get her home safely. Then that was it. That's all she could remember. She had a blackout until she woke up with the reflection of him in the mirrored wardrobes, on top of her, inside of her, just as he was coming.

BUZZ BUZZ-BUZZ.
BUZZ BUZZ-BUZZ.
BUZZ BUZZ

Ruby's boyfriend refilled the glasses to toast another round. His fingers were stubby; cracked knuckles and rings fused into the skin.

"I hope you don't mind me asking but what are we toasting?"

Ruby and the boyfriend exchanged a glance.

"We're a new concept in escorting: Ruby's Gentleman's Retreat!" Girlo had never seen a real-life prostitute before. She expected them to be skanky smack heads, riddled with herpes and plastered in bruises. This woman had come straight off the Hollywood red carpet. "In London we had a spa with Jacuzzis and everything. That's what we're aiming for here. This pretty shitty city won't know what's hit it!"

"I don't suppose you need a receptionist?" Girlo had always fantasised about working in an escort agency. Nannie

Pearl told her once that she'd left for London with nothing more than a couple of pairs of knickers, half a bottle of brandy and a five-pound note. Then she'd met a woman who was setting up a 'bona fide escort agency', and Pearl had worked the switchboard. They took out a dozen ads in the paper: 'City Goddesses,' 'Diamonds,' 'Starlets of the City,' 'City Diamonds,' 'Kittens,' 'Elite Company' and the two of them dominated the escort scene in '70s London. On her days off, Pearl would wander around the streets barefoot, wearing multi-coloured theatrical gowns and drinking creme de menthes at Christine Keeler and Mandy Rice's favourite London haunts.

"Be careful," interrupted the boyfriend, "we don't know who the fuck she is!"

"Have you worked on the phones before?"

"I've done plenty of bar work."

"She's not a bad looking girl… wha' you reckon?"

"We need a new name for you though."

"What's wrong with my real name?"

"You think Ruby is my real name? In this game nothing is real, it's all about the performance, the show!"

"We'll call you…"

CRYSTAL CLEAR

When Crystal's leg got better she took the kids to stay with Scottie, who was okay whilst sober, but terrifying when drunk. His blue lips rippled like a deflating balloon as he jabbered incomprehensible shit to the un-trained ears of Girlo and Eddie. Scottie was Crystal's oldest drinking buddy. Dicky was Eric's, whose vernacular was less decipherable than Scottie's, but he did cool tricks with fag packets, so the kids liked him better.

"Are ye takin' the pish, Scottie? Get that slug oot o'ma drain!"

They had all met in service: The Imperial Services, a hotel where Crystal was a waitress, Eric, a kitchen porter, Scottie the chef and Dicky, the barman. Dicky had tried to get fresh with Crystal quite early on in their acquaintance.

"See this?" Eric had growled, holding the stem of a wine glass firmly up to Dicky's left nostril. "If you touch her again... it'll meet your brain!" After that, Eric and Dicky were the best of mates.

The Imperial Four, as they'd refer to themselves, always had a blast. Dicky and Scottie would go out 'Shop-PING'. Shop-PING meant shoplifting for booze, and after a quick spree in the local offie, they'd always bring back the same order of three 40oz bottles of Smirnoff, a bottle of Malibu for Crystal, and Bells for Dicky.

"Did you remember the pineapple juice, Scot?" called Crystal. Malibu, vodka and pineapple juice was her favourite tipple.

"What dae ye tak' me for, Lassie?"

"I wouldn't deprive 'er of her fancy punch butt, God only knows what she'll doo—"

Once every drop of booze had been downed, they'd hit the clubs. Dicky was a good asset on the piss because he could act the hard man, but really he was soft as shit. Years later he'd gotten into a fight on Christmas Eve, or maybe it was Boxing Day, and

71

had his two front teeth knocked out. 'All I want for Christmas is my two front teeth. My two front teeth, my two front teeth.' The last time Eric saw Dicky he was sleeping under a bridge, and the last he'd heard, Dicky was dead.

Scottie had two volume settings: loudspeaker when wankered, silent when hungover.

"Crysieee, Crysieee, Crysiee," he'd cry like a dying Hoover when Crystal was on the turn. Girlo's parents had a turning point when drinking. One minute they'd be the centre of attention, entertaining the crowd with outrageous anecdotes—then one of them would have that one too many, and

BANG

On many occasions, they'd fallen into the alcoholic abyss, and all hell had broken loose. On one occasion, Eric's 21st birthday, like a scene from Eastenders, Crystal had shoved a whiskey tumbler into his mouth, blood gushing down his new denims.

"No more designer jeans for you, Sonny Jim!" she'd sneered after their divorce went through.

> *Happy Birthday to you.*
> *Squashed tomatoes and stew.*
> *Bread and butter in the gutter.*
> *Happy Birthday to you.*

Meanwhile, instead of playing in the promised: "just the three of us," lush-green park, Eddie and Girlo had a day out in the concrete jungle with the herds of tourists who'd flocked to the square on this typically British overcast day. And instead of a picnic, they got a flimsy bag of bird feed that they pretended to enjoy thrashing over the lion statues.

"You've never been here before, have you, kids? Look at all those pigeons!" Crystal tossed some seed into the air. She was half-cut from downing two pints of cider en route. At least her mood had stabilised.

"Mankee fukin things! Ah'll rip their wings aff!" blurted Scottie. "Rats o' the sky! Watch oot, or they'll drap fleas on yer… yer heid'll be loupin."

Why did everyone hate pigeons so much? As the under-valued lumpen proletariat of the avian world, they're resourceful, resilient, community spirited and monogamous to boot. Crystal sang, "Catch the pigeons. Catch the pigeons. Catch the pigeons! Ah ooh!"

The kids were being eaten alive. Once their palms were empty of feed, the birds dispersed and pecked the ground with their barnacled beaks: pink feet, malformed and bubbled up like burnt plastic, the odd toenail poking out.

"Look kids, there's 'Op-it!" Eric used to say, pointing to an old moulting pigeon, who, like a retired army general, hobbled about outside the train station. Girlo often wondered how their feet came to be so mangled. One time, while she waited for her dad at the ticket office, Girlo asked 'Op-it if his feet were bad from carrying special messages in a little satchel over the sea. He told her, no—his feet were bad from walking up and down the high street all day looking for crumbs to eat. She suggested that he fly elsewhere—"you got wings 'aven't you?" Dicky had told her that their feet were 'fucked' because some 'rich fuckers lace their windowsills with acid.' It made her feel sick to the stomach.

"But why? They never done nuffin to no-one!" She could just see those rich fat cats with spiky grins in their monochrom-atic suits, spraying the sills of their castles to protect the facade from streaks of pigeon shit.

The lion sculptures were also drizzled with plops of poo and teemed with beaming kids who scrambled up for a souvenir snap. As Girlo and Eddie sprung around the square—tossing feed like it was fucking fairy dust—Scottie and Crystal had 'words', Crystal cwtching into the crook of Scottie's bony neck.

"I don't know who he is any more, Scot. Ee've changed. I carn go back. Not this time… an' anyway, I've moved on. We've moved on."

73

"Changed, yer say?"

"He was always away, mun... an'... I know that he wants to do it for the kids, but we had no money all the time... an' I didn't see him... I was on my own all the time, mun. He dun seem to realise that I am the one at 'ome with the kids all the time. I would've loved to have gone off myself. I would've loved to have done more with my life. I had to get off that fucking Rock!"

"From whit he's said, Crys, he's daeni it fer the weans an' fe ye. Education's the only wey oot, there's nae'thin' left, noo... Och, these thin's are neever crystal clear, dear!" Scottie passed her a cigarette. They shared a light and smoked and waved at the kids.

"Take a picture of us!" the kids cried, but nobody had a camera.

"Right kids, time to go. It's getting cold," Crystal said, stubbing out her ciggie. They didn't want to go back to Scottie's because he lived in a high-rise in a rough area where the kids were unfriendly and spoke funny. Last time they'd been there they'd encountered a rogue pit-bull terrier who chased them around the block: a haunting memory which spawned a deep-seated fear of all fighting dogs.

"C'mon kids, it's starting to spit!" Crystal was starting to get her hair off they could tell—the faint curl of her lip quivering to expose her scary-toothed-face. Scottie stood up, still dodging the pigeon flocks and their fleas.

But the kids didn't move from the lions. They felt like the Pevensie children from The Lion, the Witch and the Wardrobe—crusaders for all that was good, riding Aslan to victory against the White Witch and her minions. Crystal wasn't best pleased and eventually had to bribe them with a Happy Meal to "get off those fucking Lions." Instead of the Happy Meal they each got a clip around the earhole.

"We *have* been here before!" Girlo spat in a burning strop as they weaved through the crowd at the square's edge. "DAD brought us here... AND he bought us a Happy Meal!"

"Well, yuh farvuhz got more money than I have. I got you two, haven't I?!"

But before they were on the tube Scottie bought them a Happy Meal each.

"There yuz go. Don't say I niver buy yuz nothen." Scottie wasn't that bad after all.

He had a high-tech intercom phone for a doorbell: you could see the pixelated face of a visitor, or in Scottie's case, the face of the skip-rat kid who terrorised him on a daily basis. He lived on what felt like the 50th floor and they all had to squish into the lift, which stunk of burn and piss.

"What's that?" asked Eddie, pointing to what looked like the door to a furnace the minute they got out of the lift.

"That's where the devil lives!"

Girlo pushed passed to investigate.

"Leave it! It's just a rubbish chute—never mind!"

It was too late. She already had her head in. "Blurgh! It stinks! I can't see the bottom. Where does it go?"

"It gaes aw the way tae hell! An' if ye fa' in, naebody wid ever find ye." Scottie grabbed her and played at pushing her in. It scared the living shit out of her; she never knew with him. After they'd calmed down, Scottie fished his keys out. Two glass bottles clinked in the plastic bag he was carrying as they all pushed to get in. Scottie's flat was like the set of a film noir. The kids had never seen anything so extravagant in their whole lives. A long black leather sofa and a big sheepskin rug spread out in front of a glass-stoned gas fire; all shoplifted stuff. He jabbed the button on the side of the fire with his thumb and it coughed a few times but then...WHOOSH! Turquoise flames flooded the iridescent baubles. The kids gasped with delight! They weren't used to this. Nannie Pearl's coal fire took ages to light with matches, firelighters, newspaper and kindling.

"Yew are, Cariad," she'd say, holding a strip of vinegar-soaked newspaper like a piece of battered cod. "Use this to clean all the soot off the panes." This fire was flashy but it couldn't replace the toasty smell of good ole coal. When coal was short, Eric would buy a sack-full for cheap off the boys, who burrowed and picked what they could find from coal slurries. With loaded sacks, they'd walk a good few miles to get it back to hard-up striking families living on the Rock. Eric and Crystal could only have one fire a day. That's probably why they fought all the time, thought Girlo—to keep warm.

Crystal busied herself with Scottie's L.P. collection, gulping vodka and Malibu from her tumbler while Scottie went to take a long piss.

"Why are menz weez so loud and take forever?" asked Girlo.

"They have to stand up, that's why." Crystal snapped.

Girlo already knew that.

"Stick the bath on for the kids," Crystal called out to him.

She put the kids in the bath to 'wash away the dirt of the Big Smoke' but really she wanted to get rid of them so her and Scottie could get on it properly. As Duran Duran began, the kids played their favourite bath-time game of 'Pubs'. First, they placed flannels over the side of the bath to resemble the towelled spill-mats you'd find on a bar top, then they filled cups with bubbles, using water from the tap, (their beer pump), to pour pints. Eddie always played the customer first, freezing his arse off outside the bath, waiting for service.

"Say, 'same again please, love'," instructed Girlo.

"Same again please, love."

"Wanna fag?" Girlo passed him a toothbrush and pretended to light it with the soap.

Eddie took a handful of bubbles from the bath and placed them on his dimpled baby-chin.

"I'm an old man, look!" he said, before sucking on his frothy pint of pretend lager. Their bath-beer tasted like soapy air—nothing like the real thing—which Girlo had tried once before; a stolen sip from the summer slurps of a neglected beer-glass. It had burned the back of her tongue, but the warm, fuzzy residue it left behind her eyes was strangely enticing. She never really got the appeal, but it seemed to be her mother's get-out-of-bed, put-a-smile-on-your face tonic: a necessity that Girlo grew to accept.

"Can I wear your silky dressing gown, Scottie?" called Girlo from the bedroom.

"Whit ye up tae in there noo? Dinae tooch!"

"Please Scottie? It's like a princess dress."

"Och, it's ma genuine silk kimono. Ye'll get Tizer aw doon it!"

"I won't, I promise… pleeeease."

"Och, aw richt then. If it'll shush ye up."

Girlo flounced into the living-room, which was cosy because it was lit with a lamp behind a Geisha's parasol. Crystal was cwtched up on the couch and was being nice. "Come and cwtch up with Mammy, kids."

"Can we watch Dumbo, Mam?" Eddie asked.

"Daena hae Dumbo, Laddie… jist 101 Dalmations. Ye an' yer seshtuh can watch tha' in the marning."

"Unlee if yuh good. Now get in will, ewe?!" Crystal always made empty promises. "Come and watch a film with me and Scottie."

"It's ma favourite," he said as he pushed in the video cassette with a clunk-clunk noise.

The film opened with a portrait of a woman with dark doughy eyes much like Crystal's. Then there were pictures of elephants marching towards her. One of their trunks struck her. In slow motion she screamed, her face turning blurry. Then, there was a huge puff of smoke, the cries of a newborn filling the room. The camera cut to a spooky carnival.

"Ant-nee 'opkins, inni' Scot?"

"Aye… Eric met 'im in the lift at the club… when they wez felming dint ee?"

"Did eee? He nevah tole me that!" Crystal scrambled for her fag-box and lit up.

Behind a gold curtain there was a hullabaloo, and a man blew a conch. The film cut to a large vat of vinegar where a giant foetus bobbed, then a woman with a beard laughed hysterically.

"Life is full of surprises!" chimed Scottie in line with the film. The kids watched with disturbed curiosity as the Elephant Man appeared from the shadows. A close-up shot zoomed in to his grey face, pale and bumpy as though he had hard-boiled eggs stuck under his skin.

"What's wrong with him, Mam?" cried Eddie, "Did Dumbo jump on his mother's belly when he was in there?"

"Sssh now, will ewe?!"

As the film progressed the tears began to flow. When the Elephant Man got locked in a cage with baboons, Scottie jumped up and walked over to the window. The Lego warren cityscape below felt alien to him. Figures, like specks of undissolved vitreous gel floated between the incessant snakes of fierce fluorescent cars. "Look at thaim doon there. Mindless machines, dinnae ken how lucky thay are."

Crystal went to his side and lit his cigarette from hers.

"They ca'ed *us* EVIL... it's like the fuckin' Holocaust ... wipin' us oot thay are."

"I know Scot, and we miss him every day. It's a fucking tragedy."

"Kept me, his only love, awa'. How dare they. How fuckin' dare they."

Scottie was swinging his glass between his thumb and forefinger—swinging it, then swigging as he spoke.

"But you are a'right. You survived!"

"D'ye ken whit it's like, Crystal, tae be persecuted? Tae be locked awa' fae the fowk ye love? No bein' able tae haud their haund."

"The numbers have dropped now and there's things they cun doo these days..."

"Na, it winnae bring him back, will it?"

"Have you had your results back yet?"

"Such a damn waste... D'ye ken whit it's like, Crystal, tae be persecuted? Tae be locked awa' fae the fowk ye love? No bein' able tae haud their haund."

"They can do things now, Scott. It's better now. You'll be ok, no matter what... you'll see."

"Och, anyway, ye're damned if ye bone an' ye're damned if ye dinnae."

At that moment there was a rat-a-tat at the door accompanied by an angry voice through the letterbox: "Oi! Fucking poofter!"

"I amnae an animal," shouted Scottie in time with the film. "I ama human bein'."

"Fuck off you little bastards or I'll tell your mothers!" shouted Crystal.

"Ooz that Mam?"

"No-one love, just kids."

Two hours later they were dancing around the living-room, singing Gloria Gaynor's, 'I Will Survive,' Scottie twirling in his silk kimono, Crystal singing into a hairbrush. Girlo stole one of Scottie's cigarettes and smoked it in the kitchen. He called out to her to get him a drink while she was there. She stared into the empty fridge; there was plenty of vodka, but no mixer left.

"Use waa-terrr," he shouted. So she filled the glass right up with vodka, adding just a splash of water because Crystal had said the water was poisonous in London. Scottie came bounding into the kitchen and snatched the glass out of Girlo's hand. "Whit's the hauld up, Lassie?"

"Are you a woman or a man?" asked Girlo. She felt she needed to ask since she'd noticed lots of people on the television who didn't sound like they looked, or didn't look like they sounded, even. Boy George from Top of the Pops had long multi-coloured hair and sang like a woman. Then, there was Tracey Chapman, who had short, cropped hair, and sang with a baritone voice. Scottie looked Girlo straight in the eye and said: "does sss'et… matter?" Girlo didn't know how to answer that. Boys seemed to have all the fun and get away with murder.

"Ye can be whaever the fuck ye want tae be, lassie. Dinnae let naebody tell ye who ye should be. Naeb'dy!" Scottie took a large slug of straight vodka and Girlo honestly thought he was going to drop dead right there in front of her. He staggered over to the kitchen sink and snorted. Then coughed. Then gasped for air. He coughed again for some time, then eventually raised his red face to reveal a worm of brain creeping from out of his right nostril. He held a finger over his left nostril and blew the worm into the sink. "Whoosh! Rocket fuel! Chin chin!" He took another large slug from the tumbler.

The next day Girlo saw Scottie's brain-worm still clinging to a sponge floating in the shallow water of the washing-up bowl.

LADY MUCK

Girlo was still tamping about being banged up. The more she thought about it, the more it riled her and the more it justified her bender. When she got into work, Ruby was on break. She was running a bath and had popped in a Big Blue bath bomb from Lush. "Strip off," instructed Ruby.

"I'm a'right," replied Girlo, still half-pissed.

"Get in! I got a client in an hour, and you need to do your fucking job," she said flouncing off. Girlo undressed and sat on the edge of the bathtub watching the bath bomb bob and hop under the force of the running water. "Yewuh fuckin' lucky I knew that copper, you know? Very fuckin' lucky!" called Ruby from the kitchen.

Girlo dipped a toe into the water. "How did you find me?"

"A little birdie told me." Nannie Pearl used to say that. Girlo lowered herself into the water. "Which one, Peter or Paul?"

"Shut up smart arse! Get in the bath, you stink like a raw steak."

She lay back, allowing the liquid to fill her thrumming eardrums but she could still hear a client being dutifully punished by a vixen in the next room and in the kitchen below, the voices of men and tinny pans clanging, cupboards slamming; all amplified by the enamel vessel in which she lay. The water held her: a nubile figure shimmering beneath silver and blue, sweat and steam as one. She felt at peace, almost herself. And then came the urge to scratch her unshaven legs. In her Nannie Pearl's bath, she'd scrape the skin, peeling layers back with an old pumice stone. She started to scratch, wide raking scratches up and down her legs. As she scraped, the vampiric grin of The Snot appeared in her mind's eye.

"Oh Moosh, leave those lovely pins alone!" Ruby had poked her head around the bathroom door.

Girlo shot up and smoothed her shins.

"C'mon Lady Muck! It's showtime!" Her Grandmamma used to call her that.

Downstairs, jewelled eyes and high-glossed lips made up the wall paint. The playgirls bound in a huddle of giggles, bodices, and body-glitter while Girlo recited her beguiling phone-script. "We've a selection of delectable delights… Luxury Apartment… Discreet Service." The inquirer's shy telephone manner shifted to guttural grunts and moans… "We have another time-waster, Ladies!" Cocking her wrist, Girlo curled then shook her fingers to indicate that this one was a wanker trying to score a freebie. She switched from headset mode to speakerphone: a cue for the playgirls to tease—a warm-up for what Ruby called: "The Full Girlfriend Experience Extravaganza!" She cranked up the tunes, Drum & Bass filling the space.

BOOM—wah wah wah!
BOOM—wah wah wah!
BOOM—wah wah wah!

Raunchy Ruby took centre stage with a floppy rubber butt plug, flat-side pushed onto pubic bone, thrusting herself across the playhouse. Moonshine and Candy's throaty cackles between Corky shots and fast fag-drags drowned out the insults of the flailing telephone inquirer. Enter Suzie (the Floozie), who playfully sucked Ruby's rubber softie until the wanker cut the line.

BOOM—wah wah wah!
BOOM—wah wah wah!
BOOM—wah wah wah!

Popped cork to blur the edges.

BOOM – wah wah wah!
BOOM – wah wah wah!
BOOM – wah wah wah!

Champagne to whet the lips, strictly Bucks Fizz to follow Madame's orders: The Full Girlfriend Experience minus the hangover.

BOOM – wah wah wah!
BOOM – wah wah wah!
BOOM – wah wah wah!

"Be real, playgirls! Suck him in and keep him coming back for more."

DOORBELL SCREAMED

A mad rush for stilettos, KY Jelly and Max Factor touch-ups. Music—Air Freshener—Lights—Action!

Client number one. Tied, gagged and blindfolded. In a two-girl, Ruby and Suzie, fondled the cock. "Makes a nice change from packing factory chickens." They give him the fingers and clenched-white fists mock-punch the tight air he sucks. "This one likes us to leave marks." *Just numbers. A game, it figures.* Moonshine in for a quick nine o'clock, not on form from the day job, floor-buffer hum still running up her. "Credit cards sky-high from La Senza and tuition for the kids." Candy works number two, a real softie who buys her trinkets from the high-street. "Married. Workaholic. Tiddler who can't squirt." She sticks to the no rush policy as front-of-house juggles walk-ins. Diary backed up.

Discretion is a priority, especially in a poky flat above an Indian takeaway.

Client number three has a bit.

BOOM – wah wah wah!
BOOM – wah wah wah!
BOOM – wah wah wah!

He likes tit wanks. Suzie's swing from side-to-side, so Candy made the earner, and skags her fishnet on the Claire's Accessories anklet from Tiddler. "Worth it for that distinction in Linguistics?" *Just numbers. A game, it figures.* He likes to lick her. BOOM— wah wah wah! Bites until she pisses. Sometimes it feels nice pissing in his face. Instead of working the tills for six-quid-an-hour, work the fellas! As dawn drew in and the drunken, shy, and lonely had been milked, Madame Ruby appeared. She sniffed the curried air, counted the cash, drug-checked the designer bags, and extinguished the candles on the private bar. Then she turned to the playgirls with fizzing Champagne flutes: "Let us toast to The Full Girlfriend Experience Extravaganza!"

Once Girlo had cleared the boudoir, placed the last nappy sack of used condoms in the bin and the last aubergine towel in the machine, she paid the girls then kissed them all goodbye.

Ruby went into the bathroom to peel off her false lashes. There was something sullen about her, something Girlo had never seen in her before. "You ok, love?"

"Can you stay here, with me, tonight?"

Girlo wasn't used to seeing Ruby like this; frail. She hadn't worked at all that day. The last time she'd taken any time off was when Girlo naively wiped her vibrators over with Zoflora and it had given her thrush for a week. Ruby took off her underwear and filled the sink. "Don't worry about these delicates… I'll hand-wash them in the morning."

"What's up, love?"

"I had an operation."

"An operation? When? On what?"

Ruby stood before her; small, about to burst. "They had to take off the neck of my womb."

"Oh god! Why?"

"Cancer."

Girlo did stay that night. It was just like a slumber party, watching Pretty Woman in fluffy pyjamas. "It smelled like burnt pork," Ruby said, over the piano scene.

"What smelt like burnt pork?"

"When I had my op. Burnt pork and iodine."

"You'll be alright now though, won't you? You'll be alright?"

Ruby sparked a fag. "I fucking hates the stink of 'ospitals, I do..."

Girlo reached for the remote to reduce the volume.

"When I was a little girl my mother's boyfriend used to kick the fuck out of her. Not constant, on weekends mainly, after the pub. Until one time he pushed it too far, and cracked her head open, right down there—" Ruby used a red fingernail to score the skin of her forehead. "I remember her running at me, head cracked in half. I tried to push it back together but the blood just kept on comin'." She sat up, pulling her knees into her chest: "Anyway, he come with us, in the ambulance, to the 'ospital, and they left me in a room with 'im and he told me that if I ever breathed a fuckin' word, he would personally finish her off and then come for me... I didn't say a word, but the cunt still come for me."

Girlo gently stroked her arm.

"After that, she was in a wheelchair, and because my grandfather had a used car business, he stayed and pretended to be the perfect fucking husband. But he wasn't. He had his bitch-uv a sister come up and do most of the dirty work, and I—" she swallowed back her words.

"You don't have to talk about this if you don't want to Rube. It's—"

"No, it's fine. I dun mind. I was about twelve by now, and because my mother was "a dribbling mess," uz ee used to call her—he'd come in my room and touch me up."

"That's terrible."

"But you know what the worst thing was?"

"I—I don't—"

85

"It wasn't the fact that he'd put my mother in a fucking wheelchair or that he used to do what he liked with me—the worst thing was the look in my mother's eyes. She saw what he was doin' t'me and she could never forgive 'erself, and there was absolutely fuck-all she could do about it."

"Fuck! I'm so sorry. Where is she now?"

"Oh... she's dead now. Not long after my grandad 'ad a 'eart attack. Broken heart, I reckon. They were so close. She inherited the car lot but because that bastard had married her after the 'accident', he got the fucking lot! He didn't need me there no more, so when I was 14 he chucked me out. I went to live with my grandmother. I soon fucked that up though."

"Why, what happened?"

"In the end I just couldn't keep it in. It had to come out one way or another. I was mitching from school, drinking, smoking, fucking about with boys an' tha'. My head was fucked right up! I just had to tell someone so I told my granny, and she threw me out. Said she'd had enough of my filthy lies and thieving."

"I left my mother. Mind yew, she wasn't the most loving. When I told her that I was being abused by my uncle she didn't believe me," added Girlo.

"Ha! 'The Abusive Uncle.' Textbook! They tell us to watch out for the Big Bad Wolf or warn us about Stranger Danger, but the real monsters are lurking under our own roofs!"

"Luckily, I had my Nannie Pearl. I went to live with her. I haven't looked back since."

As they talked through the night it occurred to Girlo that despite its function, the name Retreat was exactly that, a place where the lost belonged. The lonely could escape, forget themselves, give up their identities to live out hidden fantasies, nurture needs, find solace in the comfort of a warm bosom. Girlo thought of it as a place where identity became lost in transaction, a welcome distraction. *Identity lost in transaction.* An extraction of self. *Identity lost in transaction.* A counteraction to the chains of marriage. *Identity lost in transaction.* A reaction to the climate of hyper-sexualisation. Identity lost in transaction. Attraction to the bad girl, naughty girl, dirty girl, good girl, girl next door. *Identity lost in transaction.* A fraction of power, paid for by the hour. Erection. Cure for hypertension. *Identity lost in transaction.* A fleeting, no-strings interaction—inner-beast subtraction. Identity lost...

IN TRANSACTION

Her eyes, like a girl's best friend's, made your member grow. Your secret friend, her furtive foe. Blow your job, your wife, for her rented belle. Your pin-up heaven, her lucrative hell. Un-taxed. Waxed. Slender with curves in all the right places. Lipstick snack. Turn you on, turn around. Upside-down and on your back. Discreet service. Guaranteed satisfaction. A mutual abstraction of feigned attraction. Their heterotopia, lost in transaction.

SHEWOLF

In true tribal style there were three *boss* families who ran the Rock. Son-strong, each family scrapped for the daddy's share of what was left in the former-pit village. Jack was the head of the Wolf family. He and his wife, Pearl, and their four sons, Eric, Jimmy, Micky and Bobby frequented The Muni opposite the castle. A haunt for travellers, boxers, gangsters, miners and punks, The Muni had a brutal reputation. As soon as it was Open Doors, they could all be found in the murk of the bottom bar—it was like a den of iniquity in there—and among the beef and sharp suits lurked a few nasty characters who the Wolves came up against from time-to-time, including the infamous 'Dobby 'Ole in the 'ead', Eric's nemesis. After a row over money, he and Eric had come to blows in the men's bogs: 'Ole in the 'ead had Eric up against the concrete urinal by the scruff of his shirt. "I'm warning you, pretty boy. You bettuh get me tha' money." Eric scrambled around, feeling his way for a weapon, and managed to pull a piece of copper piping off the wall, prising it from its shoddy installation. He whacked Dobby over the head with it, dragged him to the stinking toilet bowl and shoved his head in. "Dobby 'Ole in the 'ead iz it?"

'Ole in the 'ead tried to push off, his hands pulling off the fag-burned Bakelite lid of the cistern. "Dun worry about it, Butt…"

Eric tried to hold him firm but the grease from his Brillo cream and leather collar made it difficult. He stretched up to pull the chain, shoving Dobby's head into the water. "Dobby 'Ole inne 'ed iz it? No, Dobby 'ead in the 'ole!"

The Wolf's connections gave them the edge on the Rock. Jack Wolf was a cop-hating ex-coal miner who darted around town in his Savile Row suit like a lost boy on whizz. A local celebrity, he'd often get mistaken for Tom Jones, who he claimed he'd worked with. Jack's hands were as rough as sandpaper, reddened from cement burn, knuckles tattooed with the obligatory blue-ink dots. He'd ride around town in a white convertible with his dogs hanging out of the back windows, tongues flapping in the breeze. He'd been chucked out of 'everywhere' "because of those fucking dogs!" On its opening week, Jack parked up in Asda's freshly tarmacked car park. "C'mon en, boys," he'd said, as he held the dented passenger door open for his canine rabble. Through a swathe of puzzled housewives, he'd led the unleashed dogs straight up to the meat counter: "Which one do you want boys?" He'd pointed to the steaks on display. Jack was swiftly removed and banned for life.

He was also banned from The Arms (several times), the bookies (for creating a ruckus) and the coffee shop at the top of town (for bedding the owner's daughter). Jack had fathered Eric at seventeen so was more like a brother than a father. Eric usually bore the brunt of Jack's temper. When he came home wired from a ruckus he'd start on Eric, who in turn would punch his brother Jimmy, who would give Micky a wallop. Micky would kick Bob and Bob would kick the dog. But it was Pearl who always took the biggest hit. Every bit of cash she managed to scrape together, Jack squandered on drink and women and gambling. Whenever she saw a piece of land or a big house at auction, she'd plead with him to invest. All she needed was his signature; she had no right to buy without her husband's say so.

Later, when video cassettes became popular, Pearl had the bright idea of opening a video rental shop before Blockbusters had even come out with it. "It'll never catch on," Jack laughed, bereft of Pearl's foresight and strategic capability. He was impulsive—a fucking show-off. But people loved him, and when he climbed the Cenotaph, he was revered as a working-class hero. He was a scaffolder by trade so skilfully managed to mount the flat-surfaced Cenotaph, (the height of a council house) without any ropes or foot-holes. He'd stayed up there for three days.

"What's ee doin'?" asked a member of the crowd who had gathered to see the spectacle.

"He's protesting, ee iz."

"That's my father, that is," said Micky, trying to winch a Chinese take-away up to him. "Good on you, Dad!" When the police came with their megaphones he pushed them away. "Fuck the Pigs!" he shouted. "Fuck the Police! Fuck that Witch, Thatchuh and Fuck the War!" Jack was a baby-boomer, an original Teddy Boy who'd been too young to enlist in the Second World War but his father and three uncles had served, fighting for King and Country. All three of them had come back unscathed so their names were not etched into the Cenotaph stone. But Jack had scratched his own name beneath those who had fallen: "Jack Wolf Woz Yere '75."

Eric remembered seeing Jack's father, a WWI veteran, folding up cardboard boxes and sweeping in the market. He'd ask him for a shilling and every time, his grandfather would find one behind Eric's ear. Now, his own father, Jack Wolf, was perched on top of the Cenotaph speaking on behalf of the boys about to be sent to war by order of the Iron Lady. He knew that Bobby and Micky, who were in the T.A, would have to fight. That wasn't really a problem though, they'd been brought up to fight. "We are the Wolf Warriors," Eric hollered as he made his way to The Muni.

Crystal didn't want to go up town on her own so she convinced Beryl to come. "Come on, Ber, I wanna show off my new red rhinestone platforms!" She really fancied this fella who drank in The Muni. So, off they went, with hair backcombed and flares pressed so stiffly you could slice a tomato on the crease. As they swung around the corner on the shed-of-a-bus they could see the sinking turret of the castle. Despite the weather, town was as busy as ever. Crystal always loved the weekend buzz. But the entrance to The Muni was like the front-door of Bilbo Baggins', and inside, a row of flat-caps mushroomed along the top-bar. "I think I'll have a Cinzano and lemonade," she said, removing her coat and fluffing her hair.

"I think I'll have the same," said Beryl. "Can you see him?"

"Not yet, no."

"Are you sure he'll be here, Crys? If you've gone and dragged me up here for nuthin' in this fucking rain, I'll—"

"Ellor Lair-deez." A man with some nerve swooped in. "Can I get you a drink, twinkle toes?"

Crystal pulled a face at Beryl. "We've already got one thank ewe."

"Er, sorry. I'm Eric... and you are?"

Beryl giggled. She didn't get out much. She spent most of her time at home making dolls' clothes with scraps of fabric. At that point, the leather-patched elbow of another young man appeared at the bar. "I see you've met my buttie, by yere... A'right, Eric boy?"

"A'right, butt! You know these two, d'you?"

"We do now," said Crystal.

"So, what brings two lovely lairdies like yuh-selves into town?"

"Well, my sister wanted to see if you—"

Crystal dug the toe of her red shoe into her sister's leg.

"Just wanted to get out of the Village for a bit like. Wha' about you?"

"Well, there's a bit more life up yere, I cun ashoo-wer yew of that!"

"Where you from 'en?"

"He's from the Rock."

"Oooh, we've heard all about you Rock boys!"

"Crys... Mam and Dad says we mustn't bother with Rock boys."

"We been warned t'stay away frum ewe lot!" Crystal took a sip of her Cinzano and turned her barstool to face Eric.

She was soon captivated and followed Eric to the forbidden Rock: a place so deep in the valleys it wasn't even on the map. It wasn't long before they started courting and the following month they went up the Checkmate with a few of Crystal's Aber friends who'd heard about "this Eric," and wanted to see what all the fuss was about. Crystal wore a blue blouse and underlined her bottom lids with an azure liner that made her eyes pop. Eric made an effort too, wearing his tan leather shoes. Crystal was a good-looking girl and got a lot of attention on the dance floor. As she spun round, some random bloke came out of nowhere and grabbed her by the waist. Eric, who was standing at the bar, saw this chancer grab his new girlfriend and ploughed his way across to them.

"I know he's mixed up, but I think I've fallen for him," Crystal told Beryl in the girl's toilet. "And I'm late…"

"Dad will fucking kill him!"

"Dad will fucking kill me!" Their father was a drinker who'd warned them about Rock boys. "Eric's not like the others though. You know, all fists, an' tha'. He's got a good head on his shoulders *really*. He went to grammar school and everything."

Eric and his father never saw eye-to-eye. It was a wonder the two of them survived a six-week job in the West Country without the buffer of Pearl and his three brothers. Eric's last job had been at a cider factory but his mother had nagged him to pack it in because he was losing weight and constantly pissed from the free cider and weekend filching. One of the lads had been stupid enough to drink directly from the tap of the 30ft cider vat and the force of it killed him. "Now, that's a way to go!"

His new job was to steal diesel to fill the generators on-site. He'd scout out huge trucks parked up in lay-bys and with a long plastic straw suck the fuel out into barrels stolen from the cider factory, a good little earner: "The 'undrud quid a week was like gagging money. If caught, the bosses knew *nothing*."

Their digs were in the Lodge Inn, a pub run by the middle-aged Mrs. Tucker. She kept birds out back and Georgie, the Alsatian, out front. Each room was decorated in one single colour. On arrival, Eric and Jack were given the keys to the twin 'Blue Room,' where everything from the bedspread to the bog-roll was a shade of blue. "It's like a fucking morgue in yere, all this blue," Eric said, hanging up his shirt in the wardrobe. "She's no' all there iz she? Le's 'ope all the women dun't look like her, boy."

Their first port of call was to check out the local. The Stag's

Head was in pissing distance, full of wax Barbours and fraying Dai caps. "Fucking 'ell. Iss no' much bettuh in yere, iz it?" Jack said picking a strand of curly tobacco out of his bitter. "Must liven up on the Friday, surely..."

The 'bonk-eyed barmaid' tried to wink at Eric when he approached the bar for his round. "Alright, me loov-er? You ain't frum these paa-rts, uh-yuh?"

"Orvuh the border weyar, love. Wayulls."

"Ere tha' Jerry? These boys uh from Wayulls."

An old sod who'd been falling asleep in his tankard looked up. "Why, why, why Delilia?" he sang, before slumping back into his drink. "Jerry 'ere luvs t'do a Tom Jones numb-err." The barmaid pointed to a tattered poster that had been fixed to the wall with a variety of tapes. "Tomorruh."

"He'll 'ave a run for iz munee, love: Jack loves a bit of Tommy Jornz ee do."

The barmaid tried to wink again as she placed two pints on the counter.

After a week's work, Jack's hands were chalky and pinched from handling the scaffolding rods. Eric's diesel breath could've set a fire alarm off. The two came back to the blue room and got ready for Friday night at The Stag. "This shirt alright, Dad?"

"It'll do... c'mon, stop faffing about like a woman. I'm gagging fuh ruh pint."

The Stag had burst into life. In the lounge big groups of people were sitting around a single table covered in soppy beer mats and an overflowing ashtray, dropping fag ash all over the place as they laughed and larked around. Women with set hairdos sipped Babychams from lipstick-rimmed glasses while men supped pints crawling with curly brown tobacco stands. There were a few young ones, looking cool in their bell-bottoms and shell lippie, hanging around next to the pool table in the bar so Eric joined them. "This ain't gunna be forever, this. I got dreams!" He took his shot and potted a red.

"Ere tha' Cherry? This one by 'ere is gonna go far!" A Bonnie Tyler lookalike blew blue dust from her cue tip.

"I got a place in Coleg Harlech."

"Never 'eared of it."

"Part of the Worker's Education Association."

Jack did a lap of the pub, noticing Eric from across the room.

"He's not boring you iz ee, love?" Jack was always a lady's man, envious of Eric's raw youth. "He's only fourteen, you know that dun ewe?"

Fourteen pints later, they got back to the Lodge. Georgie the dog's ears pricked up at the clinking of Eric's keys as he struggled to find the keyhole.

"Give um yere, fuh fucksake. Gotta do everything myself, mun," Jack snapped before falling through the front-door like a Weeble Wobble. Georgie shot up from his bed in the breakfast room and caught them in the foyer, barking his head off.

"Shush! Fuck off, fucking mutt!"

But the dog was livid and he set the birds off in the back. A cacophony of barking and tweeting started as Jack and Eric felt along the skirting boards and door frames for the switch. "What idiot puts a dog in the front room of a guesthouse?!" There was a big kerfuffle as the two men tripped up the stairs, clinging to the spindles. Georgie's jaws locked on Eric's leg. "My jeans! Get off! These are fucking new, these are!"

"I'll 'ave 'im now, come yere boy," Jack grabbed the dog by his shoulders.

"Get 'im off me, Dad!"

Then, without hesitation, Jack sank his teeth into the dog's fur. It was at that moment Mrs Tucker flicked on the landing light, illuminating the scene.

"What *is* the meaning of this?" Eric tried to mumble an apology while his father continued to scrap with Georgie. He had the dog in a headlock, trying to force its jaws shut while the dog was losing the plot. In true Wolf style, Jack wrestled him to the floor and bit a chunk out of his ear. Mrs Tucker let out a wail: "Get off my Georgie!" The dog whimpered and darted back to his bed.

Jack stood up and spat out a bloody bit of dog ear. "What? He bit me first!"

"Out! Get out! Both of you, out!"

Jack was a helluvah boy and managed to find a warm place to get his head down that night. Eric had to sleep in the van.

The next day they drove home, Jack bringing Pearl a little unwanted gift.

WIFE

After sitting up on the GP's couch, Pearl pulled on her undergarments.

"Have you *been* with anyone lately?" asked the doctor.

"*Been* with anyone? Oh, only my husband, Doctor, why?"

"It seems we have a problem."

That fucking bastard! Pearl decided not to let on but instead, bided her time.

One chilly November night, the estate globed in coal smoke, Jack was laying low after a run-in with a Cardiff bruiser. He was in the house, for once. After he'd polished off half a bottle of Hennessy with a pot of tea, he stoked the fire, chucking in coal stolen from some posh house. Pearl had been out that night, for once, and came in half-pissed and happy.

"And what time d'you call this?"

Pearl didn't respond. She was fed up with his antics. She was the only one trying to keep things together and everything she built, he went and smashed up. "Been out screwing all and sundry, 'ave you? Like the village tart you are." She was in the hallway, removing her fur-trimmed coat and gloves. "Aye… yew cun fucking talk," she said in bitter jest.

"Where've yew been then?"

She knew where this was going.

"I been out with Coral, I told ewe this before, Jack."

"'Oo thuh fuck iz Coral when she's at 'ome?" Jack sat back in his club chair (found in a skip the previous week) and hand-rolled a cigarette.

"Jokeus' Missis."

"Jokeus izzit?? Joke is on us! Joke is on me!" He was spitting his words, working himself up.

"I thought you an' 'im were uz thick uz thieves last week in The Muni?! Thought ee wuz 'elpen ewe out with some bother."

"Dun fuckin' menshun that to me. Where's the dinner then? Starving in by here."

"I'm going t'bed Jack, I'm tired. Do yuh self some beans on torst."

"Yewer meant to be my fucking wife! Where's my fucking dinner?"

The fire was smothering so Jack got up, leaving his cigarette smouldering in the cut-glass ashtray; a hunk-of-a-thing nicked from a cocktail lounge. He picked up a poker from the fireplace companion and started to prod at the black husks—pushing at them to reveal their glowing underbellies. "I'm here, keeping the fucking fire lit, and you? You are out *fucking* gallivanting: making a name for yourself, and a show of me... and the boys... what kind of a mother are you?"

As he poked away at the embers, Pearl snuck into the living-room. She had noticed the empty bottle on the table and had heard he'd taken a beating from a few scabs, who he'd gone to 'paste' for crossing the picket line. She'd knew she was in for it before she even stepped foot in the house. She should've got out of there. But why the fuck should she go and sleep on her mother's settee and make out she'd lost her fucking keys again? This was her house. She kept it.

Jack stabbed at the coal. Spits of flame leapt up the chimney. "Yewer a slag. A village bike. And everyone round yere knows it!"

He had a fucking cheek calling her out on monogamy. He'd given her the fucking clap! She tiptoed over to the table while he angrily punched at the fire. The ashtray gleamed in the firelight, edges beckoning her closer.

"You are nuffin but a fuckin' slag. A woman of the night. Wait until I tell your mother."

"My mother has got nothing to do with it! And anyway, I'm not the slag in this house Jack Wolf. I know what you've been up to. You must think I'm stupid. You think I don't know you're playing away?"

"I don't know what you're talking about, Pearl."

"LIAR!" she screamed, and without a moment's hesitation picked up the ashtray and lifted it over her head. "Have THAT. You lyin' bass-tud!" Just before she smashed the thing over his head, he looked up in total disbelief.

The force of it knocked him clean out. He fell beside the hearth in a cloud of cigarette ash, butts lying around him like stuffing from a soft toy. The ashtray had split precisely in half and there was blood everywhere. Pearl panicked. She grabbed the keys to the Mini and bombed it up the Cop Shop.

It was an unusually slow night at the police station, the officers playing Crib and supping on tea in front of the coiled bars of an electric heater, when in flew a crazed woman with blood over her hands and face. "Officer! Officer, I think I've killed my husband."

"Calm down now, Madam. Let me take your name." The police officer shrugged and smirked over his shoulder at his colleague while he removed the notepad from his top pocket. He licked the tip of his stubby pencil.

"But you don't understand. He's just lying there next to the fire. I think he's dead!"

"Yes, yes, we heard you. Now, what's your name?"

When the police eventually arrived at the house, all was quiet. Pearl turned her key in the door expecting Jack's body to be stretched out like a slaughtered stag in front of the hearth. He wasn't there. The fire was on its last legs, the teapot and bottle of whiskey cleared away. There wasn't a speck of blood to be found. "Well, he was right here! I hit him over the head with the ashtray while he poked the f-f-f-ire."

"There doesn't seem to be anything suspicious here, Madam. Are you alright? Would you like to sit down?" Pearl hadn't noticed but the sleeves of her sheepskin were soaked in blood. It hadn't come from Jack; it was coming from her. She found a tea towel in the kitchen to stop the bleeding. *Where the fuck was that bastard?*

"Are you ok in there, Madam?"

Pearl managed to pull herself together. "Quite ok, thank you. Would you boys like a cup of tea?"

They heard a toilet flush upstairs. Footsteps descended into the hallway. "Hello, who's there? This is constable Davies and P.C.—"

"Well, well, well. What's going on by yere, then, Officers?" Jack standing in the doorway, immaculate, wearing his Sunday Best, not a scratch on him. Pearl came out from the kitchen cradling her swaddled wounds. "Jack?! How the... what the...? You were—" She pointed at the fireplace.

"Is this your wife, Mr—?"

"Yes, when she wants to be, Officer."

"Your wife claims to have killed you this evening."

"She's always trying to kill me over someink, Officers. That's what wives do, issunt it?"

"But I... I... I smashed him... "

"Shush now, love. Let's let these policemen get on with their work, shall we?... Thank you for your concern, Officers, but she's not quite all there if you get my meaning."

"You might want to take her up the emergency room to get that hand seen to."

"We'll be sure to. Thank you for your concern, Officers. Goodnight now. Goodnight."

At the hospital, the nurse stitched up Pearl's little finger. She had sliced right through the ligaments, so it had to be dressed in a splint. Jack stood over her, his wandering eye undressing the nurse. "I've told her before to be more careful with the peeler."

"Just make sure you keep it out of water, Mrs Wolf," insisted the nurse as they left.

"I tell you what, Pearl, you're gonna have a helluvuh job doing the dishes with your hand like that, now, in ewe? Silly girl!"

"I won't be doing no dishes. I'm leaving you."

"Where you gonna go?"

"London... just like Christine."

"Christine, who?"

A HAND TO PLAY

The hand built her a bike before she could ride it. She took it to peddle it to the corners of his grainy world. The hand opened her up to boys. She breathed fires, conquered trees, rough 'n' tumbled with tombstoning Tom, Dick & Harry. The hand stuffed her with fibreglass, then stitched her with thread so, she daren't tread, beyond hunger of his bed. Until, teen-bled, no script, unwed, she ended up with a baby. Gin dead. With the hand's final word, she rode across borders without tracks, to the window of eyes, to be a fashion sketch, of Mary Quant size. But the hand of rule caged her, paraded and staged her for the scalps and suits who slapped her gem-wax buttocks, smoothed her polished thighs. A mannequin, a plaything for snollygosters in loose neckties. The fateful dip in a skinny pool, nude, beneath a lecherous moon. She was handed to the stiff with an upper-crust lip. Was it kismet? Was it just a blip? After her postcoital cigarette, slithers of glass pushed from within. Grew from her cheek, from her lids, from her tits, to score the crease of his pillowed peck. Cold blood cast a shadow of war between them. She invented sex in the sixties when the odd squeeze, translated to sleaze. And news-hacks picked at the lauded titles' bricked wounds where landed ranks of peevish prudes were toppled by a tiny teenage termagant from the wrong side of the divide.

for Christine Keeler.

CARIAD

Nannie Pearl's always smelt like real home-cooked chips. On the stove there was a large black pot full of hardened lard which would be fired up on the arrival of any of her grandkids. In would go handful after handful of chips until the bubbling cauldron worked its magic, transforming potato slithers into crisp, golden morsels to be devoured with lashings of vinegar and dipped into a creamy egg yolk. As soon as those potatoes hit the hot fat, it would scare the shit out of them. They'd be banished from the kitchen.

"Stay in by there, kids—Burn!" Pearl would say as she put a lid on the chip pan. The kids were not allowed beyond the beaded curtain, which swung like painted dreadlocks over the kitchen entrance. To Pearl's annoyance they'd swing on it and wrap the raggedy strands around their heads like hair. "Look at my long-long hair, Nan."

"Lovely, Cariad. Now take Eddie in by there while I do this food, will ewe!?" Since they always found themselves waiting in doorways or by windows, Eddie and Girlo had developed a range of games centred around windows and doors. Nannie Pearl's living room curtains were always great for giving dramatic musical performances to a tipsy audience. Nannie Pearl hated net curtains—notorious dust collectors. They could only be used for ghost games or when playing practical jokes anyway: "Suck through that Eddie," Girlo would dare, then laugh her head off as he'd burst into fits of coughing from breathing in a shitload of nicotine. Blinds were to be used with caution; they always had a tendency to break from a mere touch. However, the vertical blinds at the Doctors were fantastic for 'knock-knock, who's there?' Doors were of great interest—especially ones with knockers— or better still—ones with bells! They'd take pleasure in ringing doorbells as many times as they could, until they were threatened by either a visit from The White Monkey, a stint in the coal shed, or worse still—being sent to 'the 'omes!' The 'omes was what the adults threatened as a last resort. Kids in 'the 'omes' had no shoes or socks, were naughty little children who Father Christmas forgot all about.

"What about Annie? Did Father Christmas forget her? She wasn't very naughty, was she?"

"And Oliver Twist? He wasn't naughty neevah!"

"Eat your Weetabix!" or "Go out and play!" was the usual retort. Letter boxes were a good source of entertainment, providing a means of pain and punishment, especially if stiffly hinged.

"I dare you to put your hand in there," Eddie would say before releasing the letter box on Girlo's pudgy fingers.

"Nan! Eddie just slammed the letterbox on my finger!"

"Come away from the door you two. Just bee'ave will ewe?!"

As much fun as doors were, the games were loud and annoying. With curtains and door coverings there was a bit more leeway. Adults allowed the game to go on because "they're doing no 'arm."

Out of all the curtains, Girlo was particularly fond of the plastic ribbon ones found at the bookies. When it was her father's turn to 'watch' them, he'd pop into the Bookies before dropping them off at Nannie Pearl's. The Bookies was much like the pub, except the bar was behind glass and the punters were green-eyed rather than red-eyed. They'd lose themselves on little tellies pushed into corners between blackboards. Blueish smoke lingered and rested like a film of oil over the crowd of Dai caps and bald heads when the race was being run. It burned Girlo's nostrils and made her eyes stream so that she was ordered to stand by the door. There she'd plait the plastic ribbon curtain meant to hide all the gambling men from their nagging wives. When the race finished the smoke dispersed and swirled, and the still figures became animated, shouting and throwing their betting slips. By the time Eric had ripped up his last slip and was ready to go, Girlo had almost plaited the entire curtain into a rainbow braid, like one of her Little Pony's tails.

"Come on, you two!"

"But I need to finish the hair!"

"It'll be there next time."

"Will it? Do you promise?"

"Yep… come on. I'll get you a pack of crisps in the pub on the way."

Girlo tried to braid Nannie Pearl's kitchen curtain too, but the cylindrical beads would have none of it.

"Can we see how tall we are, Nan?" In the doorway of Pearl's kitchen were the markings of all her grandchildren's heights. They were always so proud to stand against the exposed plasterwork and let her chart their growth.

"Put your feet down!… Nan, she's cheating. She's going on tippytoes."

"I'm not. I'm not. Look, see? I'm much bigger than you are anyway. He's still a baby isn't he, Nan?"

"I'm not a baby, Nan, am I?"

"Shut up both of you and keep still!"

Girlo and Eddie could make a competition out of *anything*. And they did. On those rare occasions when they were given a treat they'd try to out-do each other, eating what-ever-it-was at the slowest pace, so that one would be finished before the other, leaving the other to beg. Girlo had a set ritual for eating sweets and chocolate. She'd bend Chomps back and forth until the chocolate had flaked away, then the caramel could be rolled up to be eaten whole. Twix had their biscuits bitten off so the caramel could be stretched and wound around her finger then licked to nothing. Strawberry Millions were eaten individually. Whistle Lollies worn down to glass shards then used as a poking implement.

Girlo preferred to eat a whole pack of crisps all in one, creating a sticky paste that coated her tongue which she'd duly present to her brother. Eddie licked the flavouring off each individual crisp before popping the soggy remnants into his hamster pouch, creating the same disgusting paste to be displayed.

"Errr. Nan? She is showing me her food."

"I nevuh, Nan. I just offered him a crisp, tha's all!"

Nannie Pearl always had crisps—in fact, she'd stock them by the box. She had a sandwich run and would serve the factory workers of the valleys with her fleet of sandwich vans. Every morning at 5am she'd be up, frantically buttering bread. Then she drove off in her little white van stocked by her grandchildren the day before.

"Can I have a Toffee Crisp, Nan?" Girlo asked, carrying a box of chocolate bars up the banking.

"If you do as you're told." (That was her answer for everything; they knew it meant 'no'.)

Her house was at the top of the Rock. She'd park the van in full view of the living room window on the mount on the grassy banking.

That was until one freezing cold day in early December when she woke up late to find she'd run out of cling film. She spent an hour scraping ice off the windscreen with her credit card, then the bloody van wouldn't start! She had a 'funny feeling' about the day ahead but ignored her instincts. Christmas was around the corner; she needed the trade. So, she ploughed on. When she got down to the industrial estate, there was a queue as-long-as the eye could see and she flipped up the hatch to start the day's work. While her back was turned an officious voice called, "Pearl?"

"Won't be a minute love…"

"Mrs Pearl Wolf?" That was it. The jig was up. She slammed down the hatch and jumped into the cab but the 'bastard engine' was playing up again. It was too late; the extra Thousand quid a week for her nest egg was gone. "Some snake us grassed me up to the Sorshul," she hissed as she came through the front door.

YOUNG LADY

Groggy and Beryl moved to a new flat. Crystal followed them, taking Girlo and Eddie from their shitty bedsit hole to a slightly less-shitty basement flat on a hill. There was a forecourt outside to play on, with kids on both sides. Girlo and Eddie were chuffed. They still had to share a bedroom, but it was bigger than the cupboard. The front-door led straight onto a sharp concrete staircase that nosedived into a musty cave of a kitchen, living room and two bedrooms. Their bedroom had a small window, thick with mould, which looked out onto a scrapyard.

Crystal bought them a telly for their room to "keep um quiet in the mornings." They were over the moon! She had kind of got her shit together, securing a day job as a private cleaner. She still did the odd shift at the bar, but at least she could get them to school on time in the mornings. School was still a struggle. Girlo tried to keep up, but she was so tired all the time. She would shake if the teacher called her in front of the class, a sweaty heat crawling all over her, making her feel like she'd been trapped in a cooking pot with the lid placed firmly on. "Have you completed your Friday Journal this week?" She hated the Friday Journal. She had to lie in it all the time, pretend she was a *normal* little girl, living a *normal* life when really all she wanted to do was tell the truth. She wanted to write what was happening in her own words, the words she kept secret in her mind, the words she scrawled in the back of the cupboard, using a pencil she'd filched from the bookies.

Girlo was late. Her mother had fallen asleep on the settee and missed the alarm going off in her bedroom. Girlo was up, dressed, and had got breakfast for her and Eddie by the time Crystal surfaced.

"Argh… waz the time kids?"

"We're gonna be late again, Mam!" Girlo hated being late because she hated how the teachers would penalise her in front of the other kids. "Come on, slowcoach, we haven't got all day!"

"You'll have to have a taxi!"

The taxi drove them right up to the school gates. It was Autumn time, her 'lucky' seventh birthday over. The sycamores were shedding their seeds in the form of aeroplane propellers, conkers dropping like spike bombs. Girlo loved to peel back the thorny skin of a conker to find the polished mahogany inside. The schoolboys strung them onto shoelaces to play with in the playground; the aim to smash them to bits. Girlo never liked this game. Instead, she cherished her conkers, treasuring them as good luck charms, secretly smoothing them in her blazer pocket. Her blazer had cat hair all over it that morning. They'd recently got a cat named Molly, who Girlo and Eddie made run through a maze of boxes under the bed. The cat got her own back though by giving them worms.

"That's what you get for kissing the cat on the lips all the time. I told you!" Crystal said passing them a glass of water to wash down small white pills.

Girlo's hair was all skew-whiff again. Crystal had cut her fringe too thick this time and it stuck up all over the place. Girlo had toothpaste down her jumper and a stripe of grime on the collar of her shirt. *Why couldn't her mum be like Bambi's?* Girlo thought as she sat down at registration. Bambi had shiny hair, braided and finished with bows. She also had the new Magic Steps shoes from Clarks with diamonds in the soles. Girlo had had to leave her red shoes at her Grandmamma's. She really *really* wanted Magic Steps.

"Shush-shush. Magic Steps is on," she'd shout whenever the advert aired; a young girl with long, flowing hair, swaying on a swing in a magical secret garden, the diamond soles of her patent red shoes glittering. "I wan' them. I wan'them. I wan' them so bad! Can I have them, Mam?"

"You'll have to ask Father Christmas," was the usual

answer. But Father Christmas was a tight bastard. He never brought her anything she asked for, even when she tried her best to be a 'good girl.'

There was a new boy who had started that day at school. His parents owned a florist. *What a lovely life he must have, living in a shop full of flowers,* thought Girlo, as he introduced himself to the class.

"Why does he keep looking over here?" Girlo whispered to Bambi behind her hand. She was worried he could see the toothpaste down her jumper.

"I think he likes you."

"Me? No... not me... must be you!"

He glanced over again, and the girls giggled.

When it was playtime and they'd finished their bottles of milk, Bambi told her that the new boy *did* like her, and that he wanted to kiss her in the yellow submarine. The yellow submarine was a play den featuring a variety of knobs and buttons made from foil milk tops and egg cartons. Girlo felt very hot and needed to use the toilet. There she wet some toilet paper to put in her knickers; her foof was still sore, and she'd weed her pants a bit, making it burn. After flushing she didn't know what to do next. *Should she just hide until the bell went?* She paced up and down the row of cubicles. She didn't want to kiss him, but she didn't want to look silly in front of Bambi either. *What could she do?* Pretend to be ill? Maybe jump through the gap in the wall behind the fig trees and into the beer garden where her mother sometimes drank? She could say she wasn't feeling well and her mother could take her home.

Then it hit her! Nannie Pearl had given her a pin for her blazer. "To remind you of who you are," she'd said, proudly planting the pin in her hand. It was an inexpensive piece of pewter cast in the shape of a running wolf with enamelled green eyes. Her mother warned her not to wear it to school because she'd lose it. In the cold, echoey toilets, Girlo hesitantly slipped the pin from her blazer and danced it around the plughole. Then she blasted the faucet so hard the water would be responsible for losing it—not her. As the water increased in speed, it took the little wolf from her pincered grip and there… it was gone! Girlo instantly regretted it.

She'd been told *not* to lose that pin and now she'd lost it on purpose. *No-one must ever know the truth,* she thought as she ran to the school office.

"As I was washing my hands it just fell off in the sink," Girlo told Mrs Pilgrim, who seemed unconvinced.

"Ok, we'll ask the caretaker to unscrew the U-bend in case it's got caught."

Girlo burst into tears.

"Don't cry, child. Hush hush. We have church after break. You can share your loss with God. Perhaps he will return it to you." Mrs Pilgrim gave her a tissue and sent her back out into the playground.

School was a weird one. On the one hand it was nice to be somewhere safe, but on the other, Girlo had to wear a bloody beret, which was too small because her mother had shrunk it on a hot cycle. It itched like mad and left a stripe across her forehead. On top of that, the teachers would call her 'young lady', which made her feel like she was being told off. The dinner hall smelt of wood polish, plimsoles and spew. As the kids lined up against the radiator for their dinner, a gigantic portrait of a someone important watched them, eyes following them around the room. There was a rumour that he haunted the school. He had the same middle name as her grandad Jack, who she never really knew. She'd been told that her grandad had died crossing the road to get a pork pie.

"Hiya bairb'z!" He'd said on the only occasion she met him. He'd been surrounded by a bunch of old fellas who were slapping each other's backs and laughing between gulps of bitter, a skinny roll-up hanging off his lip. She didn't have a clue who he was.

"This is your Grandad Jack, Cariad," Pearl said.

"You are… " he said, digging in his pocket. She knew what was coming next; a quid, maybe two. "Go ge' yuhself some sweets bairb'z." He passed her a five-pound note—a whole fiver all to herself! Not to be shared with Eddie.

"All for me?"

"Aye, all for you! Get someink nice with it." He smiled, then returned to his pint. Before she could stash it in her pocket, Nannie Pearl had whipped it out of her hand.

"I'll mind that for you!"

It was the only thing her grandfather had ever given her and Girlo never saw it again.

After he died, she'd stare at the brightest star in the sky, imagining it was him watching over her. She'd ask him to make it all stop. She stared so hard that her eyes ached in their sockets. She wanted her pupils to jump right off her eyeballs and rocket to the star and hit it so hard that he would listen and do something. Then she'd recite the Lord's Prayer, begging God to help. After that she would take out her Guatemalan worry dolls and tell each of them everything, whispering so that Eddie couldn't hear. After she placed them under her pillow, the long night of waiting and wondering would begin.

The dinner queue had gone down a bit, but Girlo kept moving back a space. It was treacle sponge day. She wanted the scrapings off the tray where all the gooiest bits were. She loved the puddings and hated the dinners but at least they were better than her mother's spam and beans or her Auntie Beryl's dry chicken dinners. The teachers would practically force-feed the children. They weren't allowed to leave the table until their plates were clean. And church! They made her go to church three times a week! It was so flipping boring that she couldn't stop yawning throughout the whole thing. They'd have to sit on these awful, hard pews and watch a shrivelled man in a mountain of robes talk in a pip-squeak voice for two hours. He reminded her of one of those voodoo shrunken heads stuck on a pyramid of antique curtains.

"Stop yawning!" hissed Mrs Pilgrim. "Hear our prayer," she repeated in chorus with the rest of the congregation.

Girlo wasn't sure if she liked God much anymore anyway—he had not heard her prayers, neither had her grandfather or those stupid fucking worry dolls.

"Hear our prayer," she mumbled, too scared to stop praying 'just in case.'

"Hear our prayer," she said, louder, hoping God might hear her better in church.

As the schoolchildren filed out, a thought struck Girlo: maybe she'd have to tell a real person. Maybe she could tell the priest. She had seen confession once on telly; it was meant to be kept secret. *But what if he didn't believe her? What if no-one believed her?* In the 'Good Samaritan', the injured man was helped… maybe she'd be helped too. But the priest in that parable had just walked on by when the injured man was in need. *Who could she tell?* She would have to tell Mrs Pilgrim. Mrs Pilgrim had big soft boobs like Nannie Pearl's, and she cuddled her if she fell over in the playground.

Later that afternoon when Girlo had finished sticking dried pasta to Queen Elizabeth's dress to "make it ornate," she pulled Mrs Pilgrim aside.

"Yes, young lady, what is it?"

"I need to tell you something… it's something bad…"

Mrs Pilgrim led her into the stationary cupboard and leant her pillowy buttocks against a filing cabinet, while Girlo struggled to speak. The thoughts were there but they got lodged in her throat like word-shaped burps.

"Well, speak up! What have you got to tell me?"

Girlo's hands were sweating streams and she could feel her bowels dropping. All manner of different variations of the truth raced through her mind.

"When Groggy and Auntie Beryl got back from Calais he brought me a Skippit. I'd been nagging my mother for one for weeks."

"I'm sorry, who's Groggy?"

"He is my uncle—my Auntie Beryl's boyfriend."

Finally, the whole story came tumbling out along with her treacle pudding, which splattered over the floor and the toes of her shoes. Mrs Pilgrim—who had been silent, staring at Girlo stony-eyed for the last few minutes—dashed for paper towels. Then Bambi popped her head around the door.

"Is everything ok, Miss?"

"Everything is fine, thank you. Please go and fetch Mrs Dunstable from the staffroom."

Mrs Dunstable was Mrs Pilgrim's opposite. She wore a tweed twin piece and the shiniest shoes in the school, the Trunchball to Mrs Pilgrim's Miss Honey. Mrs Dunstable arrived and whisked Girlo off to the school office where she was told to wait.

"What's the matter with her?" asked Crystal over the phone.

"She's a little bit sickly so you'll have to come and collect her."

"But I'm in work. Can you keep her until the bell goes? I don't have anyone else."

Crystal was telling the truth. She wasn't in the pub. She really was in work and Groggy and Auntie Beryl were out of town.

"Well, it's highly inconvenient. Can't her father come, or perhaps one of your gentleman friends?"

"Her father isn't here. And I don't have any gentleman friends!"

Mrs Dunstable replaced the receiver. "Looks like you're here until the bell goes. You can't go back to your class in case you are infectious. You'll have to remain and complete some handwriting sheets."

She left.

Girlo felt clammy all over, full of shame and doubt. Her hands were dripping wet so she wiped them down her skirt but the plasticky fabric wouldn't absorb it. She wondered if Mrs Pilgrim would tell Mrs Dunstable. She didn't want Mrs Dunstable to know about it. She didn't really want Mrs Pilgrim to know about it either. But it'd just had to come out. She couldn't sleep any more. She couldn't think straight anymore. The secret had been eating her alive. And now it was out. Now it was out. They would rescue her, anoint her with oil and pour wine over her wounds just like in the 'Good Samaritan'. Girlo tried to phone Bambi when she got home but there was no answer. She changed out of her school clothes, ran over there and knocked on the door. Bambi's mum opened the door.

"Is Bambi home?"

"She's upstairs revising for her 11 plus."

"Can I come in and wait?"

"You can't... her father and I have decided that she has to concentrate on her schoolwork from now on. We want her to go to the grammar school."

"I want to go to the grammar school too. We can revise together..."

"I'm sorry, but Bambi doesn't need any distractions. Go home to your mother, now, Poppet." She closed the door in Girlo's face. She didn't know what she'd done wrong, maybe Bambi had overheard her telling the teachers about Groggy, and it had frightened her. She walked down their windy path out of the garden. She didn't want to go home. She needed her best friend and as she sobbed along the pavement, it started to rain. She found a phone box for shelter. Beside the receiver was a poster for Childline. She could phone them. Tell them. She'd called them before on reverse charges.

"One Nine Two... Hello, can you connect me to Childline?"

"Hello, before we begin, we need to make sure you know that all calls made to Childline are one hundred per cent confidential. You do not have to give us your name if you do not want to."

Girlo didn't know what *confidential* meant.

"Hello, my name is Sapphire," she lied, scared in case she get into trouble. What if they came looking for her? What if *he* ever found out she told? Her mum wouldn't love her. No one would love her anymore. But it was rude. It was wrong. She knew this now; it was all rude and all wrong.

Groggy was meant to be babysitting that night. Girlo was terrified that he might want to "see her." She'd had an itchy foof for ages and when she looked at it in the hand-mirror all the skin was cracked like something you'd see on the heel of an old woman in sandals. It was *so* sore. She went into the bathroom and ran the tap as hot as it would go, filling up the sink. She hoisted herself up and in, bare-bummed. She sat for a while, holding her breath, wondering if the little bubbles might fizz the itch away. Despite the pain, she convinced herself that it was doing good. It certainly stopped the itch but when she hopped down from the sink the itch started up again. She refilled the sink with freezing cold water.

"What are you doing in there?" It was her mother. "You should be in bed by now! Auntie Beryl will be here in a minute."

"Auntie Beryl? I thought Uncle Groggy was babysitting."

"He's got a job. Beryl is coming instead. Come on now, brush your teeth and get ready for bed." Girlo was relieved. She couldn't bear to put all of those tights and knickers and pyjama bottoms on again for bed.

"Trah kids. See you in the morning… and be good for your Auntie Beryl."

Even though she knew she'd be safe with Beryl, habit prevented Girlo from going to sleep. She lay wide awake, listening for every sound from the door. Silence consumed her, every slight noise echoing through her. Eddie was still awake too, afraid of the clown from the horror movie IT.

"It's ok Eddie, he can't get you. He's not real. It's just a film."

Then she heard the front door slam. Maybe it was her mother back early… maybe she forgot something. Then she heard his voice reverberate through the walls and up through her spine. Dread hit. Her first thought was for Eddie. Was he still awake? Her second thought was to grab the pyjama bottoms and tights, but it was too late… he was in the room.

"Yew ussleep keds?"

Girlo always pretended to be asleep. She could smell his breath.

"I've got a little present for you."

June 26th 1992

Dear Friday Journal,

Yesterday
I went over Bambi's for tea and the day before that
and the day before that. We found an old trolley and
pushed each other up and down the road in it.
Then we saw a creepy looking man all dressed in
black and stuff. He was hanging around outside
the phone box. He was very, very very scary so we
went home and told Bambi's mum.

Well Done. You
did the right
thing, telling an
adult.

July 10 1992

Dear Friday Journal
we only have twenty move sleeps until the
summer Holiday. Bambi is going to France, I will
miss her very very very much but I am
happy because I am going to stay with my
nannie Pearl. I can't wait to see all my cousins
and hunt for the nasty who white monkey up the
foot ball Pitch. We will find him one day!!!!!!!
Here's a poem I wrote Hope you like it!!

Pearls of wisdom

Across starry skies on her magic wings she flies.

Her mission is to see the lies

She swoops here and there spinkling
seeds of Joy upon lost girl and boys.
As she flies, she hears their their cries.
then she helps them exscape the lies her
seeds give courage to their needs and
all of the word's memories.

I hope you catch that
Monkey!

V. Good, but try not to forget your attention
to grammar and punctuation.
Also, please refrain from using your
Friday Journal for anything other than
the events of the week.

117

CHAVETTE

Girlo first met the Lighthouse Bard when, after reading her portfolio, he requested an informal interview. She was surprised he'd even replied. *Was 'informal' code for a grilling? Were they trying catch her out?* She'd done a quick search online, "a national icon." *No pressure, then.* She clicked on a video of him. There he was reading a poem in front of a spindly lighthouse in the choppy sea, a proper Swansea poet.

After her Cymraeg friends secured internships in media and politics, she felt her undergrad was defunct. She decided to take a punt at a Master of Arts. Despite her political activity as an undergraduate, Girlo felt that the Socialist Students were just ideological tourists who, in the name of revolution, sought to change society but never really had the time for the people they claimed to represent.

Girlo found herself on the periphery again. She'd managed to get an education but after so many rejected job applications, the twenty-grand piece of paper seemed worthless. She supposed that maybe the Rock boys were right, *it's not what you know, it's who you know,* and education didn't have anything to do with qualifications. At least she'd found her way out and a place in the world. She felt she had two options: go into some form of politics, a cog in the system essentially, or use her art to make her mark.

The Lighthouse Bard beckoned her into his grotto workspace, an incubator of greats filled with book-lined shelves, and piles of papers and pamphlets reaching up like mini skyscrapers. The smell of earthy coffee instantly put her at ease.

"Take a seat," he said.

She shifted a few pamphlets; one entitled *Welsh Pub Crawls*.

"Have you done the Mile?" she asked him.

"Well, I'm not as young and buoyant as I once was, but I can't deny, I like the odd local ale."

Girlo instantly regretted prying. This guy was a famous poet.

He cleared his throat and leant back in his chair, taking a sip from a thick mug, his beard collecting a few coffee droplets. He seemed totally unpretentious, a normal bloke; someone to have a good chinwag with over a pint.

Beards usually intimidated Girlo. A beard, in her mind, stood for men in power which—in her experience—meant a struggle. Her heart was rebellious, but her mind was tortured with a chronic pressure to people-please. She didn't have the best track record with men in positions of power. Their long-winded speeches bored her. As they took their time speaking, she could feel points firing off in her head, shooting out of her mouth. Exchanges were lightning quick where she was from: you had to fight to be heard.

They were always *too* interested in her and often inappropriately *cosy* with her. After the abuse, this all-too-common scenario made her uneasy. She knew of lots of women who had 'put out' to get published or win the job, but her Nannie Pearl taught her "not to owe anybody anything," and her father had encouraged her to establish autonomy. She stood her ground and freed herself of compromising situations. She knew that no-one was better than anyone else—so kowtowing was not an option.

But this man in authority was different. He made her feel as if he wanted to hear what she had to say. *His* beard gave him a certain sense of nobility. His office smelled like home to her, old books and well-worn leather shoes.

"I've had a look at your portfolio, and firstly, what you have given me here is *not* a monologue…"

Girlo squirmed under the softness of his glare. *Who did she think she was, rocking up here, thinking she could do this? Who would give this rude girl chavette a chance?*

"It's a story. *That* said, there is some potential here; with some strong imagery—although you do tend to overload your adjectives. I especially liked the adjoining poems…" his voice was like velvet.

"Oh right, well I wrote them in the voices of people from the Rock."

"The Rock?"

"Yes, it's where I grew up. It's a pretty bleak place these days, but the community is still strong."

"I do find the sense of community in Welsh pit villages far outshines those of say, new developments, which essentially become enclaves for the rich."

Girlo felt a pang of affinity, but she was fearful of using academic language.

"It's a shame, because there is something so comforting about growing up on an estate; it's like having a big family to look out for you. I don't believe that people were meant to live in little segregated suburban houses, isolated from each other. Human beings were originally tribal nomads, tribal. But my father always called the Rock, Alcatraz... once you're on it you can never get off!" She laughed.

"There's a Spanish poet, Lorca. Have you read his work?"

"I can't say I have, no..."

"He's been described as a folk poet. He wrote the 'Gypsy Ballads.' There was a real passion for the individual in the human world; an exploration of the marginalised fighting against the social order thrust upon them... persecuted because they have their own culture, and he ultimately threatened the stability of the status quo. Some can be fearful of people they cannot relate to."

"We'd welcome them. People on the Rock were always skint, and the travellers were always selling something on the cheap. From us, they'd buy our homegrown skunk."

"A union of the underdog, of sorts?"

"Yeah. Exactly!"

"And, I see you have included a poem here which is written in the dialect of the southern valleys. It is important to capture the true essence of a language. Warts and all. I would urge you to go further with your phonetics to really capture those voices in all their glory."

"I just wanted to convey the injustice from our point of view.

People on the estate get a rough deal. The lack of regeneration under Thatcher and New Labour basically ghettoized, demonized and scapegoated us."

"It has been a cruel inheritance for the sweat and toil of our forefathers in industrialised Britain."

He reminded her of Richard Burton, who spoke of the miners with such passion and fondness.

"Lorca celebrates the fire of the human spirit, exonerating the mis-represented. I'm sure I have a copy here somewhere for you to borrow." The Lighthouse Bard stood and ran his index finger over the spines of his books.

"You know, I attended Boarding School in England, which was very unpleasant, but a useful experience of totalitarianism. There was no court of appeal… here!" He passed Girlo a small pocketbook, "you were completely at their mercy." He sat back down and poured himself another coffee. Tapping his brown Moccasin on a flaking box beneath his desk, he began to recollect: "I was fairly unconscious that I was Welsh when I got there, then it became quite clear that I was Welsh. Some of the boys could be quite bullish. When I went to work in England too, my colleagues made it plain that I was Welsh in a way that I wasn't really conscious of."

Girlo understood what it was like to grow up in England.

The Bard's face brightened. "Then when I went to University I began to investigate my Welsh literary background. I became much more methodical."

"I was hoping to do the same. I thought university would stop me settling for a dead-end job. I've never wanted to be rich; I just want to make a living from something I love."

"I mean financially, it's always hard for any writer to piece together a living… but for me, I just didn't want my kids to scrimp and save."

"You're doing well now though, aren't you?"

He laughed. Girlo felt she'd put her foot in it again.

"I mean yes, I earn a good living, but I don't have much time to write."

"Do you think I'll have a chance to earn a good living?"

"Well, that remains to be seen. That remains to be seen."

"I'm not really your typical writer, though, am I? I suppose it's the only place I feel I belong. I've always been the outsider."

"Truth is, we're all outsiders." He picked up Girlo's portfolio and flicked to the back.

"Perhaps you would like to read..." He held out the rolled-up document as though it were a baton.

She unfurled the paper, took a deep breath and began...

THE WASTED PLACE

Slag spoil seals his pebbledash prison once built to ensnare his grandad: a worker, who slogged to make his country great, to give his kids the chance he never had. The Wasted Place: a law unto itself. One way in and one way out. Damage control. Made to contain the blue-blood-thirsty, grass-roots masses, anti-fascists and now a ghetto for their wasted off-spring. Lost streets veined with cryptic clues, tales of change hide in plain sight. Great Expectations, a shit schoolbook but he knows *Hard Times* and the 'Dickens Court' flats, where he wastes his place, saving face. Fading race. Shot blind, his mind in concrete; a graffiti graveyard scratched with the rudeboy tags who'd lost before they were even born. He waits for his go on the circulating bong as Tupac's truths beat his box. This brother from another mother, feeds his need to be freed. *All eyez on me.* He exhales smoke and his Reebok sole slips from the grime stripe of the wall. His beliefs in a fog, unclog, then he leaps over the empty flagons, past the inky arms of dragons, through blown spew chunks. *A coward dies a thousand times, a soldier only once*

WANNABE

It was slightly sunny so Girlo thought she might nip to the pub on her way to the interview with Earl. She foil-wrapped a couple of cheese and onion sandwiches to conceal her lager breath. *Why couldn't she stay out of the pub?* It wasn't so much the alcohol that appealed but more the pub itself, the people in there. It didn't matter which pub she went to; she'd find people like her. It was home to people like her; lonely, lost and without purpose... people just *existing*, wanting to while away the otherwise empty hours with their pub family. It was the best place to tell and to gather stories, populated by the most interesting characters, the most tragic tales, the place where the biggest laughs were to be had. Girlo could strip herself of her masks there. Somewhere where all those scraps of somethings and nothings, snapshots of being, and confetti words from so many mouths-and-hands-and-brains—finally came together... where connections were made, and theories came into being. Immersed in pub life, Girlo felt the somethings and nothings could become something tangible... anecdotes, folklore and jokes spun from lips like lines of runaway stitches. The more she drank, the faster they'd come. The pub was her playground. Even though her words were lost on the ears of guzzlers who literally saw her as 'a piece of skirt', she enjoyed the banter. In her naïve arrogance she never backed down from a fight.

Pint number one up at the bar, she was charming with her easy back-and-forth. By pint number two she'd taken it up a notch, progressing to jovial banter, intimidating her audience with her knowledge of current affairs. By pint number three, she'd almost certainly be challenged in a pub game—usually pool—which she'd accept, sufficiently tipsy to hustle whichever poor fucker had taken her on. By pint number four she'd have already won two games. Pint five had her feeding the jukebox with her opponent's coin. After pint six, kindly purchased by her opponent, came the return of the original discussion: *always* politics, despite having been warned over the years never to talk about politics in the pub.

"No point in voting, they're all the fucking same, politicians eez days."

"Think of the sacrifices made for you to have that vote!"

"Not in this lifetime... and anyway, what's a booful girl like yew talking abow politics? Everyone knows iss just showbiz for ugly people!"

Sitting in the beer-garden, one pint slipped into three and before she knew it, Girlo was gliding down the road with a bit of a head on. *Life looks better after a couple,* she thought as a fuzz of bloated geese paddled across the dappled light on the pond. As she passed the football pitches, she realised that she hadn't actually been to the posher end of town before. They always talked about doing the infamous 'Mile' over a round at the student bar but were too busy chugging Reefs at Ritzy's to soak up the coastal civility of the continental style culture. As the houses grew larger and grander, Girlo started to think she might be lost. She dug in her pocket for the ripped newspaper margin where she'd scrawled his address. It led her to a private cul-de-sac, lined with forecourts big enough to park four or more cars. Eventually at the end of the street she found the bungalow of Earl Newman. *He must be a old rich fucker*, she thought, *just like Nancy said.* She knocked on the door. There was no answer, so she knocked again. *He must've forgot.*

"Hello," said Earl when he answered the door.

Shit, he was not old! "Oh, hi! I thought I got the time wrong for a minute then!"

He was in a bit of a tizzy, wanting to tidy up a bit before she arrived, but his V.C. had kept him and he'd hit the rush-hour traffic.

"Nah, nah, come in," a cockney accent with a patois twang. He stepped back to open the door wider, still in his work clothes. As she stepped over the threshold she could smell new wood. On the breakfast bar was a dirty plate and an Ikea wineglass with a drop of Shiraz glazing the nippled bottom. Behind the bar, a pile of scrunched-up cotton shirts. She hoped to God he didn't expect her to iron them all! Earl held one in his hands: "I... er... I was just trying to get the ink out." A pen had leaked onto the top pocket.

"Let me take a look," she rubbed the back of his hand as she took it. "Vanish might do it. Ink is the worst. I can give it a go, if you like?"

"That would be very helpful." He tossed the shirt onto the pile with a smile and rubbed his hands together. His nerves activated the butterflies in her stomach. *This felt more like a date than an interview.*

"Would you like a cup of tea, coffee?" He would've liked to have offered her a beer, and sat in the evening sun, talking, taking pictures...

"Tea please, two sugars." Girlo suddenly became self-conscious of her onion breath. She spotted a four pack of Peroni as he took the milk from the fridge. Her buzz was starting to sink and she needed a top-up. "Lovely day today."

"It is, yeah, but I've been cooped up in work for most of it, unfortunately."

"Oh no, where d'you work—"

"So have you come far?" he said, colliding into her question. "Sorry!" He turned to fill his illuminating glass kettle.

"Oh, just from the student area."

"So, you're a student?"

Girlo was having trouble figuring out his age. *Did she fancy him or not?* She straightened up, trying to appear respectable.

"Yes, but I'm taking a gap year at the moment." She followed the lines of the tiles with the toe of her silver wedge, catching Earl's eye. "You got a lovely place, here."

"Thank you. It's taken long enough to get it to this stage... a lot of hard work."

"It shows."

Earl only lived a quarter of his time at his painstakingly renovated house, and mostly asleep. He said he felt like a hotel guest. There weren't any pictures on his white walls. Just one photograph of himself wearing the traditional shirt and shorts of King Baba.

"Where's that?" Girlo asked him.

"Oh, it's from a trip I went on, a remote village in Borneo."

Earl's lobster tan made him look like a superimposed image of a well-meaning white man, surrounded by women from the Kubu Dayek tribe. Despite the tribal wear, he reminded Girlo of a florescent price sticker crudely plastered on a picture-perfect postcard.

Earl explained it was one of his longest and most extravagant holidays and then he told her how he was truly moved by the experience. He had found something, a sense of solace in the simplicity of basic village life. "I bought a traditional Dayek sculpture. It's on the table in the lounge."

The sculpture was perched on the corner of his coffee table with a selection of coffee table books; 'Norman Foster's Architectural Works,' 'The World's Greatest Art: Kandinsky,' and some Lonely Planet city guides. Budapest, Barcelona, Paris, Milan and Amsterdam—some of which he had visited, some he planned on seeing when "work eased off a bit." The only Lonely Planet guide he didn't have was Istanbul where he was born. He'd lived in a village with his mother on the outskirts but always dreamt of visiting the heart of the city.

"What was it like?" Girlo asked.

"I wouldn't know, I was locked up indoors most of the time." Earl often browsed online, imagining himself exploring his birthplace. But he said he was so pedantic with his travel planning, he'd always buy several books to study over the course of a month or two, compiling a list of his must-see attractions. Then after many calendar checks, some further toing-and-froing, several telephone conversations with his mother and assistant, he'd make the booking 12 months in advance. And his holidays were always booked for *just* a long weekend: four to five nights, tops!

He poured the tea.

"That's a lovely kettle,' Girlo said. "Nice lights."

"Er, yeah – B&Q, I think. Please, take a seat."

She pulled up a barstool.

"I know that you are a cleaner, but do you have much experience in ironing?"

"Yeah, I can do your ironing. I used to iron for my nan's friend's when I was 7 for fifty pence a black bag! Not a problem."

"It'll just be the shirts, and a general clean of the bathroom, lounge and kitchen. It still needs some work in here though."

"It looks okay to me."

"There are still a few bits to do on the finishes." Earl was a self-confessed perfectionist, and his unfinished kitchen really, *really* bothered him—to the point where it would sometimes keep him awake at night. Instead of the mosaic backsplashes he planned, raw salmon-pink plasterwork chequered with pencil lines and spurts of grease—from his 'naughty' Sunday morning bacon sarnies—confronted him each time the sun slicked over the second skylight. "I really need to get someone in," he said draining his disposable coffee filter. "I go through at least twenty of these a week."

"Maybe you should get yourself a big-ass coffee maker!"

Earl laughed out loud. "Maybe I will!"

Girlo could see this was going to be a cushy-little-number. There was hardly any mess! Her last cleaning job was at a local comp, a soul-destroying job, a joke! If two or three cleaners didn't show, the rest were expected to pick up the baton and work on with no extra pay. Some days she wouldn't get out until 2 hours after her shift, others she wasn't even called in for a shift. Cab fare wasted; she ended up out of pocket. The teachers barely acknowledged her. They didn't seem to differentiate between her and the bins she emptied.

But cleaning the student nightclub was even worse. With a decrepit vacuum cleaner from the '90s she'd have to suck up pieces of glass the size of marbles and scoop orange puke from the cubicle walls with her hands. It was the same club where some dirty cunt had decided to slip a finger up her while she waited for a drink at the bar and when she'd slapped him, the bouncers had removed *her*—throwing her to the ground in the rain. A van had almost run her over. It turned out the boys in the van were researching for an article on student life. She told them everything, but never saw her name in print.

But now she was standing in front of this nice, rich man who wanted her to clean his already spotless house and iron a few shirts for nine pounds an hour.

"Would you like a tour?"

"Er, yes please."

Earl took her through the open-plan living-room featuring a custom-made steel staircase that spiralled up to his mezzanine master bedroom. From his sleigh bed there was an unobstructed view of a roving stretch of football pitches, which attracted troupes of sunny American sweethearts studying at the nearby university. Unlike the boozy British girls, they chose the campus for its sporting activities and proximity to the sea. Girlo could imagine Earl lolling in his duck-down, Egyptian cotton duvet on a Saturday morning, waiting for the gym-vested girls to bounce into view.

Back in the kitchen he bragged about how he'd renovated his bachelor pad using only the finest, purest and most locally sourced building materials.

"It's like a palace," said Girlo as he spoke of its bespoke design. Granite worktops reflected the masculine lines of his imported American fridge-freezer and eight-ringed Rangemaster, which he only used for his nightly meal of Thai Green Curry straight from the jar. No rice since Earl followed the Atkins diet.

"I like to cook," Girlo told him.

"I wish I had the time to."

"Maybe I could cook for you sometime," she said, gathering her things to leave.

The following Wednesday Girlo returned for her first shift. Once she'd finished the dishes, she helped herself to some lunch. She flicked through a magazine while she ate, imagining herself in the various outfits featured; a white linen suit, a two-hundred quid bikini, a beautiful pair of red leather platforms:

"£1,089 for shoes?!" Girlo bought all her clothes from charity shops. That had been her favourite pastime with Nannie Pearl, who'd taught her to rifle through rails of clothes to find the designer labels then haggle with the shop assistants. She felt quite traitorous, sitting in Earl's plush pad fantasising about being wealthy.

Girlo had become aware of the dangers of inequality after reading a copy of Dr. Seuss' *Sneetches on the Beaches,* given to her as a child by her dad's black feminist girlfriend, Heera. She had thought about how stupid the Sneetches with the 'stars upon thars' were, how they had segregated themselves from the Sneetches 'without stars upon thars,' excluding them from their 'frankferter parties.' *Snobbery is the epitome of cruelty and stupidity* she thought, remembering the McMonkey McBean character, 'a fix it up chappie' with a 'star-on machine,' who'd ripped off *all* of the Sneetches on the beaches. Once he'd rinsed them of every last dollar he'd driven into the sunset with a vanload of cash. Girlo had always identified with the Sneetches 'without stars upon thars.' Earl was a star-bellied Sneetch.

She read his note again:

If you could give the kitchen and bathroom a once-over and have a go at that shirt, I'd be very grateful. Also, I hope I'm not being too forward, but are you free for dinner tonight?

Best, Earl x

She felt conflicted. Of course, she yearned for an easier life but could she really carve out a wannabee WAG lifestyle for herself with Earl?

She found his feather duster in the oak cupboard.

"Fluff in the buff," she sang, as she dusted his stack of DVDs. He had every *Frasier* box set in existence. Too bad she preferred *Cheers*. She started to think about how audiences' tastes had changed as she'd grown, comedies like *Bread* and *Porridge* replaced with *Two Pints of Lager* and *Little Britain;* the repellent Vicky Pollard representing working class single mums. *Yeah but, no but!* Salt of the earth had become scum of the earth.

She pressed play on Earl's CD player. *The Best of the* 'Beatles' started up with 'Paperback Writer.' She pulled out the ironing board to make a start on his shirts. She sang along as she ironed, '…can't buy me love, everybody tells me so.'

DAUGHTER

Eric and Crystal were married in a registry office. She wore a black-and-white striped dress that made her look more like a chain-gang prisoner than a bride, with scarlet lipstick to match her shoes. The reception was at The Muni. Nannie Pearl had once been banned for protesting her right to drink in the bar, which was off-limits to women.

"Let's raise our glasses to the happy couple!" announced Pearl, who'd returned for the birth of her first granddaughter.

"To Crystal and Eric," echoed the room of well-wishers.

It wasn't the wedding Crystal had planned exactly. She'd had dreams of something much fancier. But they couldn't even afford a house so it would have to do.

"At least we got each other," said Eric, as they cwtched up on a mattress on the floor. "I wonder what she'll be when she grows up," Crystal said, stroking her belly.

"She or he can be anything she wants to be."

"An artist, or singer, like me?"

"An artist, like you... or an activist or academic like me. I'll make sure she has a chance to be anyone she wants."

Girlo was born and Eric peered down into her cot, "Look at my lickle Girlo. She's going to change the world."

"There we are, my Cariad." Pearl gave her a Cabbage Patch Doll from America. "No-one's seen one of these here yet."

"You're always ahead of the times, Mam," said Eric. He kissed his mother then his newborn and packed his books for night school.

On a clear January day on his walk home from his slog onsite, whispers of his New Year's resolutions still in mind, he headed up through the lower estate known as Wunny, (or Number One) on the other side of the train-tracks. He marvelled at the drive-ways of working cars as he went, a contrast to the rust buckets he was used to seeing in his neck of the woods. A private coach pulled up, dropping off a troupe of patent leather-shoed school kids swinging satchels full of shop-bought books. The Rock kids' faces were pinched from malnutrition and worry.

When he got in, Crystal told him that she had just put the baby down. He gently took off his boots. Up the wooden hill he went to the cot he'd made with his own hands. The baby looked nothing short of angelic next to her ugly Cabbage Patch Doll, sound asleep.

"No," he said softly. "No, we don't want this for you, do we, Girlo?"

Everyone had gone to the Forge & Hammer halfway between the Rock and the neighbouring parish where Pearl was born. The pub had been converted from a real working forge. It was only accessible via a haunted country lane. The story was that a man and his wife had broken down and the man had gone for help. But when he'd returned his wife had disappeared and was never seen again. The White Monkey was said to lurk around there.

Inside the Forge wacky-backy was smoked freely. Leonard Cohen played loudly, hippies, bikers and workers blithely socialising.

"Where's Eric, Crys?" Jack, who'd been propping up the bar all night asked.

"He's popping in for a quick one after work..."

"A quick one?"

"He've got night school, 'aven't he?"

"An' where's tha' gunna get him?" Jack grumbled.

Eric landed at the bar that very moment in his cement-crusted denims.

"Out of this place. Pint please."

"Oh, yere he is, The Professor! I just don't understand why he's going out of his way to go to this night school. What's the matter with the job he've already got?"

"He've got to get on, Jack. He've got a baby girl now."

"I know, Pearl. And they're looking for boys down the industrial estate. You should pop your name down there."

"I will do, Dad, and I can still do night school."

"Doesn't matter what you do, won't make a blind bit of difference. You think you're someone now because you stood on a few pickets. Socialist, be fucked! You gotta get on in the real world. College isn't the real world. You can't get your bread 'n' butter from a piece of paper, can you? Face it, we're fucked. The Iron Lady rules us now, and you can thank yer mother for that."

"She was a woman, I thought she'd make a difference."

"She made a bloody difference, alright."

When first built, the estate symbolised hope and modernity a world away from what its new residents were used to; houses luxurious in comparison to the bathroom-less tin prefabs and farmhouses they'd came from.

"I couldn't believe it!' Pearl, one of the first women to secure one of the new purpose-built council houses, said. "I had a cooker, electric lights *and* a fitted kitchen." She later purchased the house under the Right to Buy scheme.

In addition to the assumed role of 'mother', Pearl had two career choices: secretary or hairdresser. She became the latter and was seduced by Jack Wolf over the stile near The Run. A shotgun-wedding sealed her fate at the age of 17. She lived in a stone-cold cottage and had to get up at the crack of dawn to light the fire, starting the day's cooking for her three infant sons, her mother, father, grampa and blind grandmother sitting in the corner.

"My poor Mamma had a dog's life. Grandpa was a bastard, stomping around the kitchen in his big thick boots, frightening her to death. Every time she needed a pee, I'd have to take her out to the toilet in all weathers. She was a lovely woman, but she had a dog's life. Thirteen children she had, and by the time she was fifty she'd gone blind."

Every Monday Pearl boiled the cloth napkins in a pot on the fire. If the tiniest speck of soot came away from the chimney and landed in the water, she'd have to start all over again. The neighbours would talk if they saw the nappies had turned grey. In the evening, the family would sit crouched around the table with a jungle of electrical wires plugged into a sole outlet above their heads. When there was a storm, the outlet would crackle and hiss, making them spill spoons of cawl down their chins.

When she finally got the keys to her new council house, she turned the central heating on. It was still on when Girlo came to stay years later, the soothing lull of the boiler humming through the chipboard walls. The pint of water Girlo took to bed zinged with bubbles throughout the night as if the heat was slowly boiling it.

WISTFUL

Girlo loved bold colours, but Earl only liked white. His whole house was painted white.

"They're all different shades," he announced with a sense of accomplishment.

"You can't even tell!" Girlo said. She'd come to his house this time in her new role as a 'professional model'.

"Well, this is Chalk White," he said pointing out one of the chosen shades. "Cloud Nine. Chantilly Lace. This is Dove White."

"Yeah, ok, but, really? There's not much difference, is there? White is white."

"There is! If you look closely you can see a very subtle difference."

"Oh, yeah, but it won't matter too much when the light changes though, will it?"

"I have designed this whole house within a well-thought-out specification as to where the sun rises and sets." Earl gave her a tour of the places where each source of light 'settled'. Why had he even bothered? The only visitor he got was Girlo. She supposed he'd designed it as a studio space for his string of 'professional models'.

"Yeah, I get it, but I think it could do with a few little touches... you know, to make it more homely. Maybe a rug... a plant, perhaps."

"It's minimalism."

"Feels a bit clinical."

Earl wasn't paying any attention to what she was saying.

"This massive wall behind the staircase could do with a splash of colour. There's so much light in here, the space could handle it. You could paint it deep red. That would make such a bold statement, don't you think?"

"If you could just take a seat by the window we can make a start."

Girlo worried she'd offended her employer but before the anxiety could kick in, she settled on the belief he was being professional.

"Look wistful," he instructed.

Girlo sat up on the back of the sofa. He was paying her £50 an hour to take some 'tasteful' photographs. She'd agreed because she was skint as usual, but also because the idea gave her a little thrill.

"Like this?"

"Try to think of a time when you felt... melancholic."

Girlo didn't know where to begin; there were so many times when she felt *melancholic*, or devoid of any feeling, or frequently, suicidal. She looked out onto the overgrown garden and thought about how lonely she'd felt as a child lying on her plastic covered mattress, the lingering, cloying odour of Zoflora and damp piss. She remembered the pain in her scalp, the throb from one of her whacks in the mirror. A stream of itchy tears tearing the sides of her face as she worried over who or what she'd have to pretend to sleep through that night. The dread of waking, perhaps to a house full of wasted wankers? A stranger on his way out of the front door? A snivelling Eddie, wanting his nappy changed or bottle filled? The unwelcome warmth of her own wee. The prospect of having to confess to her mother that she'd peed the bed again only to have her mother shout at her for drinking too much before bed, for not "getting up to go." Bedtime was the worst time of day. At least when she was awake, she had some level of control over what happened to her. When she was asleep, she was powerless. A person's bed is supposed to be their sanctuary but, in *her* bed, Girlo felt like a prisoner; a scab of a girl left on a forgotten slab.

"That's great. Good. Hold that thought... You are very beautiful." Earl weaved around her as her eyes bulged with tears.

"Very emotive!"

Even though she hadn't spoken, Girlo felt like she'd shared this memory with Earl, that he had understood her. There was a connection between his camera lens and her core that hadn't happened with anyone before. Since it all came out when she was seven, she'd been tip-toeing around. Girlo had pushed the memories down, pretending to be okay for the sake of everyone else. She acted like a survivor, walking around looking perfectly normal, but with each new encounter with emotion, the pain sutured inside; multiplied like a box of venomous snakes. As she grew, they hissed and twisted, becoming ever more toxic. Her only defence was to push her entire childhood down. She didn't know how to untangle the whole festering mess of it. If she opened that box, she knew the tears would come and she was afraid they'd never stop.

When Earl finished taking his shots of her, they had dinner. After they'd polished off a bottle of tequila, she let him take her to bed.

ROCK GIRL

Crystal and Eric's split was abrupt. One moment they were all living in the city—Girlo was in a good nursery school, learning how to say the colours in Cymraeg—and the next, her mother was packing up their ground floor flat. Girlo had one vague memory of happiness. It was Christmas Day and she woke up to find a plastic inflatable wigwam in the living room. Initially, she was petrified of it but the pictures of bears on its sides reminded her of Yogi and she soon warmed to it. In fact, she fell in love with it when she found all her presents inside. It was Eric's idea. He was like that, young at heart. Her mother and father had seemed in love then. They weren't arguing. She could feel the love—she had to treasure that.

Girlo would try to brush her hair like her mother in the mirror with her mother's silver hairbrush, but the brush got caught every time in her fine blonde hair. Her mother was very impatient; no time for gently removing the hair from the brush strand-by-strand. Instead, she'd instantly take to the scissors, cutting the thing right out and leaving an awful tuft that stuck out of the side of Girlo's head like an antenna.

"Keep still!" she'd snap whenever she did *anything* to Girlo's hair. She pulled and ragged the brush, whispering: "Ratsss' tails. This hair is like rats' tails!" She had a way of hissing her 'S's' which brought the rats to life.

Girlo wasn't sure how her father felt about her. Part of his parental role was to play referee, which seemed to encourage him to refer to his kids as 'nuisances'. She supposed that was better than what her mother called her. She'd hear him more often than she saw him, his booming laugh bellowing through the flat, or his shout of "up the wooden hill" after they'd gone to bed.

"Where's Daddy gone, Nan?"

"He's gone to see a man about a dog."

"Are we getting a dog?!"

Girlo never saw any of the men of the family really. They were always out looking for dogs but they never brought any dogs back, only 'off-the-back of a lorry' pairs of trainers two sizes too big.

"Don't worry, you'll grow into them. Shove a bit of tissue in the toes."

"Does Daddy love me?" Girlo asked Nannie Pearl.

"Of course, he does, yuh daft apeth! He loves you more than anything in the whole wide world."

"All the ice creams and lollipops, and sweeties in the world?"

"Yes, yes, yes. All the ice creams, and lollipops and sweeties in the world. He loves ewe a million pounds, and so do I, my Cariad."

But Eric had a crazy temper.

He'd be all smiles one minute, and the next—he'd flip his lid. It would make the kids jump something terrible. Such a shock to suddenly feel your brains and bones momentarily dislodge beneath the skin. They never got used to it.

On Bonfire Night Crystal made toffee apples. After Eric had burned his mouth on the molten sugar, a row erupted that culminated in Crystal's own little bonfire of Eric's university books, retribution for his decision to sell the video recorder. He left the house. Once the fire had fizzled out, Crystal packed up all their belongings and fled, leaving Eric with nothing more than a couple of cushions and a crusty flannel on the radiator.

After the breakup, Eric found solace in his studies. He learned about literature, working-class history and despite just scraping his first year, he found himself in the Socialist Worker Party where he first met Heera. He tried to knock her down on the entry fee to his first campaign meeting.

"Pay the fiver or do one!" she'd asserted.

The kids became key weapons in Crystal's arsenal as she

relished and exploited every opportunity to twist the knife in Eric's back. At the start of each school holiday, he'd pick them up, travelling with them by train. He couldn't drive so relied on the trains to get him from Harlech to Newport and Cardiff, then Bournemouth to Folkestone, later Bournemouth to Whitley Bay, then East Anglia as his academic career progressed and he moved around the country's universities. He knew all the stops, links and routes by heart. But with two feral kids as travel companions, a quick hop over the border was practically impossible.

"Will you kids just sit still and be quiet?" he growled the moment they sat at a table seat. They'd be flipping the lids of the ashtrays and flapping the buffet cart menu about the place, demanding anything and everything.

"No. No. No. The answer is no!"

"Please, Dad? Pleeez. Just a chocolate bar to share?"

"Lemme 'ave a look?" he said, snatching the menu.

"One-pound-twenty? You gotta be jorking?! That's daylight robbery. Wait till we get tuh yuh Nannie's."

"Argh Daaaad, but..."

"Shush now you two, will ewe?"

"But we're bored!" They loved to push their father as far as they could—especially in public places. He had nowhere to hide on the train and had to be on his best behaviour under the judgemental gaze of onlookers.

"Yew are..." he said, frantically dislodging a matchbox from his jacket pocket. "I'll show you a trick!"

"Ooh a trick... what is it? What is it, Dad? What's the trick?"

"Hang on a minute and I'll show you now... in a minute."

As the train cut through the landscape, Eric took two match-sticks and wedged them into the drawer of the matchbox forming a triangular shape, which served as foundation joists. He snapped a bit off a fresh match and set it perpendicular between the joists, pincers to hold the phosphorus head in place. Eric was ready to work his magic.

"Right! Watch *this*, kids!" Like a couple of chimpanzees

they bashed the arm rests, barely containing their excitement.

"Careful mun, you two! You'll ruin it!" The careful arrangement had taken the form of a horse-shaped structure, the pink match tips like muscles on the outside of the horse's skin.

"Tudd-dah!"

The kids became transfixed.

"What is it? Is it a horse?"

"No, it's a dog!"

"What does it do?"

"Watch now." Eric took a final match, striking it on the zip of his jacket and lighting the joint above the dog's front legs. They watched as the entire thing swooshed up into a pink flame and a poof of smoke.

"Watch now," Eric said again, pointing to a match supposed to replicate the dog's leg that was curling under the heat. "It's a dog having a piss!"

Girlo loved the Rock as much as Nannie Pearl did. It wasn't a prison to Girlo at all. It was her one true home. The Rock in the Summer was like Butlins on marijuana, The Stretch lined with postage-stamp gardens full of Rockfolk; barbecuing, smoking joints and drinking dumpy bottles of Belgian beer—kids and dogs everywhere! UB40 and Bob Marley blasted, and they sang songs of struggle and solidarity to the valley. Every morning Girlo would wake to the smell of toast and cigarettes, the hubbub of a living-room full of chaos—uncles and aunties dropping off their kids for a day of daredevil adventure! After breakfast Girlo was pushed out of the door with a pound coin squished into her palm and five cousins to watch over until the streetlights came on. They were the Rock Ragamuffins with Tyson the Alsatian as their mascot. He'd herd them like sheep and nip them if they strayed too close to the edge of the quarry or went too fast on their go-karts. On their treks through the maze of tarmacked alleys, they'd recruit more Ragamuffins, their mission to hunt for The White Monkey. They'd steal tarpaulin and timber from gardens to make bivvies, light fires under tree swings then whoosh through the flames with invincible gusto.

They'd swim in the foamy fluorescent river alongside the factories and ride the Shetland ponies bareback on the wild fields opposite.

Nannie Pearl's council house was as irresistible as an Aladdin's Cave. The kids were encouraged to explore the "magic drawer" in her kitchen sideboard. They couldn't resist rifling through the family artefacts, a wondrous source of curiosity. Every time they'd go straight to the drawer, which smelled like Grandad Jack's Old Holborn tobacco, and find old mobile phones left over from Uncle Jimmy's door-to-door enterprise, Grandad Miles' postcards, plectrums and harmonicas, loads of old car keys from Uncle Bobby's car selling enterprise and various pairs of antique spectacles.

"What's this, Nan?"

Nannie Pearl was chopping potatoes on the kitchen top, scoring the Formica as she went.

"He's the Drunken Prince, he is."

Girlo picked up a squidgy cotton wool man stuffed into flesh-coloured tights. She lifted up his grey beard to reveal a scrunched-up willy.

"Ooooh—it's his willy!" Finding the Drunken Prince was a ritual conducted by all the grandkids.

"Willy? I can see his willy! I can see his willy!"

In another drawer was lots of ANC paraphernalia that Eric and Heera had brought back from the marches for Pearl.

"What does your name mean?" Girlo had once asked Eric's girlfriend.

"My name is diamond in Hindi."

Heera was an open book. On returning from a canal walk once, Girlo had found her knickers soaking in the bathroom sink, blood in the gusset. Heera had sat her down and told her all about menstruation. "You see, we shed our womb lining once a month and if our little egg hasn't been fertilised it goes with it."

"Where does it go?"

"Into your sanitary towel."

"And boys?"

"They get away with it!" Heera told Girlo about the differences between men and women, as well as all the different people in the world; how some were treated badly by the people who were in power. She asked Girlo why she'd called a man the N- word on their walk beside the river. Girlo told her she'd heard it in the playground; she didn't understand what it meant. Heera gave her a book about two little black children, a brother and sister just like her and Eddie. Heera seemed to make everything so clear.

"You see, we are all the same. You are no better than anyone else, and they are no better than you, remember that for me, Girlo." Girlo did remember it. But the other children in the playground had no idea. They thought she was worthless because she didn't have any money and because her mummy and daddy lived in different houses. They said they loved Michael Jackson, but they still used the N-word. They said Girlo talked funny.

"What's this, Nan?" Girlo asked, holding up a brass badge.

"That's the official Anti-Nazi League pin, babe. Heera brought it for me."

Girlo knew what it was. Heera's flat was plastered in campaigning stuff. Every summer Eric took them on the Tube to a big Marxist festival of talks and protests. On arrival Girlo and Eddie were dropped off at the crèche. At Heera's she remembered sneaking down to the secured door there to play with the intercom. Determined to see the main entrance on the little screen, she pressed the button. A fuzzy black and white picture of a skinhead appeared; a large Swastika tattooed on his head. With a swift jerk, the skinhead head-butted someone off screen. When he'd moved away, Girlo saw a man in a turban. His nose had been smashed all over his face, a splatter of greyish-looking blood dripping down his chin. He pleaded with the skinhead to stop but the skinhead started wrestling him to the ground. Girlo pressed the button. With a low, grown-up voice she shouted, "Stop! Police!" The swastika man ran away. Girlo ran to tell an adult, but she never did find out if the man in the turban was ok.

Those were the 'turbulent times', her nan said.

"Right, put it all back now. Go and wash your hands. Dinner will be on the table in a minute." Girlo climbed the stairs, the smell of chip fat giving way to the trustworthy trace of the Wolf family, a comforting ensemble of incense, tobacco and Imperial Leather. Not sticky clean like the English boy her mother made her and Eddie play with (who was sick in his hands every time he came to the house). Not sweaty, but toasty like the towels on the radiator—even when they were fresh, the familiar biscuity smell remained. A smell so distinct, it must have been distilled in the womb sealing the tales of the family's battles, triumphs and losses.

"What's going on up there?" Nannie Pearl was halfway up the stairs, hippie skirt wafting like a loose sail. Girlo'd been absent-mindedly plunging her hands into two giant tubs of E45 Cream.

"Nothing, Nannie! Don't send me home!"

"Why would I send you home? What are you doing in there?"

Girlo opened the door, hands thick with the cream, eyes filled with tears.

"Come yere, you daft apeth." She wiped Girlo's hands with a flannel and cwtched her into her boob. "There we are, Cariad… shush now!"

"Can I wear your T-shirt, Nan?"

"Of course you can, Cariad." She went to the bedroom to pull out Girlo's favourite T-shirt, which commemorated Nelson Mandela's 70th Birthday. On the front was a grainy close-up of his face, eyes more knowing than the blue-eyed Jesus Christ. On the back was a list of the Artists Against Apartheid who'd played at the concert. The grown-ups would play their songs all the time, a mark of solidarity in future hopes for their struggles. Crystal always played Joan Armatrading when she was getting ready to go to work. Girlo sang along with her: *I belong to me, I belong to me.*

"I don't want to go back, Nan, I want to live with you."

"We'll see, my Cariad, we'll see now."

Brown & Stuart
Solicitors with Notaries

Ref: 1lb/Thw/W1983
Date: 2nd June 1997

Dear Mr Wolf,

We refer to our discussion on 9th April and are sorry to hear your concerns regarding your daughter. You explained the situation to us in detail in that, following certain difficulties last year, your former wife agreed that your daughter should stay with your mother.

Your former wife now wishes that your daughter return to live with her, the reasons for this being unclear. You and your mother feel that following your daughter's difficulties last year, a move would not be in her best interests because she is settled in school, has made friends in the area and her behaviour has considerably improved. We feel that it is relevant that your former wife's new relationship may have failed, she has a new baby to care for together with your son, Edward, and this being the case, she may feel that were your daughter to return to live with her this would give her help in the home.

From what you have told us, we do not feel this would be in your daughter's best interests. After what she has been through, she needs to feel settled and secure, which is the case now. It would seem that her mother did not protect her, and we suspect that your daughter is aware of this. Your daughter has indicated that she wishes to remain living with her grandmother but possibly have some contact with your former wife. In that connection, whereas you remain in constant touch with your daughter, your former wife has not, only seeing her a couple of times in a period of 12 months. We feel all of these factors are relevant and would be considered by a court were the matter to come before a judge.

If an application to the Court were made, then your daughter is of an age where her views are taken into consideration. She would not be required to attend Court in person but would have the opportunity to discuss how she feels with Social Services or a Court Welfare Officer. No one would consider forcing your daughter to do anything she really did not want to, and we imagine if this was attempted, she would react very badly.

There's one option that we feel you could consider, that your daughter makes an application to the Court in her own right that she be permitted to remain living with your mother. This is rarely done, and the child has to be of "sufficient understanding" but at the age of nearly 14, you may feel she is old and sensible enough to give proper and firm instructions to a solicitor to act on her behalf. Her solicitor would need to obtain leave of court to make such an application, and this could be considered by her solicitor at the time. If your daughter has no income or considerable savings, then she will be granted Legal Aid to pursue the case.

You told us that you wish to discuss this situation further with your mother before taking any further action. Should that be the case, we enclose a second copy of this letter should you want to send it to your mother for her views.

We await hearing from you further once you have considered your position.

Yours truly,
Brown & Stuart.

PROBLEM CHILD

Eric popped one of the upstairs doors in his mother's council house when Girlo ran away. Nannie Pearl was used to covering the holes from heated family rows, blue-tacked prints of Siddhartha Gautama and Bob Marley covering hexagonal cardboard like someone had chucked a grenade at a beehive.

Girlo had only been living with Nannie Pearl for just over a month when she'd got in with Wild Child, a sixteen-year-old girl so fucking deranged she'd been excluded from school. Even the official Rockcrew wouldn't bother with her. Wild Child was a rebel Girlo idolised because she'd given her a belly top stolen from New Look. Wild Child was a pro-thief who robbed her drunken mother blind. She'd nicked the video player, the Teas-maid, and everything in between. She'd taken a shine to Girlo the first day they'd met down by the river.

"Oo uh yew 'en?" she said, skimming a stone across the weir. Her front teeth were butterflied, green gunge along the gum-line.

"Pearl Wolf's granddaughter."

The fact that she was a Wolf didn't bother Wild Child.

"You talk funny. Where you frum? D'you smoke?"

Girlo wasn't sure what she was talking about. If she meant fags, then yeah. She fiddled with the stolen fag gripped in her clammy, pocketed hand—retrieved from her secret spot, the finger shaped space at the foot of the toilet bowl—which she'd nicked from her mum's boyfriend, Doug. He called them 'tabs' and kept them under lock and key in the bureau: stacks of twenty-pack Regal Blue and Focus Points, collected to exchange for extension leads, garden hoses and everything else Doug held dear, piled alongside the entire collection of *Fawlty Towers* episodes on VHS.

"Yee clothed-eared bint!" he liked to shout. He liked Motocross too. He'd bought Eddie a Kawasaki 360 in lime green and every weekend Girlo'd be dragged off to the scrambling pits to watch the bike shows with them, the razz of the bikes and pump of petrol and testosterone making her feel on edge.

When Girlo'd first moved in with Nannie Pearl, she'd asked her to paint a pair of red lips around the letter box. She'd taken real pleasure, long, slow brushstrokes to create a big red pout to make the postman smile. But Crystal went mad when Girlo painted her wardrobe with silver moons and stars. Life with Crystal and Doug was institutional, especially when their new baby came along, whereas Nannie Pearl's was like the Green Fields at Glastonbury, full of Nag Champa and colour. Girlo liked to explore her library at the top of her stairs. One of her favourite books was a small poetry collection by Ella Wheeler Wilcox, bound in a soft moleskin cover, mossy green with embossed gold lettering. *Poems of Power*. It was singed at the edges. Girlo held it to her heart, trying to channel its history. She imagined it had belonged to a spirited young woman whose strict father or husband had thrown it into a fire. *Laugh and the world laughs with you. Weep and you weep alone,* she recited. Amongst the dusty classics, Blake and Shakespeare, she found a curious text called the *Women Who Run with the Wolves* by Clarissa Pinkola Estés. Someone called Alice Walker described it on its cover as, 'A gift of profound Wisdom.' Girlo'd end up with carpet indents on her bum-cheeks from sitting on the stair reading it all day. *What was this 'soulful reclamation' she spoke of? And what did she mean about stories being lived not studied?* Girlo was living a story. She needed to write it but didn't know where to begin. She found some yellowed file paper and a bitten-down biro. She began with Clarissa's words: "There is an integrity to a story that comes from a real life lived in it." The following day she gave her story, 'Uncle A. Buse', to her teacher to read. At first, he seemed impressed— this wasn't a prescribed homework task. But after reading the title his gaze dropped. He hid the stapled papers in the top drawer, and it was never mentioned again.

Girlo ran away when she had a bollocking from Nannie Pearl for filching two quid from her handbag—she'd wanted to buy ten Lambert & Butler to impress Wild Child—but Nannie kept a close eye on the purse strings. She'd noticed almost immediately. "Stick out your tongue. If it has a black line on it, I know you're lying." Even though Girlo was almost thirteen she fell for the trick. She poked out her tongue.

"It's got a black line! Yewer lying, Girlo. Now if that two quid isn't back where it belongs by bedtime you're grounded for a month!"

After tea, Girlo packed her rucksack with the essentials. She'd got better at it over the years; she remembered a toothbrush and bar of soap as well as clean knickers. When her nan went outside to natter to Coral over the road, Girlo made a run for it.

"Oi… And where d'you think you're going?!"

She bolted into the maze of back alleys then hid under the honeysuckle bush that hung over the fence of the prettiest garden on the Rock. She plucked a few petals and sucked the nectar while she waited to find out if she'd been followed.

Wild Child would be hanging round the shops, probably on the rob. *How could she get to her?* The Stretch was the obvious choice, but she would be exposed, grassed on by one of the mothers. Her nan would know before she even reached the phone box. The Stretch was like the lifeline which ran through the centre of the Rock. If you were up to anything shady, it was the last place you'd want to be seen—news travelled along it like wildfire. She'd go through the lanes but there were obstacles everywhere. Firstly, the nasty Pitbull allowed to roam on the green. It'd chased Girlo and Eddie up a tree once and they'd had to wait until dark to come down. (Nannie Pearl never believed that one, but it was true!) Then there was Nannie Pearl's friend who often popped in for a joint or pack of Rizlas, which Girlo would be sent down to collect. His kitchen window had a clear view of The Stretch. He'd be sure to ring her. Girlo'd have to cut across the lane which was in the direct eye-line of Nannie Pearl's kitchen window, and risk alerting the nasty Rottweiler in the process. The poor thing was tied up and condemned to tramping in its own filth all day. No wonder it was livid.

She cut across the carpark. There was a skip she could hide behind until the coast was clear. To avoid the courtyard area, controlled by two identical Spaniels, was the refuge of number 17: home to the woman Girlo used to iron clothes for. The Spaniels were snoozing on the patchy piss-stinking grass on the far side of the court. Girlo slipped by, taking a sharp left past the flats.

Finally, she felt a wave of relief roll through her. But then she heard the cackles of a clan of notorious kids, seven of them in total, all under the age of 10. They were perched on the wheelie bins like a flock of scrawny jackdaws, scruffy and slit-eyed. As Girlo flew down the steps they took their positions: each armed with a weapon. One of them was holding a small kitchen knife, which he thrust into the air, the blade winking in the light. Another, a stone too big for his tiny hands. Another of them held part of a broken drainpipe. Another, a scratched length of four-by-four. The last kid was wielding a good-sized shard of broken glass.

"No trespassers!"

"Fuck off, I'm coming through," Girlo had learned early to stand her ground.

"What's the magic word?"

"Get outta the way."

"Gis a fag!"

Girlo tried to hold her nerve, using the same lines the adults used on her.

"D'your mothers know you're up to no good?"

"Got a light?" One of them took a dog-end from his pocket and straightened it out. Girlo held out her Clipper and he snatched it from her grip.

"Have it!" She darted down the lane dodging handfuls of their hurled pebbledash.

She made it out over The Stretch and into another warren of lanes. This end of the Rock wasn't quite as treacherous. There

were a few shops to pop into to break up the journey. Wild Child
was in the park making spit puddles. (The park wasn't much more
than a crumbly patch of tarmac and a helter-skelter slide, reduced
by a torching, to a molten, yellow candle.

"Hiya!" said Girlo.

"Alright? You're out early. Finished your homework like a
good girl?"

"I've run away!"

"Yeah? That's the 'ammer! Have you got any money?"

"Just pinched two quid f'fags. Will ewe go in for me?"

"Unnee if I can 'ave one?"

Wild Child had already helped herself to a cigarette when she got
back. Girlo took the box and turned the middle fag over for luck.
At least Wild Child wasn't as bad as the Berghaus crew she'd left
behind in Whitley Bay: if you asked any of those to go in the shop
for you, they'd jump at the chance and then after buying whatever
was requested, they'd keep the goods for themselves. It was
always a risk asking someone to go in the shop for you, and on
those occasions where alcohol or cigarettes were successfully
purchased, there was always the risk of the police catching up
with you. Girlo used to knock about down the sea front, outside
the Rainbow Arcade. The Berghaus crew thought they owned the
place. They were solid and if she got in with them, she'd be
sorted. They were proper street kids, and because they hung about
in minus conditions, all night every night, they wore outdoor
Berghaus coats. It was difficult to become a fully-fledged
member: there were certain initiation tests Girlo had to overcome
before she was allowed to set foot inside their territory (the
Rainbow) where they'd gamble their pennies on the Tupenny
Nudger. Every time she asked one of them to go in the shop,
they'd skank her. Once she'd had her third pack of fags and litre
of Merrydown cider stolen, she kicked up a fuss and was swiftly
punched in the face by a scrappy girl who was obviously new to
the gang too. *This was Girlo's chance.* She gripped the girl by the
hair and slammed her onto the floor where they punched and

scratched the shit out of each other, until the head honcho's sister, decided to break it up.

"Hauld on. Hauld on, wuss goo-win on by heeyuz thun. Coom-an... howay wiv yuz, man! Yull huv the fookin' filth sniffin' aboot uz." The hood of Girlo's coat had been ripped clean off, but in her hand was a clump of the girl's permed hair. She'd won!

"Cheeky mare. Lemme at her! I'm gunna kill uh!" Screamed the defeated girl, scrams all down her cheeks.

"I didun na... yuz uv gotta a left hook on yuz there, Lass!" The head honcho's sister took Girlo under her wing and they went into the Rainbow. *She'd made it – the first step in with the crew...*

Inside, the arcade was lively: full of people in raincoats, slotting coins into blinking machines. Girlo could feel her hands warming up. It had been sleeting that evening and she had been stood in the doorway for the past three hours, freezing her arse off.

"Let uz show yuz how tuh pley this," beckoned the girl, who unzipped the multitude of pockets in her coat to find some change.

"Yew are! I've got some munee," said Girlo who held out a hand of two-pence pieces. She had got them ready for her admittance.

"Fook, where yuz fram pet?"

"Wayulls."

"Sheepshagger!"

Girlo had a quick go on the Tuppenny Nudger, but then moved onto a gambler for higher stakes. She'd played a few times in the pub hanging around for her mother, so she knew the basics. After pushing in the third twenty pence, the machine gave her the option to hold two four-leaf clovers. She pressed play and to her astonishment, her luck came in—a third clover emerging. The bandit lit up and dropped its load into the cash tray. At that moment, everyone in the Rainbow turned like magpies and dashed towards her machine to take her winnings. There were so many hands, grabbing the coins as they fell. Out of a twenty-pound jackpot, she walked away with eight-pound-eighty, but it was well worth it because now everyone knew who she was.

"What you doing that for?" asked Wild Child.

"My lucky tab. I'll smoke that one last."

"Tab?"

"Fag!"

"So, we're off on the run, are we?"

Girlo remembered the last time she ran away. She'd been sleeping rough for a night when her mean friend and her kind mother were driving past Spar. They saw Girlo shivering in the sleet.

"Isn't that your friend from school?" asked the girl's mother.

"Aye."

They brought her home and fed her a huge Sunday dinner. Her friend put ketchup on her gravy, which Girlo couldn't get her head around. After dinner they gave her a sleeping bag and she slept on the pull-out bed. The weather was terrible that night and she thought the wind was going to rip the ceiling off. The next day, her friend's mother dropped Girlo home. Girlo's mother thanked them for bringing her home, casually making herself a cup of tea, completely nonplussed, as Girlo came into the kitchen bedraggled and freezing. She clinked a spoon on the green glass mug three times and didn't utter a word.

The next day her mother sent her away. Girlo stood on the bus stop with her packed suitcase, waiting for the coach for three-quarters of an hour. No one even came to see her off. Half of her thought her mother would come running round the corner, begging her to come home, but she didn't. She remembers marvelling at the window display of novelty gifts. There were clocks made of Coke cans and CDs, and a bottle of Brown Ale, which stood upright on the resin liquid it poured out. She really wanted to buy one for her dad, but all she had was her own coach fare.

"I'm wiv ewe babe," said Wild child, "we better take the quarry way down."

It was getting dark. Girlo'd never been over the fields at night.

"Will we be ok in the dark?" The last time she'd been at the quarry with Eddie and Tyson she'd lost her footing and tumbled onto the rocks.

"D'you wanna get seen?"

They shot down the side field they'd set fire to earlier that week. It had rained, so the charred ferns whipped at their legs, leaving marks on the backs of their jeans. When they reached the old oak tree in the middle, Girlo looked back at the Rock—a halo of orange streetlights encircling it. Despite the threat of danger, she felt safer with Wild Child than she did on the streets of Newcastle alone. It was pitch-black now, and they followed a secret path until they found their way to the old railway track, lit by the adjacent streetlights. They stopped for a while to lob stones at a crumpled sign on the bridge.

"I'm always on the run, me," Wild Child said, hurling a stone, missing the sign.

"Why's that?"

"My ole man, like innit. Clever with his fists and that."

Girlo had never met anyone in the same boat as her before.

"Say no more," Girlo said, "let's keep moving." She had no idea where they were going but she trusted Wild Child.

Once they'd reached the end of the track, they moved up into the woods again, taking the river path. It had started to rain, and the leafy parapet protected them from most of it. Girlo found a big stick. She used it like a machete against the foliage.

"How far now?"

"There's an old bivvy down by the horse field. We can sleep in there for tonight. Tomorrow we'll go to my cousin's."

Her cousin, Cookie Monster, had broken the virginity of almost all the boys on the Rock. She was in her late twenties, the size of a phone box. According to Wild Child, she was visiting her ex with the kids and her house was empty. Once the girls crossed the river into the horse field, they found the bivvy'd been burned to the ground.

"Fuck!" Girlo sent her machete stick hurtling through the air. The rain suddenly turned to a downpour. They huddled under a tree for shelter.

"Fucking typical! What'll we do now?"

"We'll have to sit it out. Wait for it to pass."

It didn't pass. They spent the night under the tree, Tesco carrier bags pulled over their heads, raindrops pattering on the plastic. She thought of the rain on her Nannie Pearl's tin roof, rolling over her uncle's orange canoe that had been stored there. But she wasn't in her bedroom now, she was on the run. She didn't need *anyone* anymore. Her mother was a bitch who didn't care about her. In fact, her mother couldn't wait to get rid of her. And Girlo couldn't wait to get away.

Nannie Pearl spent the night pacing. They had scoured the estate, knocking on the doors of everyone they could think of. They'd even mobilised the Rockcrew to keep an eye out around the flats and down by the shops. They'd been to Wild Child's mother. She was no use, pissed up for the seventh night in a row. The nosey woman from number 17 was on Stretch watch. She'd sent the word out around the estate.

"What if someone's had her?"

"She'll be fine," Coral said. "We look after owwer own up here, dun we? Don't be daft, now."

"I should've let her have the money. It was only a couple of quid!" Pearl lit another fag; she'd already gone through forty. "I better ring Eric."

"It'll be twenty-four hours by 5 o'clock, then the police will find her. She'll be alright, Pearl. She can't have gone far."

"I fucking hope so. Wait 'till I get hold of her: I'm gonna fucking kill her! I better ring him now." She picked up the phone and dialled Eric's number.

"What d'you mean she's run away?" he said. "Again? Fucking 'ell Mam."

"Listen Eric, it's ok. We've got a search party out for her. She won't have gone far."

"Who's she with? Who's she bothering with?"

"Just a girl from the site."

"What fucking *girl*? How old is she? Have you rung the police?"

"Of course I fucking have, Eric. D'you think I'm fucking simple? They can't do much until she's been gone for twenty-four hours."

"Well, when did she go?"

"Yesterday. Teatime?"

"It's fucking 4 o'clock now! Why didn't you ring me?"

"I didn't want to worry you."

"Christ sake, Mam!"

Girlo's muddy legs and trainers had merged into one, a wet clay sculpture.

"Right, come on, up," Wild Child said, "let's get moving."

"I'm freezing."

"Let's get back up the Rock."

"We can't. We'll be seen!"

Girlo and Wild Child busted open the Cookie Monster's window with a screwdriver, dried off and got into a couple of size 20 hoodies. They hunkered down on the sofa and slept for a while.

They didn't have any money for the telly. The Cookie Monster was the only person on the Rock who didn't use the pound coin on a wire trick to get around the pay-box. The leccy was off too. After a quick fiddle with a fridge magnet, Wild Child got the dials moving. They made some Smash in the micro.

"Tha'ss bettuh! Fucking starving, I was."

"D'you fink my nan is out looking f'me?"

"If it was *my* mother I'd say no."

"Same!"

"Fuckum! We don't need um. We got each other now, just like Thelmuh un Louise. We can go anywhere we wan' in this world. All we need is a fast car."

Girlo sang, 'You gotta fast car, I gotta ticket to any-where...'

Wild Child joined in with the Tracey Chapman number. When they got to 'I-ee-I... had a feeling that I belong,' Girlo began to cry. This had never happened before. Usually, she swallowed the tears hard and they'd resurface as spurts of anger, or she'd save them for the Guatemalan worry dolls who lived under her pillow. For some reason it was all coming up like acid reflux.

She felt real for once, not helicoptering over herself, watching her own actions from a distance. Her reality, a simulation, her body a one-dimensional player in a video game.

"What's the matter?" Wild Child asked.

The tears kept bubbling. Girlo couldn't stop. Then it erupted. She told Wild Child about the court case, how Crystal had promised her a china doll if she told the truth.

Girlo told her everything about the day of the court case. How the lucky penny she'd found had deceived her. How she'd spilled tomato ketchup down her new flowery-pocketed top. How the man in a wig on the monitor screen kept scorning her, interrogating her like she was the one who'd done something wrong. The high-backed chair they'd sat her in was like something from Mastermind, making her itch and sweat. She knew her Uncle Groggy and Auntie Beryl were in the courtroom watching her, but she knew her mother had gone to Tenerife with Doug "last minute."

She told Wild Child about her mother's father, who'd grabbed and thrown her against the chipboard walls on her eighth birthday. All she'd wanted was more milk on her Weetabix. He'd hit her head so hard she actually saw stars. She thought that only happened in cartoons. When she'd made a run for it up the concrete steps, he'd grabbed her by her belt and pushed her again, her shin slicing on the step. He gave Eddie a football coin but called her a "lying little bitch." She spent the rest of her birthday in the garage next to the scrapyard behind their flat. The guys there gave her a hot chocolate and a quid to cheer her up. She talked about Doug, who'd belt her if she gave him any backchat. How he'd cut off the plug of her tape recorder while she was taping her favourite songs from the radio. She told her about her mother's decision not to believe Girlo about everything that had happened to her.

"It's my birthday today," she sobbed.

"Happy Birthday, you soppy twat."

Girlo imagined her father, purple with rage, swear words shooting out of him like spears.

"I need to go home," she said. "I need to get back." Just then they heard a jangle of keys. The front-door flew open. Girlo leapt behind an armchair.

"Oh my god! Look at the mess in here, Sugar puffs everywhere!" It was the Cookie Monster. "Looks like they've been here."

"I take it you want to press charges, then love?" The police were with her.

Girlo felt them moving. Her heart was pounding so loudly she thought they'd hear it.

"Right, it looks like they've moved on. Let's contact the family... can we get the guys down here to dust the place?"

The front door opened and closed. They'd gone. *Fuck, she was in deep shit now. Her fingerprints were on everything!*

They got out of the back door and scarpered up the back lane, the overbearing roar of a chopper scouring the estate from above.

"They're out for you and they got sniffer dogs un every-fen. Propah celebrity yew are like," Wild Child cried. They hid in the long grass on the top field and were about to set off again, when a copper with a dog appeared from nowhere.

Girlo's thirteenth birthday present was a "lucky escape." She was arrested but not incarcerated. Nannie Pearl made her wear a gold crucifix and a full-skirted dress with a pattern that reminded her of 'ice cream castles in the sky'. It was the same dress she'd worn on her coach trip from Whitley Bay to Wales where she'd sung Joni Mitchell in her mind the whole way. The police gave her a warning tour of the cells and she was charged with a caution.

VALLEYS POET

There was a knock on the grotto door.

"Excuse me," the Lighthouse Bard said. "Yes, come in."

The head of a messy-haired male appeared.

"Oh, er... I'm sorry..."

"No, no, no not at all," the Lighthouse Bard said.

Girlo fidgeted in her chair. *Maybe she'd said too much.* It was difficult to get a word in edgeways with her. Maybe she wasn't the *right* kind of person; she wasn't exactly the literary type. She'd spent most of her free time getting smashed with stoners who claimed to have a degree from what they called the 'University of Life.' Girlo perused the book title on the shelf while the man and the Lighthouse Bard chatted. *What did people do before they could write?* They told stories, she thought. Hearing stories was more engaging than being faced with a text written in a language sculpted for someone who wasn't her, about someone she couldn't relate to. *Where were the real people in the books they did at school?* The closest she'd got to feeling an affinity with a character was Celie from *The Color Purple*. The story reminded her of the women she'd grown up around. Nannie Pearl, Grandmamma, Heera, even Crystal. All women who told stories to make things better, darning the gaping holes between what the world said about them and the lives they led.

Girlo had gut-cried over that book. She felt she *knew* Celie and was so angry when Hollywood went and tore the soul right out of the book, turning it into an oversexualised lesbian story. It was really about female love, strength, solidarity and the creativity required to overcome spiritual suffocation at the hands of an oppressive colonial patriarchy. Their patchwork quilt reminded Girlo of a story Nannie Pearl had told her about going to jail for pinching a frozen leg of lamb. 'Prison was like a holiday,' her nan said. No fights or mess or husbands to deal with, just women who struggled to keep their family benefits out of the pockets of the beer-soaked men of their house. When she'd finished her stretch, the girls had sewn her a patchwork quilt. She'd kept it as a memento of their friendship.

"Yes, all in order," the Lighthouse Bard continued chatting to the man who'd popped in. Then, "Oh," he said turning to introduce Girlo. "This is our new addition. She's a valleys poet."

What did that mean? She never wrote much. Well, not in the traditional sense. She wrote in her head, narrating what she what she witnessed, feeling her way through vision and sound, transforming them into scribbles, graffiti, verses, rants, stories to be told.

At university she became confused by the hypocrisy and duality of life which plainly presented itself. It wasn't that she *couldn't* write, just that she was made to feel like she didn't have the right to. She'd gone to a comprehensive school with its limited curriculum designed to prepare its pupils for 'useful' work. Writing was for the elite.

"Fantastic!" The man held out his hand to greet her. "Good to meet you."

Did he just say, 'new addition'? *Had she been accepted on the course?*

"This is the editor of an independent press we have here on campus," the Lighthouse Bard said.

"Yes, and we welcome submissions."

"I don't think I'm good enough to get anything published. I—I…"

The editor smiled before swiftly departing.

"Right, where were we?"

"Lorca?"

"The great wonder-working Lorca. He loved the persecuted traveller community of his native Andalusia." The Lighthouse Bard plucked a volume from its shelf. "He reimagines them in his poetry as representative of the fire blood and alphabet of universal truth."

Girlo could see how disciplined he was. Her discipline was still a work in progress. She'd spent the first two years of her degree in a vodka blur. Wallowing in her pit of a bedroom, contemplating suicide, scrawling the odd crude poem amid a dope haze. The cultural shift from lawless chavette to politics student was seismic. She'd pulled it out of the bag in her final year, but still she wondered if she was good enough.

"I think you'll like him. He was a poet of the people who put soul before profit."

"Thank you." She took the book. *Did she have the capacity, ability, mental agility, the vocabulary even, to convey her thoughts in a way that was publishable? Was she ready to expose herself? What would happen if she dug that box up out of her?*

She was shit scared. She felt like an oiled seabird, washed up by a crude-corrupted ocean, feathers bogged in gloop, only the tiniest glint of life in her eyes. Because she didn't know what was on the other side of the cliff—whether it levelled out or if there was a massive drop—it'd be easier to stay with the broken birds, too weary or heavy to fly.

"Have you read any work by Burns, Scottish poet?"

"I know Auld Lang Syne. Well, I say I do. I forget the words every New Year's Eve—"

"I think you must push the dialect stuff all the way!"

"Ok... will do!"

"And think about coming on our walk when you start in October."

"Start? You mean I got in?!"

"If you'll have us. You have a concrete foundation for something really great here."

"If you say so."

"Take this too, a few hints and tips from some of the best writers in the country." He handed her a dog-eared insert from the Guardian.

She pulled the door behind her, wondering what he'd meant about her having *them*. Wasn't it meant to be the other way round? She liked the sound of being a valleys poet. *It's got a good ring to it.* Instead of the pub, she headed to the library. In an old trolley of books for resale she found a small book with the picture of a stout, chilled-looking monkey on the cover. She began to read the introduction: "Bonobos... A matriarchal, egalitarian social structure... rather than using aggression to resolve disputes the Bonobos use sex. Therefore, they are known as the sexy monkeys. The human species is more closely related to the DNA of Bonobos than chimpanzees, thereby undermining the claim for an evolutionary patriarchal organisation of societal structures. From a feminist hermeneutical perspective, it is also interesting to note that Bonobos are described as 'pygmy' chimpanzees, reducing their status per male-centric qualities of height and strength. Such physical attributes and masculine behaviours are widely recognised as a decisive factor in the origins of gender inequality, which also carry the hallmarks of chimpanzee culture, from which we all supposedly evolved."

What was hermeneutical?

She didn't choose this existence; she'd been born into it. A toxic patriarchal world order in which her subjectivity had been severed, leaving her feeling devalued as a human being. Just like the Bonobo, she was second-class, a poor relation. She took out her notepad where she'd scribbled a quote by Sartre: *'A man is always a teller of tales. He is surrounded by his stories and the stories of other men.'* Beneath it she wrote: 'What of the stories of, or, more, precisely, my women? Erased, undermined, or misrepresented in the greater narratives of our white, privileged, forefathers.'

Girlo unfolded the Guardian pull-out and began reading the Top Ten Tips for Writing. 'Read and read and when you feel you've read enough, read some more.' *What about living? Didn't that count for anything? Never mind tips, what about truth?* She took up her pen and began to write...

THE CRAZY TRUTH

1. Take life by the scruff of the neck, live it to its fullest and write not from an ivory tower but from your sacred fount. From life itself.

2. Talk, converse and listen to everyone as true equals. We will only achieve real change through unfettered discussion and debate.

3. Forgive yourself for not reading all the classics, admit when you haven't finished reading some books or don't rate the books the reviews told you were epic.

4. Cherish those who were there for you on the way up, for they'll be the people who are there for you on the way down. Be grateful to all those who supported you.

5. Read philosophy, then seek answers through the lens of marginalised others.

6. Immerse yourself in all cultures, then find commonalities to unite, fight and write.

7. Take pride in your cultural heritage, honour your ancestors and the sacrifices they made.

8. Dive headfirst into the unknown. Embrace your wild side, challenge conventions and dare to be defiant in your creativity. Growth flourishes in uncharted waters, so take risks and fearlessly explore them.

9. Shoot for the moon and land among the stars, yet in our ascent, let's not forget: the individual is born of the collective. Our personal victories should serve as beacons, lifting communities forgotten by time. Instead of pulling up the ladder, let's celebrate our triumphs collectively and extend a hand to one another.

10. Find your tribe. In a world governed by complex networks and seemingly impenetrable structures, it's crucial to forge our own paths. Despite the obstacles, trust in the potency of your words, for they possess a depth and influence far greater than you may imagine.

BELLY FIRE

Girlo was 14 when the Youth Club closed. The women on the estate had their funding cut and were too time-poor to continue. No more tie-dying or badminton, so Girlo and her muckuz got stoned instead. They found a secret spot in which to smoke buckets by the bus stop near the woods; perfect because it had its own water supply, from a stream that sprung orange.

"Is that safe?" Girlo asked.

"Yeah, it's nature. Just iron coming out of the ground from when they mined it," one of the girls, whose dad worked in the steel works, said.

"I'm not sure about that!" But the more buckets Girlo smoked, the more she loved that sprig of sunshine popping up from below ground. It looked like an ochreous tie-dye, tinting the shallow banks. On the branches of a young sapling they placed various sized bottles, lighter-burned holes in the bottom turning them to functioning smoking devices. A one-litre White Lightning bucket, a two-litre Strongbow bucket, a five-litre Graphite Cider bucket, and a ten-litre oil container, nicked from the back of the fish shop. Plus, a slug-free pipe and lung manufactured from a lemonade bottle and Safeways carrier bag. They'd even built a platform for a selection of gauzes made from foil milk tops.

"We'll call it the Bucket Place," Girlo announced. It became the go-to hangout after school, where they competed at smoking hashish.

"Whitey! Whitey! Whitey!" the crew chanted after each creamy bucket was sucked up and coughed out. The aim was to get everybody as stoned as possible then put them on a downer. Cruel. But it was a chance for the Rockboys to demonstrate how fucking hard they were. The Rockgirls rose to the challenge, sensibly opting for the smaller buckets, avoiding getting caught out. Having had experience with buckets Girlo went straight for the ten-litre; a push-down contraption that needed to be taken in the stream. After she'd carefully roasted and crumbled the hash into the plughole-sized gauze, she gently lit it, pulling the bucket until it was fat with caramel smoke. She sucked the whole thing in one! Eyes raw and dribble pissing from her mouth, she coughed her fucking guts into the orange stream.

"Whitey! Whitey! Whitey!" They chanted as Girlo ran off into the woods.

Beneath a vast canopy of leaves the crackling undergrowth grew cloud-soft. She sped through bark limbs, whips of branches and serpentine brambles—nature's barbed wire—tripping her up and sending her tumbling down the steep Black Hill at the edge of the woods. She fell, headfirst—tit over trainer—all the way to bottom, knocking her head on the root of a tree. As her skull hit, it sent a glow up into the trunk.

"Rats' tails, rats' tails." She could hear the hiss of Crystal's voice through the leaves. *"Brush your hair. Rats' tails, rats' tails."*

The wind blew a chill, Girlo's head steadily releasing a toxic gas that had festered in her young mind since she was a dot of a girl. *"Rats' tails. Rats' tails. You got rats' tails."*

The creeping wind turned into the form of The White Monkey, his translucent skeleton flashing and flickering between the jasper-pillared trees, as though someone was lighting then extinguishing matches. He scurried up to suck the gas from her body with a whining death croak. Colour drained from her face. He looked like the infamous flapper, Theda Bara, a Goddess with smoky eyes and chalky make-up.

"I need lives. I need lives," he hissed through a vampiric grin. His bloodshot eyes focused in on her, ferreting around her rigid form—sniffing and grunting—before disappearing in a thick cobalt fog.

There was a break in the atmosphere. An eerie moment, like the split-second before a storm begins. Above the canopy, great silver clouds began to release raindrops the size of 50 pence pieces, nourishing the earth and feeding her senses. She came around and sat up, her back against the trunk—body resting in perfect alignment with each vertebra stacked in synergy. She breathed slowly, steadily, mindfully. As each breath entered her, she felt a lightness inside her chest, a space opened up around her heart. It was as though the tree was radiating, connecting with her soul on a cellular level. Her body stabilised. She found herself in a place of stillness—a place of inner silence. Her eyelids felt heavy. She closed her eyes. She was always looking, searching, seeking someone or something external. Now she simply permitted herself to turn inwards, to explore her internal world. She tuned into the quality of her breath. As the air came in and out of her, stories circulated in her head—memories and emotions bubbling to the surface as the pelt of rain washed over the deadening throb in her head. The bark warmed her back. She could smell its nature-sweet earthiness, like boiled beetroot, nourishing and sustaining her deepening breath as it inflated her belly—rising and falling—expanding and contracting—swelling and receding like the turn of the tide. The raindrops evaporated on contact, Girlo taking comfort in the knowledge that with each breath, she stoked a powerful flame residing at the centre of her being, a fire of the purest transformation. She breathed it into her belly knowing this little sun within, would be a catalyst for growth and renewal.

When the rain stopped, she got up and dusted herself down, the ground sliding underneath her like a robe of black satin. At the top of Black Hill, she took a moment to catch her breath. She noticed something glimmer on the ground. She knelt to free the shiny object from the black earth and rub it clean. The wolf pin Nannie Pearl had given her! The pewter pin she'd released into the drain all those years ago.

After their sesh down the Bucket Place, the Rockgirls went to buy a Flake in Roger Rip-Offs. They crushed it up in the wrapper and tipped it into a bottle of milk they'd pinched from a doorstep in Wunny. With a bump on her head and a rip in her jeans, Girlo made it to The Stretch.

"What happened to you?" one of the girls said as she approached.

"Fell down The Black Hill!"

"You fuckin' headcase. Have a chug of this…" she passed Girlo the bottle of cold milk. It slid down her throat, the chocolate melting all the way down to her tummy. "Best thing for dry-mouth, Babe."

"Ta!" Girlo slugged it all. She went to throw the bottle down the alley.

"Woah, save it for hot knives!" Milk bottles were always rinsed and kept for doing hot knives over the old 1970s gas fires. Girlo marvelled at the way the Rockboys could take the bottom clean off with an ornamental 'kung-fu' sword. Then they'd jam two table knives into the ceramic grate until they were white-hot, place a large lump of hash on them, and drag the creamy smoke up through the bottle. It was the most hardcore way to smoke.

The Rockboys revelled in their thuggish rep, mooching about the fish shop during the week, and gathering in their hordes to ravage neighbouring villages, fucking-up anyone who got in their way on the weekend. Violence was like a demon. Street violence was an epidemic, taking hold in every post-industrial community disintegrating under the strain of poverty.

"Anyone coming off site 'en?!"

"Where's off site?" Girlo asked.

"Off the Rock fuh the night."

As a newbie Rockgirl with a point to prove, Girlo tagged along for the craic.

"Anyone coming offsite 'en?" The familiar war cry echoed down through the estate every Friday night, justifying a week of skanking money for enough fags, booze and drugs to attend. The Rockgirls shoplifted jewellery to look good for the Rockboys. Girlo wasn't interested in any of that shit. She didn't need a Rockboy to look after her. She made her own money, selling fags down the school. She had two mates she paid with cigarettes for protection from any other cunt encroaching on her business. 30 pence apiece or three fags for a pound. Because everyone liked the sound of three-for-a-pound, no-one ever questioned where the extra ten pence went. Nannie Pearl was doing the fag run to Calais at the time. She'd come back with a load of freebies from the guy at the cash-n-carry in Belgium so Girlo could do promotions; free lighters for every six fags bought. When she knew she wouldn't be caught she robbed the odd twenty-pack from her nan's stash.

"Have you been filching again, Girlo?"

"No, Nan… honest."

The Rockboys spent their week showing off their knuckle dusters, nunchucks and daggers, gearing themselves up for their most exciting event of the week: 'going on a mission.' Come 5 o'clock they'd all be outside the fish shop: the Top Dogs and their brown-nosing joeys, eyeing up arrivals for any money owed. The Rockboys and girls were too young to buy booze. They'd wait around the corner for someone who'd 'go in' for them, everyone desperate to get their Graphite cider, ready for a mad one. The up-and-coming Ruffians came around stirring up the shit, little scrutts running up and down The Stretch making errands for the Rockcrew, and the runaway little shits who'd escaped their house for the night, hanging about for the scrumps at the bottom of the fryer and the last drag on a floor-flicked fag.

"Oh, boy! You sort tha' out fuh me, 'en butt?" One of the Top Dogs said to a Rockboy, curtains falling into his eyes, before he flicked them away with a signet-ringed finger.

"Aye butt. Yew are!" the Rockboy said.

"Oh, oh—not yere butt. Round the back." They disappeared into the small bin yard behind the flats. The downstairs flat was empty. It had been boarded up with steel window grilles painted a pongee brown colour. Beyond the wheelie bins, black bags and crushed Fosters cans piled high.

"Thass ten, twenny, thirty, forty, fifty..." the Rockboy placed the notes into the Top Dog's expectant palm. The Top Dog folded it into his back pocket. To test his loyalty, he'd given the Rockboy a nine bar of hashish to knock out. The Rockboy had sold it onto the 'young uns', too 'wet bee-yind the yers to kick up a fuss'. He'd weighed each half-half deal with his makeshift scales manufactured from an Allen key, a ruler and a half penny, which was the same weight as half a Q, skimming off a tiny bit from each deal by wrapping the cling film so thick it made up the difference.

Rockgirls were often used as excuses to start fights despite just being there, doing nothing. If they so much as thought about going with anyone who wasn't from the Rock, they'd get labelled as slags. The biggest ruckus always happened outside Spar, the Rockboys taking on the village boys who'd gathered to get their Friday night cider.

"Oh, what you looking at Mucka? Tha'ss my fucking Missis by there!" BOOSH. One of the Rockboys planted a fist into some good boy's jaw and that was enough! Everyone piled into a mangled mob of fists and legs and ripe testosterone. The Rockboys ragged them around by their hoods, while the Rockgirls retrieved anything dropped from their pockets: money, wallets, purses, drugs, booze; you name it. They scooped it up and saved it for trading. After a bust-up at the rugby club and another at the Social at the bottom of town, they'd all end up at the Checkmate, the only nightclub for miles. Access was only available via a narrow door flanked by two meat heads.

There were thirty-nine deadly steps that led up to a chequered dancefloor-cum-arena, which facilitated a barrage of guaranteed weekend fistfights. The floor was black and jammy underfoot. The bogs were stinking. The bouncers were absolute cunts, and the prices were a fucking piss-take, but anything was better than the Cardboard Palace in the village. The Checkmate was where all the action from the week's Strategising came to a vicious climax, where new alliances were formed, where babies were conceived, where arrests were inevitable… all of which provided a fertile supply of news and drama for the week's gossip in the valleys.

LIAR

Girlo came home from school and dropkicked her rucksack over the threshold. She'd spent her last lesson, maths, sucking lighter gas from a canister through the bitten sleeve of her school jumper. Now the buzz had gone, and she needed a fix. Nannie Pearl was out on the campaign trail again. Fluorescent red and yellow stickers spelling out 'NEW LABOUR,' were stuck to every door frame in the house. In the hair-stuff basket on top of the cider keg, Girlo rifled for a can of hairspray. Because she hated her greasy hair she'd slick it up into a tight bun wrapped in a pyramid of scrunchies. Nannie Pearl's hair was the opposite, a 'fruzz' she called it. Despite a few hormone-driven clashes between a menopausal Nannie Pearl and pubescent Girlo, they were bonded by their hairbrushes. The grease from Girlo's hair tamed Nannie Pearl's frizz. The static from Nannie Pearl's hair enlivened Girlo's. When they did fight, the rows were blazing. Unless Girlo bolted down the alley they ended with Girlo locked in the bathroom.

"Open this fucking door, or I'm going to kick it off its hinges!"

"I can't. You'll ground me."

"I won't ground *you*… I'm gunna fucking kill you!"

Each time Nannie Pearl kicked the lock off the door Girlo screwed it back on with the nail file. They'd have a sweet cup of tea and a few malted milk biscuits afterwards.

"I'm just trying to do the best for you, Cariad, but you won't listen! I don't want you hanging about in his flat. He's bad news. I don't want you touching that base. It's not good for you."

Girlo'd been offered a daub of sticky white stuff in clingfilm but hadn't gone for it, even though everyone said it was harmless.

175

Nannie Pearl gave her the stone-eyed look.

"Did I ever tell you about that friend of mine who took so much base she ended up with boils? Boils as big as gobstoppers—all over her body."

"Yeah, so! And…"

"All over her body! Even on her fanny!"

The bathroom was the only room in the house with a lock. Girlo would spend ages in there, valuing her little island of privacy amid a sea of family chaos, squeezing spots in the Indian carved mirror that reminded her of an entrance to a Buddhist temple.

Girlo was obsessed with picking. It was as though she wanted to squeeze all the bad out of herself. Cleanse and purge. She'd pick and scrape so much she'd end up with sores she'd have to cover with thick pancake make-up stolen from the drama department at school. And she was obsessed with clearing grime out of hard-to-reach places. She liked to pull hair from plugholes, relishing the moment the slippery clumps were freed from the drain. She loved to scrape decaying skin-cells from the grooves in the remote control. A toothpick or a bended Kirby grip guaranteed the extraction of every last trace of filth.

Girlo couldn't bear it when she found a zit on her face. A force would take hold of her making her fixate on removing every drop of pus, every blackhead root, every millimetre of scab. When the spot scabbed over, she'd start again—picking and squeezing and tweezing—until she felt it was all gone. Then she could rest easy. But the bloody holes she'd exacerbated with her picking were unsightly. *How could she be seen in public? What would people think?*

One of her strategies was to make her other features stand out to the extent that nobody noticed the imperfections. She plastered her eyes with silver eyeliner and sloshed her lips in Black Cherry Rimmel. Girlo hated her face. It was ugly. She was pathetic.

"She's a pretty little girl, isn't she?" they'd say, usually random men. "Lovely looking girl."

She could feel their eyes all over her like the filthy hands of Groggy. She wanted to pick something up and hit them. Later, when she was alone, she'd pick up a hairbrush and hit herself, crying so hard afterwards she felt like she'd spew up her stomach. The bath was a refuge. When her head was underwater, Girlo could hear nothing but the sound of her own heart beating. On the surface she had to be 'a good girl' and do as she was told. If she didn't, she was a troublemaker, a liar, a little witch, a bitch from hell, a slag, a tease, a frigid bitch, a slut. Bathwater helped to wash those cancerous names down the hairy plughole and cool her head that otherwise burned and pulsed in a tangle of persistent poisonous voices—black magic spells searing the inside of her skull, forming engraved runes that rattled and clogged her sacred chakras. These throw-away labels fossilised a malignant internal monologue, a nasty cycle of noxious self-hatred becoming preserved in her sense of self. *Are you stupid, or what? We don't want you here. You're a lying little bitch!* LIAR LIAR. Your pants are on fire. *Why are you doing this to us? Why are you breaking up our family? Tell us if you're lying. It's ok... we can all just forget about it and move on with our lives.* LIAR LIAR. Your pants are on fire. *Tell the truth and I'll buy you a China Doll. You like china dolls, don't you? You like china dolls.* LIAR LIAR. Your pants are on fire. *You smell funny! Have you wet the bed? Why do you suck your thumb?* LIAR LIAR. Your pants are on fire. *You gotta stop picking your beautiful face! Are you stupid or something? You got a weird accent. You're not from here, are you? You're just too fucked up! You belong in a mental institute.* LIAR LIAR. Your pants are on fire. *You don't know* how *to love? What's wrong with you?*

Girlo would lay in the bath for hours—incubated, trying to dissolve thoughts of coarse sea-salt. As a child, she hid in the bathroom and took the flannel, folding it into a rectangle to serve as a bra to conceal her developing boobs, not much more than sore bumps. She took the old rubber bath matt and placed it over her legs so that the suckers looked like fish scales. She'd sink down into the depths of her imagination, envisaging being at the bottom of an ocean, bubbles rising from her nostrils. She wished she could stay there, not come up for air. Switch off and die. But Crystal would knock the door and tell her to get out so her brother could get in, or to come downstairs to help with tea, or to take the bins out, polish the bureau, bring her washing down, pack up her room and move into the attic because she'd overbooked.

After puberty, the bathroom became something like a cosmetic surgery in which she was both ruthless surgeon and docile patient, her ritualistic thought-cleanse more invasive as she scrutinised and punished her developing body of the imperfections she saw in it. She scraped her skin with pumice until it bled.

"What's this?" Nannie Pearl asked, noticing her legs were tracked in scabs. It looked as though someone had attacked her with a rusty bike chain.

"Oh, nothing. It's nothing."

"Stop hurting yourself, Cariad!"

"I can't help it."

Still on the hunt for gas, Girlo found a can of mousse. She sucked the nozzle—none left. She took a can of Impulse body spray from the bin, held it under a towel and breathed in the last dregs—it wasn't enough! Downstairs she rummaged in the cupboard under the sink until she found a can of oven spray. She sprayed it into the fabric of a tea-towel, sucking the stream of gas. That hit the spot! TUH-Waaaang. TUH-Waaaang. TUH-Waaaang. There was a soothing, twanging sound that transported her from the kitchen back to the changing rooms of her old school. The schoolgirls she'd been banned from bothering with, who'd made her puff a blue asthma pump while they squeezed her windpipe until she passed out.

All went black.

A freeze-frame paused like a slo-mo camera flash.

Hollow silence.

Her eyes slid back. She found herself in infinite space—the infinite space within—gently bouncing on starry rocks of light as if they were stepping-stones made from marshmallows. They powered her soles with a diamond light the moment her toes made contact. She saw the sun, a molten inferno, dancing into its flames. She felt the warmth of the blaze in the centre of her body. She began to trust that what was within it was her personal power, her unlimited potential—she could really feel it! The weight of her self-worth. The influence of her conviction. She could see her flame grow larger, brighter, feel its heat spread around her entire physical body. *This unrelenting strength.* A capability of overcoming fear. *Conquering doubt.* She wanted to honour the strength—with courage, determination, grace. A screeching sound, familiar to her, but altered in some way, rang out loudly. A projection of human fear.

"Wake up! Wake up!" Nannie Pearl was hysterical, hitting Girlo with a tea towel.

"Are you fucking simple or what? You could've killed yourself! What's the matter with you, you could've frozen your brain cells and killed yourself in an instant!"

HOMELESS

It had started to spit. She'd better get her arse in gear, or she'd miss the bus. Despite the fug, smiling daffodils lit the roadside to the bus stop. Girlo wanted to cut the journey and be home with a cup of tea and a pikelet lashed in melted butter. She couldn't wait to be her Rock self again: down a pint of lager with an Aftershock dropped in, the traditional tipple at kicking out time.

"Hit the Road Jack. Don't you come back. No more no more no more no more…"

The station was packed with galumphing teenagers getting mowed down by the blue-rinse brigade's trolleys. Scatty shoplifting girls zipped through—all heels and hips. Screen-faced international students tried to find their way through the crowd. Girlo sparked a fag next to the Evening Post stand. 'War on Terror', the headline read so she bought a copy. She remembered the words of Bill Hicks: "How can we go to war on a noun?"

A new Muslim extremist group—"unheard of" according to the story—had attacked Mumbai, targeting seven places in all, including the Taj Mahal hotel "looking for anyone with British or American passports." She thought about the moment the Twin Towers were hit. As soon as the television broadcasted those images, everything had changed. Terror pervaded.

The conspiracy theories Girlo indulged in with her 'comrades', over a Fairtrade dark roast at the student union coffee shop, were a symptom of guilt and the loss of a romantic vision of the empire past, a savage empire, fundamentally corrupt.

"Fifty years from now we'll be under totalitarian rule," the newspaper seller said. "They've got weapons that can eliminate American GPS systems from outta space! We're being bred out! Look at the birth rates." The words curled from his bitten lips like exhaust fumes, seeping into the air like a cartoon depiction of evil.

"We are supposed to be the strongest nation in the world," Girlo retorted.

"Aye, and so was Rome... so was Rome." He lit a cigarette. "Just look at the news—British business is crumbling. Woolworths, a British institution, gone! It's only a matter of time. It'll be a domino effect. They're taking over, they are... mark my words. We're finished as a country!"

Now, he'd lost her.

"I'm not sure about that." she said. She dropped her dog-end and stamped it out.

"Mark my words. We're finished as a country!"

Were we finished as a country? Blair had said we'd 'lost touch'. The institutions meant to protect people were no more. Western leaders were short-sighted, always putting their individual interests before national safety, giving all their power away; Clinton to the markets, Blair to the Bank of England. National politics was a threat to the Global economy.

Outside knives of rain began to slash at the hodophobic buses swelling in the depot like beached orcas. The throng of people inside thickened. Girlo felt for her purse in her coat pocket, but it was gone. *Had she left it on the newsstand?* The deluge persisted in shoals of fingerlings that swam through the glass-tanked wall of the station. Frantic, she rummaged through her rucksack, sodden from her water-bottle, fingernails scraping at tobacco bits and grit until she punctured the skin of a bruised banana she'd packed for the journey. Its fudgy yellow-black flesh splurged everywhere. She was in a tizzy.

"Fuh fucksake."

The faces kept on coming, spreading through the station like there was no tomorrow. People shook their collapsed umbrellas everywhere. A hot sweat harpooned her back, the dread coming over her. A tinny command from the Tannoy. It was too much to bear. And the people just kept on coming. She needed space. Space to find her fucking purse. Space to think. She needed a fucking drink!

A group of people hiding under a nest of polyester in the Debenhams doorway were sharing a flagon of White Lightning. Girlo was familiar with the cheap cider, the go-to booze of her teenage years. She approached and asked for a light.

"You got any spare change, love?" one of the fellas asked, not much older than her. "I don't know a' minute. I think I've lost my purse. Can I sit down by here and have a look?"

"Course you can, darling, sit by here." He smoothed out the wrinkles from his sleeping bag. Girlo pulled everything out of her bag, piece-by-piece, then checked the side pockets.

"Where d'you think you left it?"

"I'm not sure…"

"Have you checked the back?"

"No, 'ang on…" She scrambled to undo the pocket. There it was. Why was it so hard for her to keep her shit together?

"Open your hands," she said before emptying the contents of her purse out into the homeless man's palms. "Might be enough for another flagon between you."

"You want some of this?" A black-eyed girl asked Girlo, having just finished slugging on the cider bottle.

"Aye… go on 'en." Girlo squeezed the cider from the bottle into her mouth. It tasted like nail-varnish remover but instantly dissolved her panic.

"Hit the spot?"

"Yeah, ta." She passed the bottle just like she would've when she was young, camping rough in the summer. "You're not Welsh, are you?"

"Nah, English 'cunts' we are." The group laughed.

"Where in England?"

"A little place on the coast called Mugsborough," said the girl.

"Robert Tressel?" Girlo said. "Have you read it?"

"Of course. It's local history, that is!"

"What d'you do?" The man asked Girlo.

"I'm a student… and I write a bit."

"Me? I could write a novel with everything that's 'appened in my life!" The girl replied.

"Shurrup! You're not posh enough to be a writer," spat another guy from the back.

"That's bollocks. The best writers are the ones who've lived, just like Tressel," the girl said. "You should read it."

"Get off your fucking high horse!"

"I remember going for a day trip once when I was a kid," Girlo said. "We bought a pint of prawns for a pound on the seafront."

"You'd be hard pushed to get a pint of prawns for that these days. It's a shithole now... the 'otels full of the likes of us. We couldn't ge' a place, cud we?" Said the man with the change from Girlo's purse.

"You wanna fag?" Girlo offered up her soggy baccy. Each of them managed to roll themselves a ciggie. "So, are you all from there?"

"Nah, London," the man at the back said, sucking the guts from his filter-less rollie through blackened teeth. "I came up here to be by the sea. Can't go home."

It dawned on Girlo then, it could've been her in the doorway if it wasn't for Nannie Pearl.

Before coming back to the Rock, Crystal moved Girlo and Eddie from Folkestone to Whitley Bay to run a B&B with Doug. Their clientele consisted of contractors and stag and hen parties. Girlo went right off the rails. She didn't feel safe sleeping in the same house as strange men who smelled of plasterboard dust and fags. So, she 'fell in with the wrong crowd', taking micro-dots and drinking Mad Dog in the graveyard. She'd come home and spew in the sink.

After sharing with her brother for years, she'd always dreamt of a room all to herself. Her mother sold the move to her on the premise that she could decorate it however she wanted. She chose her favourite colour: red, but Crystal decided on peppermint green, and stuck up a border of red strawberries as a compromise. *Sanctuary, at last!* It was her own space. A space which soon became like a prison because she was grounded all the time. But she had her stereo for company and listened to 100% Reggae Hits on repeat. It drove her mother up the wall! 'Coz we are Young Gifted and Black... You can get it if you really want, you can get it if you really want, but you must try, TRY, try and try... You succeed at last!' It was to those tunes that Girlo found her rhythm and between the odd Happy Hardcore track, she bounced around her bedroom with the window open, hoping that a big music producer would spontaneously discover her just like Kate Moss.

But that never happened,

"Turn that racket off! We've got guests."

When Doug gave her 'the belt', Girlo turned to her journal where she spilled her pain and scribbled song lyrics. When the guesthouse was overbooked, Girlo was told to give her bedroom up and move into the attic, where she'd sleep on a dodgy camp-bed. The attic spanned the size of the house and had no radiator. The people who lived there before had scrawled a Flintstones mural in crayon on the wall. The faces of Fred and Wilma were too long, and their eyes popped out of their faces. It was dark up there, with only a small, frosted window, which looked out onto the pebble-dashed wall of the adjacent house. At night, if she stretched her neck out the window, she could see a string of bikini-clad girls spill out on a surf of bubbles from the Idol's foam party at the bottom of the lane. At night, the seaside town was a smut-magnet for stags and hens, people shagging up against the pissy walls of the backstreets. But by day, it attracted family-friendly folk who visited the Sea Life Centre or rented deck chairs on the beach.

After a while, Girlo became accustomed to the attic. She could spy on the hordes of pissed-up princesses tottering down the lane, while she sneakily smoked cigarettes out of the window. Her dad had bought her an electric typewriter for her birthday, which she used to transcribe the notes in her journal. The attic was her zone: she could see and hear all the goings-on in the guesthouse and the lane below her. One day, she watched some guy smack his girlfriend full force in the face. She felt her pain. Another time, she watched as a gang of skinheads beat up Hardy, the Asian guy from the newsagents who used to sell single Embassy fags for 12 pence each. Another time, she watched her mother chase Doug down the lane, barefoot. When he jumped in his car, her mother threw her wineglass against the wall. In the attic, Girlo could hide. But she'd eventually have to come down to do her chores, which became more and more after her mother gave birth to a premature baby. This would always end in an argument, Crystal chasing her up the ladder with a broomstick and shouting from the top step.

"Haha, can't get me now!" Girlo'd taunt, slamming the hatch down and locking it.

"Stay up *there,* then!"

In a rucksack, Girlo stuffed a few pairs of knickers, a jumper, and whatever fags, cash or booze she'd managed to steal that week. She snuck down the creaky ladder and across the landing on tippy toes, extra cautious not to trigger the squeakiest stairs. The snore of a contractor came from under the door, and she could hear the scratch of an untuned radio in the kitchen. Her mother was clearing out the cupboard under the sink for the fourth time that month. Then, from the bathroom window, she had to hang-and-drop onto the roof above the living room, before carefully walking across the backyard wall, which was spiked with shards of cemented-in glass. She jumped down into the lane but, before making a run for it, took the time to go to the front door and knock the pane. She waited for the lobby door to open and for her mother to scramble to undo the locks in her yellow marigolds.

"Fuck You! I'm off!" Girlo gave her the two fingers and darted down the lane past Idols towards the Arches—a place where the kids would congregate on a Friday night and sing naughty lyrics to the melody of Agadoo.

I can do do do anything you want me to,
have a shag shag shag, have a swig or have drag.

I can do do do anything you want me to.
Have a shag shag shag, give a blow job I'm a slag.

The Arches was a derelict spot, right at the end of the promenade, cordoned off with yellow tape. Girlo and the Berghaus crew had to climb over a temporary metal barrier and shimmy along an eroded wall with a big drop right into the sea. The waves were always choppy, fiercely licking at the soles of Girlo's Nikes. It was dangerous as fuck. She bartered with a few older boys, trading what she had for a lung of hash and half a ginger ball, before letting some boy stick his tongue down her throat at the back of the piss-soaked cave. He wanted to feel her tits.

"I haven't got any."

"Fuck you then, frigid bitch!" He spat on her trainers then did one.

She spewed.

When midnight rolled round and all the Merrydown bottles had run dry, the kids stopped chanting their drinking songs and went home. Girlo couldn't face her mother. Even at the 'all-grown-up' age of eleven, that scary-tooth face still frightened the shit out of her, and she was sure to get a pasting off Doug. Instead of facing the music, she rode the Metro, past the majestic Angel of the North until it reached the city centre. The leery pavements were tanked up with pissheads, 'smashing-it-up' on the streets. She was scared, so in a subway, she found a dry space. She shivered as sheets of sleet shed from the ashen sky, only the skin of a thin raincoat shielding her. She sat down on her rucksack and pulled her legs up to her chest. She pulled her hood up and did up the jacket until it nipped at her chin, the drawstring pulled so tight someone passing by would only see the whites of her eyes. She blended into the wall, watching the waning hubbub of the city, her aching stare framed by the bunched rim of her hood, like a set of zig-zag binoculars. Eventually she fell into a half-sleep to the sway of smaze, swishing over the unwavering streetlight. Until a limacine figure in wet leather slid up the subway and toed the sole of her Nike.

"Oi! W'ass 'is by 'eeyuh thun lads?"

Another voice said, "Soom fookin' skivvie, man. How-wey, man, let's gan."

Girlo held her nerve. She didn't move a muscle.

"Eh, lass? What yer doon oot sor lairt?"

"Coom an man, let's gan yem," the sidekick said.

She could feel their stare all over her.

"I'm ok, just waiting for my dad," she said.

"Hai, pretty one... pull back yer hood, so we cun tairk a gandah."

A gust of wind blew grit into her eyes. Then, something bounced down the subway and tumbled along the floor, coming to rest next to her rucksack: a bottle. The bottom had come clean off, but the neck was still intact.

"Who thuh fook iz that, man?"

She looked up to find the outline of two menacing figures approaching. The men, who were prodding her, turned to investigate. As they did, she took her moment and seized the bottle before plunging it into his foot. She grabbed her shit and scarpered.

It was time for the bus. Girlo had one last, gassy slug of cider, sucked the final drag from her fag and bombed over the lumpy floor that stuck to her heels. She found a seat behind a group of Spanish girls who chatted in musical phonetics, pleasantly accompanying the descent of the waning Bay. She looked out of the window feeling small as a flea, imagining the coach as a beetle scuttling through the bulky furniture of the landscape. She searched for her favourite hill with its row of trees that reminded her of a barcode, too perfect to have grown that way. *Everything has a price tag*, she thought.

As they passed the caravan park, she remembered how everyone back home would cheer when they knew the travellers were in town. Travellers were always welcome on the Rock— along with their knock-off three-piece suites and Teflon kitchen knives. They'd stay for weeks. No-one said fuck all. The police were never called. And they'd party with them up the football pitch, dancing and drinking and mingling round the fire with their kids and dogs: one big family. She thought of Lorca. Maybe she could follow in his footsteps. She looked to the steel works, puffing and panting. They came alive at night—*like something from a movie set*. She thought of the men who still had jobs there, *how much longer would it last?* Maybe, the Tory boy in her politics seminar was right: a new era had arrived, no place left in it for working-class people. *Coal Not Dole*. They weren't finished as a country, but the working-class had been killed off. She couldn't help but feel that they'd taken a wrong turn somewhere.

In the absence of cider, she sank into sleep.

She dreamt she was running through the barcode forest, sun trickling like honey through flashes of foliage above. Her Rock kin followed, all grimy-faced and devilish, chasing her through the thicket. Their hands raw from the climb up The Black Hill, grabbing at rough branches. Sweat poured as they waded through brooks and leapt over bridges, howling and biting their tongues with lafftah. Then they rolled over the cowpats and down the hill and flew up to see the ochre quarry jutting out of the greenspace like the jagged front-steps of Mother Nature's porch. Farmhouses were stationary ships buttoned into the land. Fir trees lined the edge of her grand front door, watching over the ant-like villagers below. Beside Mother Nature's porch was a garden of satin fields, woven into the currents of the landscape. A sequinned river zipped through it all. She flew over the vast stretches of land: hedgerows stitching patchwork pastures like a big Welsh quilt. There in the plush grass, they landed, collapsing in a ring, slinging off their sopping-wet trainers, combing the grass with their rubbery toes.

FEMINIST

I don't belong here, thought Girlo, as she stared into the sea which had swallowed up the shitty city, again. She was gradually being ingested by a slow, encroaching horizon, its incremental crawl chomping at her like a great leviathan. Uni was getting on her tits. It was the last leg of the undergrad marathon and she still felt like an imposter. The political science boys thought their word was gold, just because they owned a Waterstones-bought copy of the *Oxford Politics Dictionary*. They'd turn up to seminars, all suited and booted, while Girlo turned up with a hangover and a fist in her pocket. They'd come out with statements like: 'People on council estates have a responsibility to pull themselves up by their bootstraps.'

"Rubbish!" muttered Girlo. She took a swig of Lucozade, a red devil from the club's entry stamp glaring from the back of her hand.

"Did you say something?" Interjected the seminar leader, his brittle Adam's apple twitching. He pointed the end of his spit-filled biro at Girlo.

"Didn't catch his name. Mr Grub Libertysnatch, was it?"

He closed the lid of his laptop and smiled.

"If you need to eat, you'd do *anything* surely!" Remarked the boy.

"And what would *you* be prepared to do to eat?"

"I count myself fortunate enough not to have to think..."

"Lucky you."

"Isn't empathy the cornerstone of critical discussion?"

"Let's just say for argument's sake, that you've done every-thing humanly possible to find food? What then? Would you allow someone weaker than you to starve to feed yourself?" The seminar leader cut in before she could go on.

The boy looked around at his peers. "It's a bit harsh to say…
but Natural Selection. There are too many people in the world as
it is."

"And, we have another one!" cried Girlo. "Malthusian
Economist, Professor Les Starvum."

"Maybe we could save the jokes for the student bar." The
seminar leader interjected again. "What do you say?" He pointed
to the boy. "Do you think that the state has a responsibility to the
individual?"

The boy looked around at his peers. "It's a bit harsh to say…
but Natural Selection. There are too many people in the world as
it is."

"And, we have another one!" cried Girlo. "Malthusian
Economist, Professor Les Starvum."

"Maybe we could save the jokes for the student bar." The
seminar leader interjected again. "What do you say?" he pointed
to the boy. "Do you think that the state has a responsibility to the
individual?"

"If the individual pays into the system, then, yes! But we
shouldn't just give them hand-outs?"

"Give *who* handouts? Who exactly are you referring to?"

"The scroungers."

Girlo had come up against this blinkered thinking before.
There was this assumption that because people relied on state
benefits, they were somehow lazy. But those whose incomes were
supplemented by the dole were the hardest workers she'd ever
met. She knew women with multiple part-time jobs, and they still
didn't earn enough to make ends meet. Community workers
volunteered their time running youth clubs, doing Avon, baking
for charity while bringing up their own kids and grandkids. Not
only did these women work flat-out to hold their families together,
but they also did so under the strain of poverty and often, abuse.

"Classism. Pure and simple. What about the sacrifices made
for industry? For war? Haven't these *scroungers* you speak of
paid their dues?"

"Yes, and they were paid wages for it."

"If they were paid so well then why are they scraping by?"

"Maybe they should manage their money better!"

"The Great Money Trick!"

"What?"

"Don't tell me you're studying politics, and you haven't read *The Ragged Trousered Philanthropists*? You'll be telling me you haven't read Orwell, next."

The boy looked around, confused.

"In one of the chapters, Frank Owen, a nineteenth century painter and decorator, tries to explain the reason for poverty. He tells his work butties that he represents *all* the factory owners in the world, and that they represent *all* the workers in the world. He holds up a butterknife and says it represents all the machinery in the world..."

"Bored already," yawned the boy.

"Please, go on," insisted the seminar leader.

"Thanks... He takes a slice of bread which represents all the world's raw materials. He hands it to the workers with the knife and asks them to chop it up into cubes. They do as he asks and hand it back to the factory owner. Frank Owen tells them the cubes represent *all* the world's basic necessities—food, clothes etc. The factory owner pays the workers for their work with a half-penny for each cube. He takes *all* the cubes, which represent the world's basic necessities—which now belong to him—and stores them in his warehouse."

"And your point is..."

"I haven't finished yet... Now, this is the interesting part... When the workers need to buy the basic necessities to live—food and clothes etc. they have no choice but to go to the factory owner who owns *all* the world's basic necessities and can sell them for whatever price he or she chooses. And because the workers, like every human being, need these necessities to survive, they must pay whatever the factory owner asks. The factory owner, who has his warehouse filled to the brim, knows he can make a lot of money, so he sells them back the cubes of bread. But he doesn't charge the half-penny he paid for them, nor does he charge a full penny, but three whole pennies per cube! And the workers have no choice but to buy the necessities they made at his price."

"That's called making a profit, a fundamental principle of modern-day economics. Absolutely nothing wrong with that!"

"Not when it comes with a human cost. Those factory workers were paid pittance and worked in dangerous conditions. From the story you can see the cause of poverty isn't mismanagement of wages, or scarce resources, or even foreign threats, it's because of the lack of wages in relation to the cost of basic necessities."

There was brief silence before someone spoke up.

"What system do you propose then? Socialism? And we'll end up like Communist Russia or Nazi Germany?"

"I am not proposing a *new* system, I am simply highlighting the flaws of the current one." She watched as they stroked their bum-fluff beards with clean, pudgy-knuckled fingers. *Had she finally made an impact? Were they mulling over what she'd said?*

"And let's not forget the real losers in this 'modern economic' system, the women with children."

"Well, let's be honest. They shouldn't be having them if they can't afford them."

"Yeah, they're a drain on the country. They think they can get pregnant and just get a council house, like that!" said some mousy-haired boy. "We see it all the time... Vicky Pollards having kids to get council houses."

"Until the contraceptive pill, working-class families were huge. They had to be to work in the factories to increase commerce and do their part in the name of progress. But those children and women were also exploited in factories across the country— which, may I add—sparked the Suffragette movement."

"God, she's a feminist as well as Marxist," someone muttered under their breath. "But that's not the world we live in now."

"It's the world *they* live in—since time forgot them."

"Maybe they should work their way out of poverty."

"Easier said than done, mate." A fire was growing in Girlo. "I think we should try to remain objective during debate, but there have been some good points raised. If you look at the Budgie Girls, for example, who worked in the municipal factories in the twenties..."

Girlo composed herself.

"Yes, I've heard of the Budgie Girls. Apparently, they were called that because the exposure to chemicals turned their hair bright yellow. Many lost fingers due to the explosions. Can't imagine what it must've been like having to lug about those huge tin baths and cook for the whole family on an open fire with missing fingers!"

The class fell silent for a moment.

"Right, let's refocus on this idea of freedom, in particular, Hobbes' Social Contract. Surely if we are willing to fight and work for our country, the state must be willing to look after us. After all, we do live in a social democracy, don't we?"

"You'd think so... our Prime Minister is busy sending hordes of working-class kids into Afghanistan for a false war."

"Well, if they haven't got anything better to do, they may as well fight."

"Most of them are used to fighting anyway," came another comment.

"Did any of *you* sign up? I doubt they'd send the scouts to your neck of the woods in the leafy suburbs of England. The recruiters specifically target the kids who society forgot."

"Strong in arm and thick in head qualifies them for cannon fodder," someone shouted.

"Wrong turn."

"What?"

"Wrong turn."

"What is she talking about?"

DIVIDE AND RULE

Western combat forces launch triumphant mission to rid the world of bloodstained dictators. Wrong turn. Vaunted weapons of mass destruction. Wrong turn. Misadventures in the East. Wrong turn. New democracy insecure. Bush's lonely refusal to heed calls to cut and run. Obama strikes a good war instead of a dumb one. Wrong turn. Sectarian bloodletting. Wrong turn. Invasion debated. Wrong turn. Bleeding economically at home. Unemployment struck. Debts as-high-as-the-eye-can-see. Yet even in the age of austerity, superpower still towers over all corners of military power. For a world to be free? Wrong turn. Iraq in the twinkle of an eye. Wrong turn. Negligible losses fly. Wrong turn. Subduing is harder. Wrong turn. We swallowed the lie. Eastern terror forces launch counter mission to rid the world of capitalist dictators. Wrong turn. Attack on humanity. Wrong turn. Attack on diversity. Wrong turn. Civil war is looming. Islam made a threat to our security, scapegoated as a public enemy, by the "Free Press" and the BBC. Narrative of hate fuelling a scripted war of ideology. Wrong turn. Power without responsibility. Wrong turn. Media control. Wrong turn. Incitement of fear. Politi-corporate forces launch surreptitious battle to rid the UK of money grabbers. Back stabbers reduce the poor to scroungers, and refugees become drowning fleas. Babies dying in freezing seas. Wrong turn. Misguided morals. Wrong turn. Obligations denied. Wrong turn. Blinded haters. Wrong turn. Divide and rule. Tory forces launch austerity to eradicate the cause of poverty. Cut deep to exterminate the poor, who are surplus to requirement in the 'Big Society.' Political Ignorance, apathy, a frightened, unthinking nation equals pliability. Tax breaks for the ruling elite and their cronies while 'Benefits Britain' deems society's poorest as takers, fakers and dirty dole-eez. Wrong turn. The deserved and undeserved poor. Wrong turn. Unashamed hypocrisy. Wrong turn. The shrinking of the Welfare State. Wrong turn. Public services starved. Wrong turn. NHS on its knees. Wrong turn. Social cohesion; a fallacy. Wrong turn. Divide and rule. UKIP nationalists launch fear campaign to rid society of outsiders. Farage forged as a working-class hero. Vows immigration will become zero if we vote to leave, we can take back the reins of our country. Wrong turn. Colonialism is dead. Wrong turn. Global nation instead. Wrong turn. Divide and rule. UK politics now in disarray, with shock resignations every day. Theresa May take the reins of the Country Yay! Time to take away the Fundamental Rights of our Liberty. Wrong turn. Reversal of history. Wrong turn. Worker's rights expunged. Wrong turn. Thought controlled. Wrong turn. Where is Labour? Wrong turn. The loss of equality. Wrong turn. A fight of the classes Wrong turn. The Orwellian Plight. Wrong turn.

DIVIDE AND RULE.

SUGAR BABE

Life with Earl was a bore. She face-planted the stale pillow on the bed in his spare room, fed up with him falling asleep on the sofa. She'd wanted to go out, but he didn't like that. Instead, she'd had to go through the usual nightly ritual of trying to rouse and get him up the tricky spiral staircase. Now she'd have to endure his half-pissed snore for the next eight hours. She burned with frustration. *What the fuck was she doing?*

She'd been busy in the house that day, arranging for the landscape gardener to measure up for a pergola. She'd run a mop over the floors, cleaned the bathroom and kitchen, and prepared a lovely meal for Earl's late arrival back from work. He'd washed down his dinner with a bottle of Merlot, barely saying two words. The spare room had been a dumping ground for years, a place for his water-powered rowing machine and a flabby futon bed, both gathering dust. Earl intended to turn it into a gym but had slowly pushed the idea to the back of his mind. Girlo convinced him to let her decorate it.

"I could turn it into an office," she said. He let her loose with a Coffee Cream matt emulsion, watching with uncertainty as she opened the tin.

"It'll be lighter than that on the walls," she promised.

She wanted to put up some bookshelves she'd chosen from Earl's favourite shop, Ikea, along with a masculine black desk with a thick glass top and an ergonomic chair with five adjusting levers.

After she'd waved him off to work with the packed lunch she'd prepared, she gathered the tools needed; a spirit level and his expensive Black and Decker drill with its selection of 24 drill bits. She'd never touched a power tool before but using it without Earl's direction would send a strong message. She was just as capable as any man, she thought, fitting the battery to the main unit. She marked out where the wall plugs would go and held up the floating shelf for a final spirit level check. It was deceptively light. She whipped out the drill, popped a bit in and cranked the chuck. Its power vibrated through her as she fired it up, but she held strong. She looked at her reflection in the window, imagining she was holding a gun. "Beast," she declared, pretending to cock an imaginary safety and blow her fucking brains out. "Now, you can have it!" She turned to the wall. The sound was delicious: BUZZ BUZZ-BUZZ. BUZZ BUZZ-BUZZ. BUZZ-BUZZ. *I am not your girl,* she shouted, pushing the drill into the wall like it was Styrofoam: BUZZ BUZZ-BUZZ. BUZZ BUZZ-BUZZ. BUZZ-BUZZ. *Not your baby, your sugar, your pearl.*

A puff of ochre dusted the clean paintwork as the drill-bit bored into the plaster. It worked. Result! BUZZ BUZZ-BUZZ. BUZZ BUZZ-BUZZ. BUZZ BUZZ. She blew away the mess, popped in a wall plug, then moved onto the next pencilled cross. BUZZ BUZZ-BUZZ. BUZZ

I am not a girl for you to call. She penetrated the wall again, the push of power running from her into his crumbling brick. BUZZ BUZZ-BUZZ. BUZZ BUZZ-BUZZ. BUZZ-BUZZ.

Nor a supplement to your respectful self. BUZZ BUZZ-BUZZ. BUZZ BUZZ-BUZZ. BUZZ-BUZZ. In a trigger-happy haze of beige dust and rage, she continued to drill, feeling positively Herculean. She didn't notice the plug point below the final cross mark and drilled straight through a wire. The snap of three-thousand kilowatts catapulted her across the room, electricity surging beneath her skin. She was awakened like Frankenstein's creation. When she'd composed herself, she checked her eyelids for singed hair, then carried on. BUZZ BUZZ-BUZZ. BUZZ BUZZ-BUZZ. BUZZ-BUZZ. *I am not a weapon to be fired.* BUZZ BUZZ-BUZZ. BUZZ BUZZ-BUZZ. BUZZ-BUZZ.

She'd show *him*! She'd make the room beautiful then she'd go to bed early in there. At the desk she'd write until her fingers bled!

I am not a girl.
Nor a shoulder.
Nor a vagina.
Nor an ear to listen.

BUZZ BUZZ-BUZZ.
BUZZ BUZZ-BUZZ.
BUZZ-BUZZ.

When she'd finished with the drill, she stocked the shelves with the books her father had bought for her from Foyles. They'd gone for a day out when she was visiting. He'd recommended Plath and Woolf. She decided not to tell Earl about the wire that sullied his wall like the frazzled carcass of a squashed butterfly. Instead, she covered it up with a poster she found in the attic. She couldn't resist rifling through a shoebox of old photographs she noticed while she was up there. One of them showed a woman draped around Earl's twenty-something shoulders, his face red with sunburn or a blush. In another he was kissing the woman outside a club. This must have been the one he talked about, the one who broke his heart. Jealousy engulfed her. She ripped the photo in half.

After time, their relationship became perforated with a series of rows over power and obedience. Despite her bloody-mindedness and will to prove every fucker wrong, Girlo couldn't escape what every fucker thought of her. The glaring indignation from onlookers and the gold-digger label that followed her around like the clag of cheap perfume. Earl was oblivious, revelling in the notoriety of getting to be a grey fox with a trophy girl on his arm. She knew he didn't really love her. She was just a trinket to be taken out and paraded at his will.

Nannie Pearl always told her actions speak louder than words, so one evening, she probed him for a plus one invitation to his next works do.

"Why can't I come? We are meant to be a couple. We live together for fucksake!"

"It's just an extension of work, you wouldn't like it."

"What's the matter? Are you ashamed of me?"

The image on the poster was a dismembered head floating in a surreal sky. It reminded Girlo of the Guy Fawkes dummies she used to make for the Penny-for-the-Guying on bonfire night. They'd seen the original work together at a Dali exhibition in Amsterdam.

"Reminds me of you, Earl," she'd joked.

When they came across a statuesque sculpture of Woman Aflame, Earl said, "Reminds me of you."

"It *really* is amazing..." Girlo said, gazing at the licks of bronze flame igniting the curvature of her spine. "You know what the crutches represent?"

"No idea."

"Middle-class trappings of security and wealth."

"Oh, come on..."

"I'm not making it up, Earl. It's true and the drawers are meant to hold her secrets."

"Every woman has her secrets."

Girlo longed to open her drawers for Earl, but she knew what they had together had run its course. He couldn't keep up with her. She didn't feel at home in herself, let alone with him. He'd modified her to his specification. With him, she wasn't human.

"I am not happy being with someone who works in a place like that."

"I'm not a fucking prostitute, Earl." She felt like a prostitute, a live-in one at Earl's house.

"I just don't want you working there anymore."

"Why? It's the only job I've ever liked."

"It's dangerous for a start. And Ruby's always keeping you late."

"It's always busy, Earl. It's actually full of men just like you, businessmen or men visiting town, lonely men, unhappily married men."

"They're not like me at all."

"You told me you'd slept with a prostitute when we were in Amsterdam. You think that choosing a woman like a Barbie doll on a toyshop shelf is better than what Ruby does?"

"That's different…"

"Yeah, it's different! It made me sick to my stomach when I saw those poor girls tarted up in the windows. I felt grubby even looking. At least what Ruby's girls do has an ounce of dignity."

"How am I supposed to take you to my works-do when you do that for a living?"

"I'm a fucking writer on an MA course."

"Still."

"The only reason prostitutes get a bad rap is because they're making money from something that men need. Men can't handle women having that level of power over them!"

"It's just not the same."

"It fucking is Earl, and you know it. We are all prostitutes in this life. We just have to sell different parts of ourselves to survive."

"Not me."

"Not at your level, no. You're a fucking pimp."

"How do you work that one out?"

"You pimp the promises of capitalism."

He laughed out loud. "Look, I really don't want to give you an ultimatum here, but…"

"And what am I going to do for money?"

"I'll pay for you."

I am not your girl not your baby
your sugar nor pearl. I am not a shoulder nor
an ear to listen. I am not a point to be scored nor a notch
to be bed-posted. I am not a weapon to be fired nor a gadget
to be poked then tossed in a cabinet. I am not a target to be
tracked then attacked in the dead of the night. I am not
your luv nor am I hun or even 'a bit of fun.'
I am not a filtered selfie bootie to
be swiped, nor a pointless
emoji to be typed. I am
not a girl for you to
call nor a supplement
to your narcissistic
caustic ego-self.
I am not a pussy
to be pounded.
Do I look like a
tissue to wipe
away your
explosion
of sorry
ejaculation?
I see the
bombshells
of nihilism
which occupy, nullify
the shallows of your unex-
plored being. I fought my way
out of the womb, past the perils
of my girlhood bed, through the
history we have read. Low-bred,
I have gone unfed. Bled for these
words to be said. I am not your
girl. I am Warman: a woman
who has *fight*.

WRITER

Girlo reluctantly left Ruby's cacophony of romping warrior women for Earl's plain shades of white. Ruby was upset but she knew it was coming.

"This isn't the type of job you can have as well as a boyfriend," she said.

Not long after, Girlo heard the retreat had closed and that Ruby was in rehab.

All Girlo had now was a phoney room of her own with a dogeared poster of a paranoid disembodied head and the tremor of his snores from upstairs.

"You're a fucking robot!" Girlo told him the next time the subject of his works-do came up. "Don't you have feelings?"

"You just waste time!"

"I don't… I'm writing."

"Writing isn't a job. It's a hobby. It won't pay the bills, will it?"

"It might, one day."

"Not for the likes of you!"

"The likes of who? It's better than what you do. Spyware pusher."

"That's a commodity."

"A commodity in Big Brother Britain. You're making money by selling our freedom!"

"It pays for this house, doesn't it?"

"Fuck you. I work in this house."

"And I pay for it!"

"Argh, it always comes down to money with you, doesn't it? Never mind the time and energy I've invested. I feel like a glorified cleaner. I never fucking see you!"

"I have to work. It's my vocation."

"No, it's a job. A vocation is writing or teaching, or being a doctor, not fucking selling surveillance."

"I've tried to explain this to you before…"

"Oh, here we go again… 'when I was your age, I had a sense of urgency…' I've heard it before, Earl. Can't you change the record?"

"When I was your age, I *did* have a sense of urgency. I wanted to do something in the world."

"You've done that, alright. You've made a shitload of money by changing the world for the worse, not the better. At least what I'm doing has some moral grounding."

"You're totally off your head! You don't live in the *real* world."

"What like you do? You call all this real?!"

"I've worked incredibly hard for what I've…"

Girlo picked up the wine bottle: "You think this is real?" She took a swig then flung it across the room. **SMASH!** It hit the canvas she'd painted for Earl's birthday, an abstract arrangement of spherical shapes in the style of his favourite artist, Kandinsky. She'd titled it 'Another World'. The canvas fell and tore on the corner of the lacquered sideboard she'd got from Habitat with his credit card for a thousand quid. That would've paid for three month's rent at her student digs!

"I am not a girl for you to call. Nor a supplement to your respectable self. Not a shoulder, or vagina, or an ear to listen. I am not a hankie to wipe away your explosion of sorry ejaculation!"

"Are you insane?"

"I am, actually, yes, I'm fucking barking!"

She picked up another wine bottle and thrust it down onto the slate floor. It popped like an oblong water-balloon; wine sloshing up his cherrywood cabinets. She continued to launch bottles, cocktail glasses and anything else she could lay her hands on, all of it exploding like Molotov cocktails on the floor.

"That's enough now. Stop it!" Earl danced like a Marionette puppet to the tune of the tinkling glass. SMASH-SMASH-

SMASH-SMASH-SMASH-SMASH-SMASH *I fought my way out of the womb, past the perils of my girlhood bed.*

She picked up a dinner plate and frisbeed it down the kitchen. It hit the cornicing and clonked to the floor.

"Stop it! They're from the Pier!"

"All you care about is labels! All you care about is appearances!"

He tried grabbing her wrists, but Girlo was still in a smashing frenzy. She escaped his grip, leaping into the living room, pulling books and LPs from the shelf.

"Not my records!"

"Anyone would swear you loved Brenda and Minnie more than me!"

"Please, they're rare!"

"And so am I Earl, so am I..."

"You can say that again."

His collection fell with a PUH-CLUNK. She snapped her fingernails with the force but didn't seem to notice... PUH-CLUNK PUH-CLUNK PUH-CLUNK PUH-CLUNK PUH-CLUNK. *Through the history we have read. Low-bred, I have gone unfed. Bled for these words to be said.* PUH-CLUNK PUH-CLUNK PUH-CLUNK PUH-CLUNK PUH-CLUNK.

"Please, just stop it now. You've made your point."

"You can't just keep me locked up!"

"I'm not. You are doing that yourself."

"You can't just take me out to play when it suits you."

"I don't. I'm not..."

"I never fucking see you. Who are you? I don't even know who the fuck you are!"

"I don't know who you are right now. Please, just calm down and we can talk things over..."

"Shut up. I'm not your fucking employee! I'm not your cleaner anymore!"

"I was going to say, be careful because you're going to have to clean all of this up."

Earl's badly timed joke sent Girlo over the top. She picked up a full bottle of Metaxa Brandy and hoisted it behind her shoulder.

"Not the brandy, no... please, not the brandy!"

She whacked it over the side of his granite worktop. It exploded like a chemistry flask in a failed experiment.

"You've lost the plot!"

"No, I lost the plot when I thought we could work! I thought we'd settle down together. Have a baby..."

"Settle down? You couldn't have a baby. You'd kill it!"

Just then, Girlo had a strange memory of looking up at her young mother's face, their eyes locking. A moment of mis-timed connection. "You can't buy me!" She opened the kitchen drawer and grabbed at some pound coins then chucked them at Earl's head.

"Woah... watch it! What you doing? Crazy bitch!"

"Yew are! This is all you fucking care about, isn't it? Have some fucking money? Have some fucking money you Tory twat!"

"Tory twat? What the...?"

The strap of Girlo's top had snapped. Mascara-tears streaked her reddened cheeks; spittle sprayed from her mouth with every catapult of venom.

"I will never be your wife. I could never have a child with a fucking automaton!"

Finally, just as she was about to topple the flat-screen television, Earl gripped her in a bearhug. They fell on the sofa.

"Stop it. Just stop. You are going to hurt yourself!"

"Get off me! Get off!"

Earl trembled as he tried to contain her. He was afraid. He'd been afraid since the day they'd met. Girlo seemed to have this effect. *But why were they afraid of her?* She only wanted to be herself. If she could just escape the uneasiness that buzzed around inside; the feeling that she was never home, a sickening restlessness borne of not belonging. She felt this was just another forced reality planned out for her, a reality the world said she should be happy in. Perhaps he was right about the baby. Perhaps she could never be a mother.

The following day, in the spare room, she lifted her head from the fusty futon to the Dali poster.

"I am a nutter," she muttered. She was good at playing the part, but only for so long. She tried her best to convince herself that she could be whatever they wanted her to be, be anything for anyone who offered any love. But their love couldn't conquer the kryptonite of her corrupted emotions. They surged wildly through her always. There was no circuit, no release, no outlet. She tried to smoke them out, gas them out, douse them with alcohol but it only made them grow fiercer and wilder. Her drawers were bursting with the forgotten secrets of a childhood that didn't belong to her. Adulthood was no better. An intricate, tightly woven tapestry of hurt. She couldn't push it down any longer. It needed to be dragged out, unpicked, examined, the blur picked and unravelled from her peripheral vision.

Amid the constant chaos, her mind was always itching, filching, scratching, picking, hunting around for something or someone who could distract her from her heavy shame and chattering brain. Her state-tamed, common sense rational looked for someone to rescue her—a Disney prince or knight in shining armour. She never found either. Tinfoil knights were all she felt good enough for.

These distractions kept her trapped in dark mind-paths, a brain-maze with no destination and no escape, a yawning chasm where she waited for a saviour, or a new identity that she could morph into. The real her never existed. She stepped into his prescribed role for her. It was easier. But after a while it just didn't sit right. She knew a life lived in submission would be a betrayal to all those who'd sacrificed so much for her independence. The self-help books told her she must love *herself*. It didn't matter how many times she read the phrase it wouldn't stick! 'Reach out to your inner child within and nurture her,' echoed the astrologers. 'Live in the Now,' preached the new-age philosophers. 'You have unrealised potential,' repeated The High Priestess of the Major Arcana. Every time she took a step forward, her demons dragged her back. The White Monkey in its many toxic guises dragged her back every time.

She was sat at her glass-topped Ikea desk in his extremely expensive bungalow, books arranged in alphabetical order, quotes scribbled on Post-its neatly blue-tacked to the wall. To her right, a steaming cup of coffee, to the left a selection of pens and highlighters. She had everything a professional writer needed, right?

"Write," she told herself. "Write, nutter."

A magpie flitted outside the window, *one for sorrow.* Everything was all wrong. It wasn't right. The following day she packed her bags and left to see what waited for her in the distant castle behind the cloth-eared, melancholic face on the Dali poster.

PREGNANT

Girlo was in no position to have a baby when she got pregnant. She didn't feel very maternal but something inside said: *this is right, give birth to me.* She'd left Earl and fallen for a proper working-class chap who worked in sales. She felt he knew her better than Earl. After all the long nights in and arguments about work, the new chap offered light relief. It wasn't long before the relief ended with a positive pregnancy test and later a string of letters regarding child custody from his solicitor.

Nannie Pearl was devastated.

"From a millionaire to a fly boy? Why couldn't you have a baby with Earl?" Girlo'd travelled home to tell Nannie Pearl the news. She'd almost fainted.

"You've ruined your life," she screamed at Girlo as she tentatively rubbed her bump.

The world told her that she'd failed, but she stuck to the decision to see this through, leaving the tinfoil knights and armchair philosophers behind. With her MA in her back pocket, she signed up for a PGCE and forgot about writing for a while, living hand-to-mouth in a strange new land called single parenthood. She loved being a mother, but the societal expectations of parenting strangled her. She'd broken a fundamental state rule by becoming both mother and father. When Sapphire came into the world, Girlo gave her the Wolf family name: Sapphire Pearl Wolf. She remembered feeling an overriding sense of strength after pushing her out, as though her toes had grown roots and driven themselves into the earth, into the shared consciousness of all who'd given birth before— a strength she'd seen in women her senior, an aura of completion, wisdom, assuredness. She had craved this secret aura as a young feminist, but never thought for a moment it would come like this.

When she looked at Sapphire's scrunched up face, blinking in the new light, Girlo discovered a reason to be proud, a foundation for love. If she could grow and birth a healthy baby from a body where toxicity had reigned, maybe she had a chance. She was adamant she wasn't going to be a victim. She was going to survive and she tapped into her warrior past to help get her through. When Sapphire was barely old enough to speak, she placed her little hand on Girlo's cheek and whispered sweetly, "I saved you, Mammy."

Girlo'd always been at war in her own head, crises upon crises piling up until she didn't know *what* or *who* was real. Her own body didn't even feel real. She seemed to watch from afar, as a detached version of herself wreaked havoc and destroyed everything. She was weaned on adrenaline, so she craved it like a drug, a substitute for life, something to fill the void. There was always a drama in her world; her own shit or someone else's. Everyone she knew hopped from one calamity to the next, self-medicating the devastation with a massive piss-up. Then long spells of the black dog, before the next booze-fuelled crisis. A rollercoaster of adrenaline, ego, and angry points to be proved.

Girlo longed to create, but couldn't find the mental energy to sit down every day like serious writers. Other women with kids got up at the crack of dawn to write but they had husbands or partners. Girlo got up at the crack of dawn to nurse her baby. If she got a spare moment, she used it to clean up, take a bath sometimes. Problems were ever-present, ever demanding. She couldn't focus on watching a television programme let alone read or write a book. Her reading material consisted of baby books which always sent her off to sleep.

On rare occasions, in the dead of the night, she'd get a eureka moment, an idea for a story like a bolt out of the blue. She'd rush to capture it. In her head it flowed so seamlessly. All the lines would write themselves—titles, images—everything would be there waiting to be committed to paper. But when she came to write, the magic disappeared, blown away like the fog at dawn. She should've got up and written it down! *Why didn't she write it down?* Because the words didn't come as eloquently as she expected and the images didn't jump from the page in the way she imagined, she'd abandon it. All those lost lines. All those forgotten titles... *where do they go?* She heard once that the heart holds memory. And she'd read about a patient, a plain food-loving, mild-mannered woman who'd undergone a successful heart transplant, the beneficiary of an organ from a feisty spicy food aficionado. When she woke her whole personality had changed and she wanted hot sauce on everything. If the heart can hold memory, perhaps the liver could too—perhaps all those blacked-out nights on the booze were still stored somewhere in her physicality. And if they were, maybe she could finally get to the bottom of where all those mysterious cuts, bruises and worrying bumps on her head had come from. But then maybe she'd discover the terribly embarrassing things she'd said or done in drink, which her brain had protected her from knowing. *Perhaps not the best idea*, she thought.

This was why Girlo found it so difficult to write. She couldn't keep her mind on one thing long enough. Her thought process was like a colony of sea anemones—opening and fanning, reaching up towards the surface in a multitude of fast-approaching lights. She hoped one day that a stream of inspired words would miraculously burst forth, that she could be a conduit, conjuring stories from the zeitgeist without barely having to think. Instead, her thoughts became wet clothes, slugging around her brain like an overfilled washing machine, mixed fibres and colours, all different stitches and weaves slopping and sloshing around, juddering under the weight of the water. After the last mad cycle, a drawer would spring open, spilling a glutinous mixture of foam and skin-cell gloop... her something that some people called a poem. All she'd ever been expected to do was swallow other people's truths. They distilled for long years in her depths, then, along with her own observations, spat up and out in words. Writing was like a sporadic bodily function, a physical, guttural reaction to living, to dying.

NANNIE

There once was a wily woman
who lived in the womb of a tree.
Each day she'd share,
with the birds on the bough,
the truths of their lost herstory.

"This getting old is killing me, aye," Pearl said, resting her spliff in the ashtray before she folded her origami limbs into the bedclothes. She had been stuck in bed 'like this' since the start of spring with her 'bastard sciatica'.

"I don't know what to do. What can I do for you, Nan?" pleaded Girlo.

"Nothing much we can do, Cariad."

The television on top of her trusty tallboy spewed all the usual shock doctrines, Pearl wondering what had come of the world. All the work she'd done had come to nothing.

"The whole thing was sewn up!"

She'd loved the badge they'd given to her at the first meeting. 'You Can't Beat a Woman', it said. She'd pinned it onto her lapel with a real sense of duty. Before long, Pearl was appointed chairwoman of a women's domestic abuse charity. She fought hard against their ineptitude and inefficiency with funds but like most charities, the management had no problem giving themselves pay rises while "the girls were left to rot in squalor—tiny bedsits, sharing beds with their kids—no protection from the bastards who put them there in the first place!"

"We just can't keep up with the demand. The council has only got a certain number of properties. It's a struggle to rehouse them."

"Women and their children shouldn't be punished for leaving their abusive husbands, they should be rewarded." Pearl told them.

"We just don't have the budget."

Pearl had read the annual report.

"Some of these women have been left in limbo for years. Where's the support? Some are so desperate for money they're selling themselves, and someone else told me the other day they're rolling cigarettes with crushed-up paracetamol."

"I'm not sure what that has to do with housing."

"It's not just about housing. They need all sorts of support services that should be provided in the 'Joined-Up' thinking partnerships you all keep going on about. I don't see anyone working together here, do you?"

After knocking door-to-door, representing the poor at laborious council meetings and the nightly phone-rants with fellow advocates, Pearl's fight had gone. Her only 'friends' now were the news presenters, who—from the epicentre of Western thought: a red-globed organ of ideology—lit the tomb of her room in a blue hue. *You* can *beat a woman in the end,* she thought while she wasted away. She shed a hardened tear, a prick of defeat pushing into the tapestry of her heart.

She'd warn of blinded battles,
and wars sunk with bellies of glee.
She danced to the innocent birdsong
that they'd coo in the light of the tree.

A gentle heat grew from the radiator and across the curtain, velvet swag blocking the strained sunbeams of early spring.

"Why don't we open the window? Let some fresh air in." suggested Girlo.

Outside in the light a flight of sparrows swarmed, like Etch-a-Sketch dust being shaken free.

"Oh, leave it will ewe! My eyes can't take it today, Cariad. Let's 'ave five minutes." Her eyelids—crinkled as cigarette-papers—closed, and she faded into the jaundiced wallpaper. An intense bile rippled up her gullet and she burped softly to quell it. Thoughts of her mother were ever-present. *She couldn't take any of it back now.* The words scorched her from the inside out like cattle branding irons. They were never the best of friends, but mothers and daughters either got on or they didn't, and her mother had made it *so* hard for her to leave Jack, but she'd tried in her own way. Maybe she just wanted the best for her and the boys deep down. Or perhaps she didn't want to have to help out— she never liked children really. Pearl could've done it on her own. She might as well have anyway. Things were changing now; you didn't need a man to have a baby.

"Just find yourself someone with a bit of nous, a bit of cash, and just have a bloody baby! It's easier on your own. You don't *need* a husband. They're nothing but trouble—believe me." Pearl said this to Girlo every time she'd watched some silly rom-com and started up about her dream wedding.

> *The woodlouse were her slippers.*
> *The leaves, her evergreen crown.*
> *The spiders were her spectacles*
> *who never let her down.*

After half-hour's kip, Pearl was roused with a cup of sugary tea, which she slurped to ease the burn. She had plenty to say but couldn't persuade her brain to carry the words to her lips. Girlo was sweating under the pressure of keeping her daughter, Sapphire, still.

"She looks like a little pixie, doesn't she, Nan? In' she bootiful?"

"Would you like to play pixies and faeries with me, Nannie?"

"Not now, Cariad, Nannie isn't her best today."

Sapphire's cordate lips puckered as she flung her arms around her nannie's clammy neck and kissed her. She had already offered her a cup of tea, which Nannie'd declined, before accepting one from Grandad Miles. Sapphire'd *even* offered to do Nannie's hair, but she didn't want to be 'messed with today'. Sapphire offered to sing her a song instead, maybe do a little dance.

"Ok, let's have a little song then." Pearl curled her lip into a smile.

"You are my Sunshine, my only Sunshine. You make me A-PEEE when skies are grey…" As Sapphire sang the sun pushed at the brick-dust curtains. Pearl clapped enthusiastically.

"That's my girl!"

"Lovely, Cariad… now let's give Nannie a rest, shall we?"

The energy in the room thinned. Pearl ferreted for the doofer beneath her stack of heavy pillows, placed to block wisps of draught from the forgotten window. Pearl never bought 'brand new' and whatever she scraped together, she stashed. She slept in 'the comfy bedclothes', sprinkled with constellations of blim-holes from years of smoking hash in bed. Girlo looked on from the stiff-backed fireside chair. It always used to be draped with her nan's jeans and jumpers but now it was a place for visitors to perch. Pearl channel-hopped until she found what she referred to as her 'mind balm'.

"Shush now… the 'owz wives is on." Her new family, *The Real Housewives of Beverly Hills*, didn't ask her any questions or tell her to get out of bed. They were as sassy and slick as she'd been back in her San Diego days.

"She thinks they're her friends," Grandad Miles said, stirring the tea in the kitchen. "It's all she fucking goes on about: 'owz wives this, an' 'owz wives tha'. I took her up a cuppa tea this morning. She let it go cold, again."

"Has she eaten today?"

"Aye… bit uv torst an' marmalade. She can't manage to keep it down. I'll go down the chip shop after, see if she fancies anything."

"Chips! You sure?"

Grandad Miles loved Pearl more than anything in the world. They'd got together after she'd split with Jack the final time.

"She walked into the Forge after she come back from America and I thought, *Woah*, who the bloody hell is that!"

Grandad Miles was a skilled carpenter. He'd worked in Canada and Saudi in the 70s.

"Can I have a fast glass please?" he'd say when he entered a bar, which meant a half pint that he'd down in one. Nobody could drink like Grandad Miles—always the last man standing. But in the end, it got hold of him. He nearly ended up dead. Pearl brought him home and cared for him until he was well. They'd argue sometimes and Grandad Miles would move out, but he always came back. He had a forked tongue, an acerbic wit, but beneath all his sarcasm, he was lovely. He stuck by Pearl and the Wolf family through thick and thin.

"Do I look alright?" Girlo'd ask him when she was a teenager getting ready to go out.

"You'd look lovely in a black bag, beaut!"

Even though her liver forbade it, Pearl snaffled a chip shop sausage in double-time, the prospect of eating something other than toast brightening her mood. Despite their initial reservations, Girlo and Miles said nothing, enjoying watching her eat normally again. The last time she'd ignored the doctor she'd gobbled down a piece of battered cod before it could touch the sides. It happened so quickly it was as if it hadn't happened at all. She'd been sick for weeks on end.

"I may as well," she said, dipping a chip in the curry sauce.

"I haven't got nothing else left, have I?"

"Suppose not, Nan."

Pearl had always had a passion for food. Her nickname was 'the Gannet' on account of the amount she could put away without gaining any weight. But she had to be a quick eater in a house full of boys. 'They'd be asking for seconds the minute they put the first forkful in their mouths!' When Pearl was flush, she prepared dishes of restaurant quality. She loved to cook seared steak with Béarnaise sauce, baked sweet potato smothered in butter and sour cream, smoked salmon sandwiches with horseradish crème fraiche, streaky bacon sandwiches with butter-soaked portobello mushrooms and crepes with cherries in kirsch and ice-cream. She insisted on grilling the bacon because that was healthier, but then she'd drizzle the dripping onto thickly buttered bread to go with it. 'It was so bad, but oh, so good.' Every plate came with a story.

"I had eggs Benedict for the first time when I was staying at the Intercontinental in California. I lived there for six months."

Girlo used to question the validity of her nan's tall tales but then she'd found evidence; a monogrammed cup and saucer from a hotel she'd mentioned or a letter from the man who loved her.

"This is how the Americans eat their bacon... over there they have it with maple syrup and scrambled eggs. I had it when I stayed with a gang of Hell's Angels. They picked me up when I was thumbing a lift. One guy's wife was a neat freak—constantly on the go—I'm sure she daubed a bit of base... anyway, she'd keep everything in little see-through Tupperware boxes... *everything* in its right and proper place. In their attic they had shelves and shelves of guns. Big guns."

"Guns?!"

"Yeah. Everyone has guns over there! And, I always remember, she microwaved a cockroach for five minutes. Zapped the fuck out of it!"

"What happened to it?!"

"It walked out alive! Tough little buggers, cockroaches are.

"When you lived up here and you used to come to me, you were such a picky child. You wouldn't eat a damn thing. When you moved down there and you'd come in the holidays, you were ravenous! You couldn't get enough food down you. And your brother."

"We were probably hungry, nan. All we had was Spam."

Sapphire was playing with her dolls in the other room. They could hear her introducing them as they arrived at her make-believe party.

"How d'you do? How d'you do? Would you like some tea? Some cake, for you? I like your dress... oh, thank you!... you look beautiful... would you like some more food?"

"'Ark at her in there."

"I know... in' she funny? God, I love her!"

"I love her too. I gotta give it to you, Cariad, you've done a good job, especially for someone who couldn't stand children."

"I know that's what I said, but it just seemed right. I knew she was going to be the making of me, that she'd keep me out of the pub!"

Pearl laughed.

"Aye, they do that, kids. From the moment you have them the years start flying by. I look in the mirror and think, *who is that old woman?* Make the most of every minute with her, promise me." She snapped her fingers. "It goes just like that!" She said in a Tommy Cooper voice. "And you should have another one. It's hard when you're an only child. Look at how I was with grandmamma."

"I don't know about that, Nan... I'm not sure I can go through all that again... I just hope I can be enough for her when she grows."

"You already are, my Cariad."

The sun pounded on the curtain, turning the brick-dust fabric rose gold, glowing brighter than the shiny housewives on the television. Sapphire had had enough of playing parties and jumped up on the bed to look out the window. She peeled back the curtain before anyone could say anything. A liquid light cascaded in, drenching Pearl and washing out the morbid news reader, back on the television. The view from the window was of the slag heaps, like two pert bosoms, a lithographed image of clouds drifting in front of the fertile hills.

"Look Nan, it's beautiful out. Let's have some salmon sandwiches and pink champagne on the lawn!"

Sapphire cheered. "Yes! Let's have a picnic in the garden. Have we got a blanket?"

"Did I ever tell you about the Legend of the Diamond Goddess?"

"Yes, Nan. Loads of times! Sapphy hasn't heard you tell it though. Come and tell us in the garden."

"You two go on. I'll be there now, in a minute."

Raspberries gleamed in the garden like Burmese rubies. From her window, Pearl watched Girlo pour the pink fizz into the bowls of three vintage champagne glasses, Sapphire picking the berries and plopping them into the drinks. Pearl hoicked open the window, the smell of young grass beckoning.

"Bugger it!" She said. "I'm coming down!"

The three of them sat in a circle. Sapphire blew a dandelion, its feathery seeds parachuting down the lawn.

"Did you make a wish?"

"Don't tell us or it won't come true!"

Girlo handed out the glasses, the raspberries magnified like little sizzling brains.

"One for you, Nan, one for me. And one for Grandmamma."

"What about me?" cried Sapphire.

"Don't worry, we haven't forgotten about you," Pearl said.

"To Grandmamma Alice."

"And here's to us."

"And me… what about me?"

"And here's to Sapphire, too!"

For she was a laughing soul
who lived to the best she could be.
And she rode the boots
of the travelling roots
of the big old, proud, soultree.

MAMA

Then, one day, lightning struck,
and her tree, it split in half.
Flames leapt up the trunk that day,
and she lost her belly laugh.

Pearl got the call on a wet-leafed morning.

"Yes, this is Mrs Wolf. Who's speaking please?"

"The nurse, love… It's your mother."

Pearl and Girlo approached the two-up-two-down, the ambulance flashing on the greasy road. Pearl's thumbs cracked like the legs of a crab as she swung the steering-wheel round. Her mother was sprawled on the floor inside, a cushion wedged under her head. Beside her knelt a handsome paramedic.

"Oh Mama! What have you gone and done?"

"I think it's a broken hip. We'll have to take her in."

"I was only trying to come down the stairs. I should've stayed in my bungalow, I should have—"

"It's okay Mama… it's alright." Pearl stroked her white-cloud hair. "What are we going to do with you, uh?"

The hospital decided her mother needed round-the-clock care and sent her to a nursing home, a fifty-minute round trip. Stocked up with sugary guilt-gifts, Pearl and Girlo made the long journey four times a week. The sweet treats were meant to cancel out the thin gravy dinners her mother was forced to eat. *Never mind her diabetes.* On other occasions she'd bring new cotton briefs from Marks & Sparks, or trousers that had been specially taken in—then let out again because they were 'too tight'—then brought back again for her mother's approval.

"They're not in season!" Alice said, opening a punnet of strawberries.

"Remember the ones dad grew at the bottom of the garden, Mam?"

"Yes, Beakie pinched um all the time."

"Who's Beakie, Grandmamma?" asked Girlo

"Beakie the Cock, he bloody hated yewuh grandmother. Every time she yewst to go out to use the lavatory, he'd go at her hell-for-leather! And of course she couldn't see a blasted thing! She gave him what-for with her stick mind yew!"

"Haha... I remember now. That was a long time ago, Mama."

"It was, yeah. It was a long time ago now..." She picked up one of the anaemic strawberries and bit into its firm flesh. "These don't have a bloody patch on yer father's." She turned to look over the bobbing silhouettes of dozing heads. Through the window—a portal onto a wall of hills—snow drifts gathered. "I wish this bloody weather would hurry up."

"Me too, Mam... me too."

Their silence was shattered by the abrupt moans of a deranged woman across the room.

"Dang and blast! Turn the telly up. She's like this every bloody day!" Pearl's mother pulled the remote control from the side of her armchair and handed it to her. "Put it back when you've finished. I don't want *her* getting hold of it again." With a bowed finger, she pointed at a raggedy woman besottedly clutching a plastic baby-doll.

"Rightee-o, Mam."

It was a sensory overload in there, the cloying mix of hot-piss, greasy disinfectant, and a ribboned waft of either faeces or cooked dinner sticking to the back of Girlo's morning-sickened gut. A clang of distant pans blended with the hollering of mortified seniors, punctuated by the cruel door buzzer sending shockwaves through the din and under the skin. Then came the booming credits of *Deal or No Deal*, Noel Edmonds opening the show doing the limbo under a broom. Girlo fucking hated that program. Sitting there, stranded, in a stuffy room stuffed with the almost-dead, watching game shows on full blast, felt a bit like limbo.

Pearl fussed over Alice, checking she had everything she needed, that the girls were treating her kindly.

There were so many things they wanted to ask, so many unanswered questions, and so many raw feelings they couldn't express without causing upset. Time was running out, but they carried on carrying on, talking about the weather, gossiping about the neighbours, reminiscing over the same memories, as though they were circling on a vintage film reel. Memories collectively churning out from the snag of an old thought, triggered by a smell or a song. Memories were all that they had now and there didn't seem to be that many of them left. The ones they did share, they clung to, finding a fleeting sense of belonging in a brief, imperfect connection.

"D'you think we could do that now, Mama?"

"Do what?!"

"The Limbo, like Noel?"

"You gotta be joking. I'd break my back in two!"

"You and me both."

Girlo noticed one of the residents had got excited, a mini tent bursting up out of the crotch of his camel trousers. She shrank under his probing stare, fixing her eyes on the TV screen. From the corner of her eye, she could see him trying to flick his slug of a tongue at her. She wondered when his number would be up.

A swipe of sweat leapt up Pearl's back. These flashes had been coming on from out of nowhere lately. She needed to get out for a minute. She went to find one of the girls, trying to find out why the hell the doctor hadn't been to see her mother about her chest.

When she got back her mother was fighting over the remote with the raggedy doll-woman. A care worker flapped through the double-doors; plastic apron ripped from the commotion.

"Bitch!" The man with an erection shouted.

"Maybe you'd like to sit in your room for a bit, Alice?"

"Yeah, let's take a breather shall we, Mam?"

"I'm NOT going *anywhere*. These are *my* buttons."

The care worker looked at Girlo in desperation.

"Let's just watch the end of this and then she can have it, is it Grandmamma?"

"Don't you want to know what's in the box?"

"Fine, weyull watch the end of this, and that's *that*."

Girlo escaped for a sneaky fag. A care worker appeared; the baby-doll wrapped up in a blanket under her arm in the hope of luring the raggedy woman away. When the No Deal credits ascended, Pearl said, "Why don't we do your nails, Mam? They could do with a polish."

"If you must, Pearl!"

She took her mother's arthritic fingers, thinking of all the times she'd watched them softly sift marge and flour for shortcrust pastry or rinse Fairy bubbles from their drinking glasses or twist and tie rags into her young butterscotch hair. Now they seemed like fossils, nails ridged like scalloped shells. She smoothed the splintered edges into rounded curves, then painted them powder pink. Before they could dry her mother gripped her hand tight.

"Thank you, my love. My little girl. Thank you."

It was just then that Pearl felt like her mother's daughter. The barrier between them momentarily lifted. She melted and fell back into the womb, reattaching herself to the umbilical cord.

"Have you been smoking, my girl?" Alice asked Girlo on her return.

"I—I—er…"

"That baby will come out without fingers and toes if you carry on!"

"We better get going, Mam."

"Well, don't forget to bring my cream with you tomorrow. It's in the bathroom cabinet. The top shelf."

The birds, they flew away from her,
and the spiders stretched their legs.
The trunk of the tree fell with a thump!
Her nest, empty—bereft of eggs.

SINGLE MUM

They say she became a songless mute,
for she'd lost her lust for learning
and she no longer played the flute,
for her heart, it had stopped yearning.

Outside, in the decontamination area of the hospital where smoking was strictly prohibited, Girlo puffed her fag. She was taking a breather from the sick-hot ward where her grandmamma lay. It was a glum day, January the 1st, New Year drunk in. Casualties, queued on trollies, spilled from the doors like cargo ships at the mouth of a harbour. She flicked her butt to the kerb. With a scrawled map of directions, she navigated her way through the labyrinth-like hospital. As she passed the maternity ward, she remembered her 23 hour 'Hell-raiser' of a birth. The contractions hit her like an orgasm in reverse. She'd jumped out of the birthing pool and ran around like a nymph with a firecracker up its arse.

"Get the fuck out!" She'd screamed at the nosy trainee midwife, some inner animal released.

"You were like a fucking camel," Pearl had said later, after they'd had to syphon five litres of piss through catheters jabbed into her urethra.

"They'd never seen someone hold so much water."

After the pethidine, Girlo was too drowsy to push. They'd found a ridge in her cervix. Sapphire's little head kept slipping in and out. Pearl could see the tiny ticker tape on her skull. Her heartbeat was accelerating. Touch and go. The epidural came in handy. Finally, the consultants burst in, demanding Girlo be sent to theatre. They cut her open sideways, plucking her baby from her with a pair of forceps.

It was like a bad trip on acid.

She was sure the surgeon had sliced a piece of her clitoris off when they stitched her up. It never felt the same way afterwards. *Perhaps that was her punishment for being a slutty unmarried mother.*

The baby flopped out like raw sausage, slimy and extraterrestrial, crying as she sucked up the cold shock of life. Girlo held her in disbelief. *Was this real?* They gave her some tramadol and left her to breastfeed her newborn in the warm-with-blood sheets. Girlo remembered her little bean head multiplying into thousands of faces, spiralling away from her in a holographic light show. The baby was slippery as a water-balloon. She had trouble holding onto her in the narrow hospital bed.

Then she remembers the string of intruders, the expensive photographers, the observations nurse, the other ignorant nurse who took the baby off somewhere twice a day to be pumped with antibiotics, the condescending breastfeeding expert who came with her knitted tit and scraped Girlo's nipple so viciously over the lip of a cup to release the colostrum, it split and remained an open wound for the next five months of breastfeeding.

She remembered her first meal as a mother, untouched because she didn't want to disturb the baby, already falling asleep on her breast. When she could eat, it was cold.

"Could you warm this up for me please?" She asked a nurse flitting past.

"We can't. It's against health and safety regulations. If you want something to eat, you'll have to go over to the concourse."

That was impossible. Girlo still couldn't feel her legs from the epidural, and she didn't want to leave her baby alone. She hadn't eaten in 48 hours, but she just had to just lie there listening to the other new mums' families arriving with gifts and delicious food. Girlo imagined dragging herself through the quagmire of corridors, limping along with the baby slung under her arm like a rolled up sleeping bag to get something from the overpriced hospital shop where, she'd realise she didn't have any money and would have to traipse empty-handed all the way back.

"Or you can wait an hour or so and have a sandwich," came the nurse's voice. Girlo'd been incarcerated in the curtained-off section of that cunting ward, right next to the constantly slamming door, from which would pour a flood of husbands and grandmothers with flowers and balloons and smiles saying,

"Welcome to this world of ours!" *Maybe if she'd had a husband, they'd have treated her better.* But she didn't so she laid there haemorrhaging blood, clutching her poor little baby who'd almost died on her ridged cervix, tripping her tits off on Tramadol.

Girlo shook the memory, returning to the directions. 'Press "1" in the lift and turn right again onto the westward.' Grandmamma was next to the window, laid out like golden tissue paper. Girlo leant down to kiss her forehead and hold her liver-spotted hands which were folded like the legs of a leopard. A red warning for snow had been issued a whole two months after their relatively mild, grey Christmas. There hadn't been snow this bad in February since 1979.

"She looks like Snow White, Mammy," Sapphire said, flapping a handmade paper card.

"She does, baby."

"It's funny," Pearl said. "The men used to call her the Ice Queen when I was little."

"The weather is quite fitting then." They smiled at one another.

Grandmamma had made some progress, her temperature had gone down. Her blood pressure was better. She was responding to the antibiotics. But the doctors were still unsure about what might be blocking the duct. They advised nil-by-mouth.

"But my mother loves her food! Look at her mouth, it's bone-dry. Please? She needs something! Water at least." The nurse promised to bring a lemon swab.

"That might help a bit."

Instead, a different nurse came to take more bloods. It was futile in the end. Her body had collapsed, a reservoir of lifeblood frozen over, frosting the network of veins and arteries that once pumped this powerhouse of a woman.

The nurse strapped her arm again. Globs of purple bruises bulged like blackberries under the skin, but the nurse kept fiddling with the syringe, looking for a way in.

"Is this really necessary?"

"I'm not sure it's going to work," Girlo added.

"We'll try again later."

"I can't watch this anymore, Nan."

"I know, Cariad. I know..."

The doctors said they'd do an endoscopic test because they were obliged to do so and because of her age they'd taken the decision not to resuscitate. Alice kept going anyway. Through all the snow she kept on fighting for her daughter and Pearl fought right back for her.

> *So, she wished upon the brightest star*
> *to open the soultree's door.*
> *For she had lost the will to live*
> *and could take the loss no more.*

PEARL

Into the divine door, she crawled,
down a sodden tunnel.
Through a glittering web, she slid,
into a grassy funnel.

Girlo and Micky, Pearl's second youngest, drove her to the hospital for an overdue scan on her liver. She'd been in bed for too long now. When Doctor Bateman had prescribed her liquid morphine, Eric had said, "Enough is enough! We need to ring a fucking ambulance."

But the ambulance never came.

This hospital was nothing like the one in the city. Its wide, empty corridors and block-colour walls made it feel like newly built student accommodation. There was artwork, good artwork; nothing like the depressing mosaic pieces at the city hospital, done way back in '97, but pictures of the climbing limbs of magnificent trees taken by A-Level photography students. Nice old ladies sat in the corridor selling silk scarves and handmade jewellery. Pearl wanted Girlo and Micky to stop her wheelchair next to the jewellery stall. She wanted to touch and absorb the healing qualities of the gemstones. She picked up a necklace made of amethyst.

"That's very good for sobriety, Nan," Girlo laughed.

"I'll put that one back then."

"Oh, look. It's a beetle! Just like Grandmamma had."

The sales lady picked up the cushion on which it rested.

"It's Jade," she said.

"For luck," echoed Pearl.

"Do you want it, Nan? I'll get it for you."

"Don't be daft, I'll get it. And choose something for yourself."

"No, Nan, I want to!"

"Listen to me, Girlo. If I want to…"

"I'll get it," said Uncle Micky. "Pick something for yourself."

Girlo chose a black pearl ring. The kindly old lady winked as she slipped it onto her finger.

"It's beautiful, Cariad," Nannie Pearl said.

Girlo pinned the beetle brooch onto her Nan's coat and a sliver of light touched it.

"I think yours is magic, Nan."

Her nan gave her a peachy kiss. "Love you, Cariad." She gave Micky a big cwtch. "Thank you, son."

Her bedroom walls had been covered with pieces like this, each one with its own unique story. After her mother's funeral she'd cleared them all away. Only their outlines were left, string-white marks against the nicotine-stained wallpaper.

Ceri, a girl form the Rock, was sat in the waiting room at the radiography department; the familiar valleys conversation distracted them from their long wait. It was just like a home-from-home, except they were stuck in a fucking hospital.

"I remember yewer mother used to collect matchboxes and stick them up the landing wall," Girlo said.

"She did, aye. She's gone now too—breast cancer."

"I'm so sorry. She used to do the best parties mind, yew."

"Best up the Rock," said Ceri.

Pearl's coccyx was penetrating her rice-paper skin of her lower back. She'd been sitting in the stiff-backed wheelchair for two hours. She needed to lie down. Girlo knew this pain. Her coccyx had been damaged with the forceps during childbirth. Someone had told her the coccyx unfurls like a tail when the baby emerges. She'd followed Ina May's advice to bring out her inner totem animal during labour but hadn't expected to grow a fucking tail. For over two years she couldn't sit. Breastfeeding in the recommended position was unthinkable. 'All worth it though,' seemed to be the common mantra, rehearsed and repeated by generations of powerhouse women. No sympathy for new or old mothers, childbirth a duty.

"I need to lie down," Pearl wailed as soon as the scan was done.
"In-a min-eh, Mam. We'll go ask a doctor now."

Ten hours later they were still sitting in the waiting room. Uncle Micky was no stranger to the scenario, having nursed his own wife fifteen years prior. He was tamping, trapped on a carousel of polite enquires, not wanting to rock the boat, waiting for results, for news, for a bed, or a comfier seat to sit on. Pearl cried out in pain.

"This is fucking ridiculous—after everything these people have given to this cuntree," muttered Micky.

"I know. Shush. Let's just wait. They can't be much longer now," Girlo whispered.

"I'm going 'ome," Pearl said, "I want my own bed.'"

"You mustn't, Nan. We have to see what the doctor says now, in a minute."

"What fucking doctor? She's nowhere to be seen, mun."

They felt like prison guards holding their matriarch hostage in some ludicrous stage play, the mis-en-scene reeking of conceit. Another hour ticked by. Patients who'd arrived after Pearl were guided to new rooms.

"You in any pain?" One of the auxiliary nurses asked a man in his eighties.

"You will be when you go with him," muttered Uncle Micky.

"I'll look after you," his colleague interjected, appearing with a wheelchair.

"Keep an eye on him, mind. He does get lost from time to time," the auxiliary nurse joked.

The downbeat audience of elderly patients let out faint laughs as the plastic-masked auxiliary nurses attempted to entertain them in the boxed-off, boiling-hot waiting room. Temperatures outside were soaring. There hadn't been a summer this hot since 1979.

"He's still got that rash, mind!" One nurse joshed.

"When's your vasectomy again?" The other chipped in.

After some clumsy fumbling, they got the man into the

231

wheelchair, and the wheelchair out of the waiting room, exiting stage left.

"You've still got your carved Indonesian puppets haven't you, Nan?" Girlo asked.

"Yeah, love. They're in the 'ouse, strung up."

"This is Mr Nice," she'd say, using the puppets to comfort, cajole or frighten her grandchildren. "He is happy all the time, even when you're feeling sad. You can tell him your secrets and he will try his hardest to make it all better. Look at his face. In ee luvlee?" She'd take his movable wooden mouth and wiggle it: "'Ello, I'm Mr Nice and I'll look after you! This is Mr Naughty! He's very naughty, he is. Watch out, because if yewer naughty, he will come and get you!" She'd take the puppet down from the hook where it hung and chase the kids around the living room.

"I'm Mr Naughty and I'm coming to get you!" The kids screamed and jumped over the furniture, cushions and cups and ashtrays spilling everywhere.

"And here is, Mr Wise." (She had a soft spot for Mr Wise.) "Mr Wise sees and hears all. He's always watching. He'll look after you when I'm gone."

"Where are you going, Nannie?"

"Nowhere yet, Cariad."

"I don't want you to go."

"I don't want to go either, my Cariad. I'll always be with you, in there." She pressed her hand on Girlo's heart.

"Does he see *everything*, Nannie?"

"Everything! So, you better be good, or Mr Wise will know."

They'd been in the waiting room for 12 hours when Uncle Micky flipped.

"This is a disgrace! She fed the five thousand during the strike! She nursed her father after the war. This is the thanks she gets."

He raised his voice so the other people in the waiting room could hear. "This 'ospital by 'ere, was built to replace ower Miners' 'ospital, which was the property of us—the Miners and their families. It was the local council who ripped it down, sold

232

the land off to private investors. The people were promised the same services, including an A&E. But surprise, surprise no A&E, and no bloody doctors by the looks of it!"

"Well said, Boyo," piped up an old chap who'd been sitting next to his wife for the last 11 hours, having been admitted with chest pains and a suspected heart attack. One of the silly auxiliary nurses popped his head around the corner to give Micky a death stare.

"We're definitely not going to get a bed now, are we?" Pearl joked.

Uncle Micky had a point. The people who used to power the country were left in the dark queuing for their Americanised private rooms with their ensuite bathrooms and personal televisions. But nobody really cared about their health with no doctor to be seen in days.

"Loneliness is meant to be the biggest killer in today's society," Uncle Micky said. "How can ower government do this to their own people? People who powered this country!" As soon as a doctor surfaced, Girlo slipped away and after mentioning that she, herself, was a journalist, Pearl was promptly seen.

Pearl landed a big room with a big telly. Her whole family fitted. Pearl even managed to commandeer the communal remote control.

"Hide that doofer," she told Girlo when they left to go for a little wander. "That bloody woman from down the hall came in to pinch it when I went for my scan."

WILY WOMAN

And when she came around,
the sun shone on her face.
She found herself in a sapling tree,
in a welcoming embrace.

"We're the next generation then Eric, boy!" Uncle Micky said to his brother, as they walked the long windless shore, a Luna landscape devoid of tracks, the sand crunching like ice underfoot.

"What do you mean by that, Uncle Mick?" Girlo asked him. She thought Sapphire was the next generation.

"We'll be the next to die," Eric said. Girlo and Eddie were breathless from trying to catch up with them while they steamed down the beach like soldiers on a secret mission. They'd come to lay Pearl to rest.

Eric was in charge—he was the oldest after all. Girlo was responsible for choosing the photos for the funeral. The only one she could find of Pearl with any of her sons was of Uncle Bobby. Out of the thousands Girlo could only pick fifteen, and that was one. Pearl loved Bobby. She was always supporting him, always defending him and bailing him out. They used to be thick as thieves, but he broke her heart in the end.

They all met at the pub in Trecco Bay caravan park. Girlo placed her nan's ashes on the chair while her dad went to the bar. She was on pins because her dad was miffed. They had to wait around for Eddie because he'd mistakenly gone into the town, and, with parking spaces hard to come by, he'd ended up parking on the beach. Uncle Micky'd had to go and collect him and his Chihuahua Louie. Girlo was afraid they'd get lost—the caravan park was the size of a small country. Sapphire instantly made friends with two girls with a Staffordshire Bull. Girlo didn't mind, the staff was only a pup; she was usually afraid of Staffs because they locked jaws when they bit. As the sun moved behind the Showdome, they swapped beer garden seats to catch its final rays—it was chilly in the shade. Girlo's beer came in a glass tankard, too cold and strong to drink. She'd got pissed on wine the night before and still felt fragile. Her nan'd always recommended drinking spritzers, but that was counterproductive because, if after the first five she didn't get a head on, she ended up doing a load of shots to compensate. But Pearl had told her once over a naughty Baileys she was the same when she was young.

It was simply a perfect day, what would've been Pearl's birthday: a sunny October afternoon down Alright Butt Bay. None of them had been to Porthcawl in the autumn before. They went when it was sunny—all six grandkids in a one-berth caravan with a red bucket underneath, to pee in. Endless summers of sandy chips, ice-cream and dirty feet. One year Uncle Bobby's girlfriend from Sweden came to visit. She and Nannie Pearl got on like a house on fire. She looked like she'd just stepped out of a magazine. Everyone watched as she plucked her way through a swathe of sunburnt miners' wives and kids, all covered in strap marks and sun cream. Pearl was sitting watching the sea when she arrived in John Lennon shades, blonde hair flowing. Her bronzed legs swept through the scorched beach blubber that parted like the Red Sea for Moses. The women stopped squirting cream on their squirming babies. The kids stopped digging in the sand. The men stopped tackling the windbreakers and untangling the kites. Then, in one slick move, she rolled out her towel, slipped off her shorts and removed her bikini top. Pearl didn't bat an eyelid. She lit two Marlboro Reds and passed one to her.

"Lovely to see ewe, Beaut." She planted a peachy kiss on her chiselled cheekbone.

"Where's the li'l uns?"

Pearl blew an arrow of smoke towards the indignant onlookers.

"Gone for chips, love. Let's have five, now, before they're back."

So, that's where she re-rooted,
in a meadow of fresh daisies.
With honeybees as her new friends
and a babbling brook, so lazy.

After Girlo read a poem, Uncle Micky took a picture, and the light from the horizon struck one of the caravans behind them. It glinted as though it were a little sun itself.

"Look Saph. That's Nannie winking, that is," Girlo whispered. Sapphire was being her usual pain-in-the-arse self. Girlo had told her not to take her shoes off and go in the sea. She'd told her *so* many times that this wasn't just another fun day out. She didn't listen though and danced on the sand barefoot; her emerald pixie dress twinkling as she leapt through the air. And, of course, she needed a pee in the rocks as they headed down to the short peninsula at the end of the bay; a spot they hadn't discussed or formally decide upon, but collectively drew them in.

Girlo could see the silhouette of her dad and Uncle Micky at the end of a trail of deep footprints in the sand. Her dad charged ahead, carrying Pearl's ashes and a box of her favourite cherry liquor chocolates. Eddie had remembered to bring a knife and a small trowel, which they didn't need in the end. With his usual gusto Eric opened the box, using Eddie's knife to try to carve off the cardboard top. Girlo pointed out the perforations.

"It's like the tomato purée again," she said. He'd told her once that Heera laughed at him every time he opened a new tube of tomato purée because he'd always pierce the foil top with a sharp knife, before she showed him the piercing nipple moulded inside the lid.

Sapphire was in the sea again, performing for the three adults looking lost amongst the rocks. When Eric and Uncle Micky decided to begin, Sapphire piped up again. Girlo told her to shut up because, "We're saying goodbye. It's just like something we'd do in Church."

It was 6pm. Pearl had passed away at exactly 6am. Eric had been born at exactly 6am. Birth and death mirroring each other exquisitely. Eric sprinkled first, then Uncle Micky, who got caught by the incoming tide, shoes soaked through.

"Typical," Eric joked.

When it was Girlo's turn to sprinkle her portion of the ashes, she was sure she saw pink amongst them. Was it the little pink ring that Sapphire'd given her for safe passage? Or the rose quartz she'd tucked into her satin gown as her body laid in the coffin?

"Goodbye, Nan," she said, letting her into the sea. "See you in the next one—love you."

Eddie managed the most spectacular throw of the ashes it almost looked computer generated. Eric gave the chocolates to Girlo. She unpeeled the cellophane and passed one to Sapphire who spat it out moments later. Girlo remembered Nannie Pearl giving her her first chocolate liquor—it had coated her brain with a film of burn.

They ate the chocolates and threw one in for Pearl.

"We should've sung Happy Birthday!" Girlo shouted, suddenly remembering the date. "I can't believe we didn't think of it." But the day had been so perfect otherwise. There was no use feeling guilty.

The sun was setting as they ventured up the beach, resting in a wispy hammock of dragon's breath as it faded into the horizon. Eddie's Chihuahua, Louie tried to eat one of the chocolates.

"Leave it, Louie!" Eddie shouted at the dog. "It'll fucking kill you."

> *There once was a wily woman*
> *who lived in a sapling tree.*
> *They say she had lost her way,*
> *but now she is happy, she's free.*

WILY WOMAN

There once was a wily woman who lived in the womb of a tree. Each day she'd share, with the birds on the bough, the truths of their lost herstory. She'd warn of blinded battles, and wars sunk with bellies of glee. She danced to the innocent birdsong that they'd coo in the light of the tree. The woodlouse were her slippers. The leaves, her evergreen crown. The spiders were her spectacles who never let her down. For she was a laughing soul who lived to the best she could be. And she rode the boots of the travelling roots of the big old, proud, soultree. Then, one day, lightning struck, and her tree, it split in half. Flames leapt up the trunk that day, and she lost her belly laugh. The birds, they flew away from her, and the spiders stretched their legs. The trunk of the tree fell with a thump! Her nest, empty — bereft of eggs. They say she became a songless mute, for she'd lost her lust for learning and she no longer played the flute, for her heart, it had stopped yearning. So, she wished upon the brightest star to open the soultree's door. For she had lost the will to live and could take the loss no more. Into the divine door, she crawled, down a sodden tunnel. Through a glittering web, she slid, into a grassy funnel. And when she came around, the sun shone on her face. She found herself in a sapling tree, in a welcoming embrace. So, that's where she re-rooted, in a meadow of fresh daisies. With honeybees as her new friends and a babbling brook, so lazy. There once was a wily woman who lived in a sapling tree. They say she had lost her way, but now she is happy, she's free.

A NOTE FROM THE AUTHOR

The inception of *The Crazy Truth* stemmed from my PhD research in Creative and Critical Writing. Originally conceived as a künstlerroman novel, its evolution during the research process led to a broader narrative that encapsulates a multitude of voices and experiences. It transcends the individual to portray the collective struggles and triumphs of working-class lives in contemporary Britain. *The Crazy Truth* is not merely a novel; it's an immersive exploration that challenges societal norms, amplifies marginalised voices and delves into the complexities of post-industrial neoliberal society. As a contribution to feminist epistemology, *The Crazy Truth* is an emancipatory undertaking, seeking to unearth discrepancies between social ontology and historical realism. Shedding light on the lives of working-class people, my novel underscores the collective transformative power of storytelling and could be said to be a work of egalitarian concern, as it draws upon the lives of many characters who have been disenfranchised by mainstream society. While tracing the creative *becoming* of an emerging 'chavette' poet, the story brings to life five generations of familial relationships and is an exploration of the rich and diverse lived experiences of working-class people, illuminating the past origins and present conditions of discrimination, marginalisation and subjugation.

As Audre Lorde states, "poetry is the way we give name to the nameless," emphasising its profound ability to unveil the unseen. In this hybrid poetry novel, the intention is to raise consciousness and shed light on hidden truths. Adrienne Rich similarly envisioned poetry as a collective consciousness-raising necessity, in *The Dream of a Common Language*, delving into new connections between consciousness and nature. In the context of my novel, the evolving relationships among characters mirror the shift from a once-fertile land to the harsh realities of the post-industrial landscape.

In *Sister Outsider* (1984), Lorde speaks of poetry as illumination in her chapter, 'Poetry is Not a Luxury', where it is "a vital necessity of our existence." She states that "the farthest horizons of our hopes and fears are cobbled by our poems, carved from the rock experiences of our daily lives" (*ibid*). Like Clarissa Pinkola Estés, Lorde takes a psychoanalytical approach, where she states that for each of us "there is a dark place within, where hidden and growing, our true spirit rises" (*ibid* p. 25)… it is here where consciousness is formed; not in the restrictive, phallic-centric world, where "within living structures defined by profit, by linear-power, by institutional dehumanization, our feelings were not meant to survive" (1984, p. 28).

Pinkola Estés uses the metaphor of a gilded carriage to describe the many traps of patriarchy, claiming that repressed states of *being* create "a devalued life" (1992, p. 223). She urges us *all* to cast off the illusions of the "gilded carriage" (*ibid*) in favour of a life authentically lived, beyond the shackles of ideological constraints. Lorde directly addresses: "the white fathers told us: 'I think, therefore I am.' The Black Mother within each of us—the poet—whispers in our dreams: 'I feel, therefore I can be free,'" (Lorde, A. 1984, p. 27). Such deep psyche connections to poetry are fundamental to transcendence and Lorde speaks of poetry as a form of distillation, "not the sterile wordplay that, too often, the white fathers distorted the word poetry to mean —to covert a desperate wish for imagination without insight" (*ibid* p. 26).

Within *The Crazy Truth*, there is the persistent reminder that women are weaker than men. The society in which Girlo grows up is defined by the needs and actions of men, who make the rules, write the books, set the agenda and control discourse. However, within these constraints, Girlo makes it her mission to take ownership of her past, present and future, dismantling the mechanisms of oppression with critical thinking, independent learning and writing. She understands that emancipation takes collective action and an imposing of the will upon the world. Her inspiration does not come from the words of those who dictate from their ivory towers, but from lived experience, her sacred fount... from the subterranean murmurs of her sister soul. Through a distillation of life through many lenses, we can free ourselves and others from the chains of power. It is through the act of writing that she becomes neither master nor slave, but an autonomous being in a constant state of transcendence.

ACKNOWLEDGEMENTS

In March 2018, I stumbled upon a Guardian article penned by Kit de Waal titled 'Make Room for Working-class Writers.' It was a revelation, an invitation into a space I had long felt excluded from. To Kit de Waal, I extend my sincere thanks for writing that article, which ignited a spark and set me on this remarkable journey.

To my supervisor Jon Gower, who has been a steady, guiding presence from those early days as a hesitant student to the writer I am today. Jon, your mentorship has been instrumental, and I am eternally grateful for the wisdom and knowledge you've imparted. I want to express my deep appreciation to Rachel Trezise, my editor and a fellow valleys writer. Rachel's work has been an enduring source of inspiration and her guidance has been invaluable. I'd also like to acknowledge my external examiner, Niall Griffiths, who paved the way and showed me that post-industrial working-class voices in Wales are book worthy. Thank you to Janet Thomas, Lindsay Ashford and Jane Aaron for your practical guidance and encouragement. My heartfelt thanks to Mick Felton, Sarah Johnson and the Seren Books team for publishing this book.

I'd also like to thank the Creative Writing Department at Swansea University, where I've been fortunate enough to encounter some remarkable mentors, writers and educators who've played pivotal roles in shaping my growth as a writer. I've also had the privilege of working with Dr Elaine Canning from The Cultural Institute who works tirelessly to support writers. A special mention to Nigel Jenkins, a champion of the underdog, whose wisdom will forever remain. Professor Stevie Davies and Fflur Dafydd and to Professor

David Britton who always pushed me out of my comfort zone. To my family, including my brother Dr Matthew E. Howell and his wife Kath, your unwavering encouragement has been a constant source of strength. My father, Professor Kerry E. Howell, your persistence for me to pursue a PhD and write this book has been a pivotal moment in my life, and your support has been a beacon of light during the challenging times. To my chosen family, Kirstie Addleton, Carys L. Romney, Adele Wild, Gareth Scott and Vici Riley, pillars of support over the last twenty years. To Troy Smith, who has helped me take the brakes off and keep the stress at bay. I am also indebted to Live Poets', Tim Evans and Rhoda Thomas as well as Mike Jenkins from The Red Poets, who provided a platform for my work. Gratitude to Rufus Mufasa, a poetic soul from a shared cultural background, whose creative journey and artistic resilience intertwine with my own. Karl Francis, who always believed in me and John Brookes who took the time to read my words. To my PhD colleagues, Raven H. Rose and Kate Cleaver, your insightful feedback and camaraderie have been invaluable. Des Mannay, Xavier Panades i Blas, Queen Niche and all of the contributors of *Land of Change: Stories of Struggle and Solidarity from Wales*. Thank you for spurring me on!

I'd also like to take a moment to honour the memory of those who are no longer with us. My great-grandmother, April Mam, and my grandmother, Gail Howell, whose life experiences have profoundly influenced the person I've become. Though they're no longer with us, their memory lives on in my heart and in my pen. My cousin Dale and friends Johnny, Pricey and Jaya who tragically left us too young, as well as fellow poets, Alan Perry who published my dialect poetry and Tim Richards who was always there cheering from the side-lines.

Lastly, I dedicate this book to my daughter, Poppy, whose unconditional love has been a ceaseless source of power and determination.

THE AUTHOR

Dr Gemma June Howell is a multi-talented writer, poet, activist, academic and editor. She is Desk Editor at Honno, Welsh Women's Press, Director of Women Publishing Wales— Menywod Cyhoeddi Cymru, and Associate Editor at Culture Matters. Her work has mainly appeared in the Red Poets, with her dialect poetry featuring in *Yer Ower Voices* (2023). She has also been published by Bloodaxe Books (2015), *The London Magazine* (2020) and has featured on Tongue & Talk for BBC Radio 4 (2021).

In 2010 Gemma was a finalist for The John Tripp Award for Spoken Word. She published a volume of poetry, *Rock Life* (2014) and a collection of short stories *Inside the Treacle Well* with Hafan Books (2009). She has a PhD in Creative & Critical Writing from Swansea University. Her research focused on the disparities between social ontology and historical realism from a proletarian, feminist standpoint and led to her debut novel *The Crazy Truth* (Seren, 2024). Her work could be described as transgressional fiction which delves into the complexities of working-class identity in post-industrial Britain. She is an advocate for equality, representation and social equality in politics, publishing and the arts.